THE BOY SHERLOCK HOLMES  HIS 3RD CASE

VANISHING GIRL

SHANE PEACOCK

Tundra Books

Text copyright © 2009 by Shane Peacock

Published in Canada by Tundra Books,
75 Sherbourne Street, Toronto, Ontario M5A 2P9

Published in the United States by Tundra Books of Northern New York,
P.O. Box 1030, Plattsburgh, New York 12901

Library of Congress Control Number: 2008909730

Library and Archives Canada Cataloguing in Publication

Peacock, Shane
Vanishing girl / Shane Peacock.

(The boy Sherlock Holmes)
ISBN 978-0-88776-852-1

1. Holmes, Sherlock (Fictitious character) – Juvenile fiction.
I. Title. II. Series: Peacock, Shane. Boy Sherlock Holmes.

PS8581.E234V36 2009 jC813.'54 C2008-902092-8

We acknowledge the financial support of the Government of Canada
through the Book Publishing Industry Development Program (BPIDP) and
that of the Government of Ontario through the Ontario Media
Development Corporation's Ontario Book Initiative. We further
acknowledge the support of the Canada Council for the Arts and the
Ontario Arts Council for our publishing program.

Design: Jennifer Lum

The author wishes to thank Patrick Mannix and Motco Enterprises Ltd.,
U.K., ref: www.motco.com, for the use of their Edward Stanford's Library
Map of London and its suburbs, 1862.

Printed and bound in Canada

This book is printed on acid-free paper that is 100% recycled,
ancient-forest friendly (100% post-consumer recycled).

1 2 3 4 5 6   14 13 12 11 10 09

To Sophie, my remarkable girl,
who will never vanish.

ACKNOWLEDGMENTS

Thanks again to editor Kathryn Cole and publisher Kathy Lowinger of Tundra Books, two invaluable allies as we together make our way through this series. I am also grateful to The National Railway Museum in York, UK, whose employees were patient with me as I pestered them with endless questions about 1860s and '70s British trains and how one might board them, jump from them, climb out their roofs, run up and down their aisles, all while said locomotives moved at top speed – I hope they forgive the liberties I took in the name of art and adventure. The Royal Naval Museum in Portsmouth, UK was also helpful as were the amazing London Walking Tours, several of which I have taken and benefited from. And lastly to my family – three girls and a boy, who are constantly subjected to my agonies of creation and are the most patient with me of all.

CONTENTS

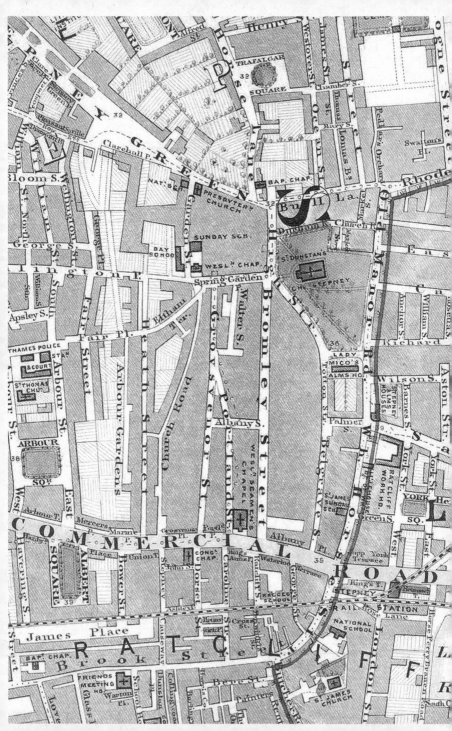

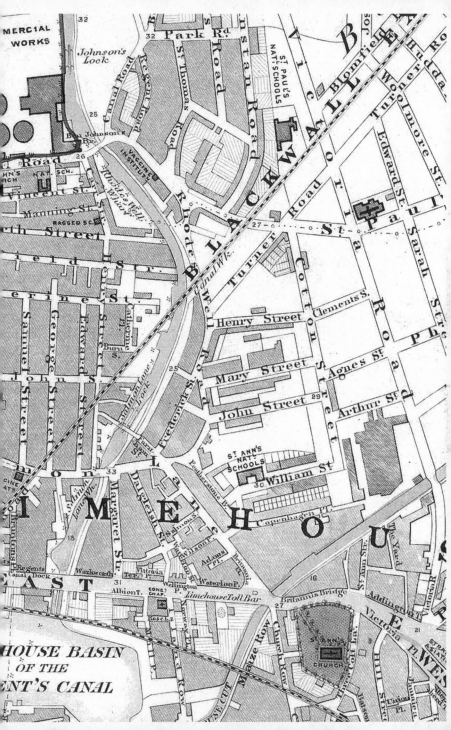

PREFACE

The wind was blowing down the hill and over the marshy field on the night they left for London. Windows were rattling, threatening to shatter. But the man with the scar and the man with the limp smiled as they rode south. They had found a girl and a victim, too. They had found a frightening place. This would be the perfect crime; make her vanish again and again, and make him vanish, too. They would all be rich beyond their imaginations. The captain's plan was working. No one could stop them; no one would track them; no one would figure this out.

Sherlock Holmes was asleep in the city by that hour, dreaming of a life in which he, and he alone, was the undisputed hero.

PART ONE

ABDUCTION

"*A flush of colour sprang to Holmes's pale cheeks, and he bowed to us like the master dramatist who receives the homage of his audience. It was at such moments that for an instant he ceased to be a reasoning machine, and betrayed his human love for admiration and applause.*"

– Dr. Watson in *The Adventure of the Six Napoleons*

DOPPELGANGER

Irene Doyle gasps. She is standing in the cavernous dining hall of the Ratcliff Workhouse in Stepney in the East End of London, staring at a little boy. A few candles dimly light the room. He is in bare feet, dressed in a ragged gray uniform, his red-blond hair disheveled; every nail on every toe is black. All the other urchins, lined up against a wall, are mesmerized by the beautiful young visitor whose lavender dress looks to them like something from a fairy tale. But the thin little lad stares straight down.

"Paul?" Irene blurts out.

The boy looks up.

"Why, Miss Doyle, 'e never responds to 'is Christian name!" exclaims the fat beadle with the fleshy face. "You must 'ave a 'old on 'im."

She puts her hand to her mouth.

"His name is *Paul*?"

"Yes, Miss, of course, just as you said, though it confounds me to know 'ow you knew such a thing."

"I didn't."

"You didn't? But —"

3

"Why does he stare like that? Why are his eyes so red? Has he been crying?"

"No, Miss, 'e 'as a disease."

"An infection?"

"Yes, Miss, a bad un. Seems to be getting worse, much worse."

"My father will help him."

"Can't be done, Miss. We 'ave lots of lads with debilitations; eyes and limbs and what-'ave-you, their little machines not workin' proper. This one 'as a certain 'aunted look about 'im, 'e does, and it draws attention when philanthropic-like folks come a-visitin'. We've 'ad a wealthy one or two in 'ere, Miss, like you and Mr. Doyle, 'o've wanted to 'elp this little scruff. But no fancy doctor they've sent 'im to can solve 'is problem. It don't seem fixable. 'e's goin' blind, poor rat."

Irene reaches out and puts one of her gloved hands against the lad's cheek. "Boys are precious."

For many years she has similarly caressed the image in a painting that sits against a wall in a closet in her father's house . . . the image of her brother. The boy had been Andrew Doyle's heir, his little man, and his death had broken the good man's heart. Her brother's life, his very existence, is something they never talk about with anyone. His name hasn't been spoken in their home since the day he died.

Mr. Doyle had been inconsolable after his loss. Nothing could make him smile. Then his step lightened when Irene's mother was with child again the following year. But the baby was a girl, and his wife, after a long labor, did not survive. It was then that he turned to philanthropy, to helping others. All he had left was Irene who, he insisted, was enough. He taught her himself, molded her to be as independent as a boy. But he never forgot his son . . . his little Paul.

"I will find a way," says Irene. "There must be people we know who can help. This little boy will *not* go blind."

♥

The following day, Andrew Doyle stands in front of tiny Paul at the workhouse, fighting back tears, unable to speak. His boy, *his* Paul, the only son he would ever have, has come back to life in the shape of a poor little waif in an East End workhouse: bone-thin, green-skinned, and cloudy-eyed. It has always been Andrew C. Doyle's policy not to adopt any of the thousands of children he aids through his organizations every year. There are simply too many: he cannot play favorites. He just tries to help. But he is sorely tested on this day. In fact, he has to turn away. The boy before him is five years old, the very age his son will always be.

"If he loses his sight . . . he will surely die," Doyle murmurs to Irene as they leave the workhouse. "I know someone who can have him cured. If anyone in England can, then it is he. We will rescue this child from darkness, or I am not worth my word."

But the very next day, a stunning incident in central London renders the boy's savior helpless.

I t happens in broad daylight.

Fourteen-year-old Victoria Rathbone steps down from her gleaming carriage as she is being promenaded on Rotten Row in Hyde Park during the last fashionable display of the season, and nears the crowd that is gazing at the rich. She pretends to be taking an opportunity to stretch her delicate legs, but is actually upset that she is not truly being seen in this evening parade of professional beauties and handsome toffs. She wants to show off her new scarlet dress to the great unwashed.

"Can't see you, Miss," someone cries. She moves closer.

A pair of thick arms appears out of the masses and seizes her. She disappears into the crowd, pulled into it as though she were a duckling sucked down a whirlpool. The culprit makes off with her, and whatever protests she emits mix with the horses' neighs and the buzz of spectators. For several moments no one misses her. Then her coachman becomes alarmed.

The girl has vanished into thin air.

The moment Sherlock Holmes reads about it in a morning paper, he thinks of it as a case for him: a notorious crime of genius and daring that rivets London's attention. But Irene's response is different: it breaks her heart. She and her father had been to see Lord Rathbone only that morning, on a mission to save the Stepney boy's sight. Now, the child will be forgotten.

But neither her reaction nor Sherlock's or even that of the Metropolitan London Police Force matters, because everything about the incident, every shred of evidence, every last player, including the victim and the criminals – even their apparent interest in gaining anything from their crime – instantly evaporates. Days pass, then weeks; the daring abduction remains an impenetrable mystery, without a ransom note, a single clue, or even public information.

Is Victoria Rathbone dead? Or are the culprits simply trying to frighten her noble family, terrify them so thoroughly that they will give in to any demand when it, at last, arrives? What is their game?

Her father is an eminent man, a member of the House of Lords and advisor to Prime Minister Derby's cabinet on judicial affairs. He is stern and ruthless, a crusader for exacting extreme punishment upon criminals. *Never give them an inch*, reads his motto, etched in a plaque on his desk.

He doesn't appear to be frightened by the silence from the kidnappers. In fact, he contributes to it, refusing to utter a single public word about their villainy, as if it had never happened. He remains aggressive about crime in general, and just a month after Victoria's disappearance, calls for stiffer sentencing in all criminal convictions. "One must be brutal with brutal people," he asserts. And he gives an example: "If we were to cut off the hands of London's thieves, there would be no thieves in London."

The summer ends, autumn almost passes, and still, Rathbone is mute about the crime. He not only puts on a brave face, but forces the police to remain silent, too. He and his household shall not play cricket with evil. It seems as though he will let his daughter die before he allows the devils who took her to scare him, to win, to have any of his money, to cause him even the slightest public grief. He goes on with his job, impressing his peers, making more jarring statements about criminal issues in the House.

"Unlawfulness," he proclaims on the two-month anniversary of the crime, "comes mostly from our under-classes. When they learn to help themselves more, to give up holding out their hands to their betters, they shall better themselves, and we all shall be better off."

But he is known to have said privately that the kid-nappers shall be caught and severely punished – and if they harm his daughter, he will personally see to it that they are hanged in the street outside the walls of Newgate Prison, before a crowd at whose head he shall proudly stand.

Lady Rathbone, of course, says nothing publicly either. But then, such statements and certainly politics aren't of interest to her. Twenty years her Lord's junior, she is still a stunning belle of the London scene at age forty. In her youth, she was known to society as "the blind beauty." Her bewitching brown eyes growing steadily dimmer with every passing year. By the time she met her husband they had become almost sightless. He put her into the hands of his remarkable personal physician, who gave her back her vision with one of his miraculous chemical cures.

No talents, however, and no one's power, can help Rathbone with the brilliant and sinister abduction of his daughter. By the time November comes and London's thickest yellow fogs with it, there is still not a solitary clue to this mystery and the police are desperate. It remains unprecedented in the annals of crime: quiet reigns unabated on all sides.

Then finally, on the third day of that month, the silence is broken. Almost instantly, everything changes.

♥

Sherlock Holmes is ready for the news when it comes that morning.

It has been four months since he solved the unusual case of the Crystal Palace flying-trapeze accident and almost single-handedly caused the arrest of the notorious Brixton Gang. But the public doesn't know the role he played, or of his earlier genius in catching the Whitechapel murderer. Inspector Lestrade and Scotland Yard have made sure of that. While Sherlock hasn't wavered in his vow to fight injustice with his very life, to avenge his mother's murder, he reminds himself daily that such aspirations will take time.

And so the boy's world is filled with frustration – it seems to be taking forever to become the man he hopes to be.

He still lives with strange old Sigerson Bell, the Denmark-Street apothecary as he continues to rebuild himself: working hard at school and studies, rereading Samuel Smiles' best seller *Self Help*, learning the fighting art of "Bellitsu," the manly art of pugilism, and gleaning all he can about chemistry.

Though the old apothecary's business was recently sagging as badly as his flesh, he is back on his financial feet these days, saved from the clutches of his miserly landlord by a steady stream of money, thanks to the young trapeze star known as The Swallow. That remarkable boy, whom Sherlock befriended after the Crystal Palace accident, has directed many of his show-business friends (including The Great Farini and his son, El Niño) in the direction of the smelly little London shop. Their sore limbs and aching backs are now the beneficiaries of Bell's often unorthodox, but always effective treatments. He requires them to spend hours locked in poses that actually stretch and loosen their muscles – it is most unusual. And sheep bile, rubbed into the joints, was never so valued by a group of patients.

"It reeks like the wrong end of a donkey, sir," said an aerialist one day, happily rotating his arms in their sockets as if they were gale-driven windmills. "But it does a powerful job making me limbs work."

"Never mind the stench, Icarus. It's the effect that matters. I pondered prescribing horse vomit for you, to be taken orally, so consider yourself lucky."

"The way you've fixed me up, good doctor, I'd try anything you propose, short of you chopping off me 'ead and replacing it with a pig's."

"Don't tempt me, Icarus. The Pig-headed Flying Man would be a showstopper!"

But such spectacular personalities coming and going from the shop haven't been enough of a distraction for Master Holmes. On the pages of the old man's *Daily Telegraph*, in the glorious *Illustrated Police News*, and the legless newsboy Dupin's *News of the World*, he keeps searching for what really excites him; for what makes his blood race. There is unchecked evil everywhere. He sees notices of robberies, assaults, extortion, and even murder – crimes in the dark East End, Southwark, Rotherhithe, and Brixton. Only one of these villainies truly measures up to Sherlock's needs; is spectacular enough that a solution would gain him his due. He first read of it nearly three months ago . . . the case of the vanishing girl.

But it is such a maddening crime to even consider solving. There is nowhere to start, neither for the police nor . . . Sherlock Holmes.

Until that morning: when Lestrade makes his move.

"Have you noticed this little bit in the *Telegraph*?" inquires Bell in his high-pitched voice at dawn on the eve of Guy Fawkes Day. They are taking one of their unusual breakfasts in the chemical laboratory at the back of the shop; clams this time, washed down with flavored ice and tea. Both partakers are still perspiring, and each sports a darkened eye, the result of a vigorous morning of pugilism during which each struck the other at least one mighty blow to the visage, scientifically delivered, but with maximum force.

Sherlock's hawk nose rises from his plate. The old man has been keeping the newspaper from him this morning, and he's been wondering why.

"What little bit is that, sir?"

The white-haired apothecary has only a slightly disguised grin on his face.

"There might be a spot of interest in it for you."

Bell knows this boy well, this lad after his own heart, and is aware that the newspaper article will fascinate him. He holds it up so Sherlock can see it, but keeps it just beyond his grasp.

"POLICE TO SPEAK ABOUT RATHBONE CASE," states the headline.

Sherlock's eyes widen and he reaches out. Bell pulls the paper back. Then he smiles and hands it over. Holmes dives into the article.

> "Scotland Yard admits that a ransom note was indeed received from the kidnappers of Victoria Rathbone yesterday, but Lord Rathbone, having refused to pay the required sum, at first forbade the message to be made known. However, it seems that the Force, and the redoubtable Inspector

Lestrade, he of the remarkable Whitechapel and Crystal Palace solutions, have convinced the distinguished gentleman to allow them to make a statement 'simply in order to aid the pursuit of the culprits.' The trail, it seems, is stone-cold and members of the public may be of help. The Metropolitan Police shall be speaking to representatives of the press at their White-Hall offices tomorrow, directly at the noon hour."

"You may be away from both school and this establishment tomorrow morning, until one hour past midday," says Bell the instant he sees that Sherlock has finished reading.

The singular boy has frightened the old man many times since he came into his employment, and not just because of those dangerous solo trips deep into spooky Rotherhithe during the Brixton Gang case, or even the growing competence of his right cross to the jaw. It's the boy's disposition that unsettles him – his moods can grow disturbingly dark. Friendless and inward, Sherlock can descend instantly into silence, his mind far away. There have been times when he has been virtually immobile, like a sort of living cadaver, sitting here at the laboratory table while they take their meals. His gray eyes grow narrow and distant, his face alarmingly pale, and his breathing barely palpable.

This lad needs stimulation, thinks the apothecary. *He needs it the way an opium addict needs the narcotic jolt of the poppy seed.*

The old man observes Sherlock as he sets down the paper. He is not frightened for him today.

The boy's face is lit up.

WATERMARK

Scotland Yard's famous offices are in White Hall not far from Trafalgar Square in the center of stinking, eardrum-popping London. But Sherlock pays little attention to the rush of rumbling omnibuses and sprite hansom cabs, the advertising signs, the desperate poor, or even the celebrated faces. His mind and his senses are riveted on what will take place outside the redbrick exterior of the Yard, and what he hopes to hear from the mouth of the police spokesman who will break the silence on the Rathbone case. He imagines what he would do *if* he were to pursue this case: he would be alert for even a whiff of a clue, of something that could open the tiniest of cracks in this mystery. This could be his one chance.

The mouth that does the announcing doesn't belong to an underling. This is not a time for those low on the pecking order to be seen. It sits under the bushy mustache of the one and only Inspector Lestrade. And the mouth is not upturned as it speaks. It is more like a line. Lestrade is not in a happy mood. And his attitude is not lightened when he notices young Holmes standing at the rear of the crowd of reporters. It is the first truly chilly morning of the season and one of those thick, bitter-tasting fogs has settled in. Lestrade squints out at the boy. If he had the time, he would have the meddlesome half-Jew removed.

"Master Holmes," says a familiar voice right next to him.

"Master Lestrade, your stealth is growing. Your approach escaped me."

The Inspector's son smiles. Though he is at least three or four years older than Sherlock, he is barely taller, and inherited, ferret-like features are unfortunately evident in his face.

"This one is said to be unsolvable, you know."

"I am only an interested observer."

"Ah! A mere observer. . . . Nevertheless, you may be intrigued to know that there are *still* no real clues."

"That may soon change."

"Were someone such as you to try a little investigating on this case, Holmes, I would wish them good luck, but my father will triumph this time, you can take that to the Bank of England."

The older boy walks away, with a grin. He snakes through the crowd and back toward a spot near his father on the temporary podium, which creaks as he ascends it.

But Sherlock is watching someone else. He's spotted a bespectacled young man in a brown coat and black top hat near the front, who turns and sees him too. There is a moment of recognition. Sherlock recalls him instantly – the reporter from *The Times*, the man who saw him in the midst of the action during the dramatic final moments of the Crystal Palace case, but then was silenced by the older Lestrade. The boy has since learned that the man's name is Hobbs.

Lives in central London, thinks Sherlock, *in the old city, age twenty-four, five foot five, not much more than a hundred-weight, perhaps nine and a half stone . . . yet flabby . . . father is a clerk . . . not given to bravery . . . could be used again for my purposes in a pinch.* He has picked up clues from the man's frock coat, the make of his spectacles, and his physical attitude. But he chides himself for making plans. *Just listen to what the police have to say. Make mental notes for future cases. Such puzzles as this aren't for you to solve. Not yet.*

"Gentleman," begins the senior Lestrade in a booming voice, "you have been called to Scotland Yard this noon hour to aid the authorities in the solution of a most heinous crime, that of the abduction of Victoria, dear daughter of the esteemed Lord Rathbone of the upper House, seized two weeks prior to the last instant of August, early evening, approximately five fortnights past, whilst minding her own business riding with her coachman in Hyde Park upon Rotten Row."

He pauses for dramatic effect.

"I hold in my hand a ransom note . . ."

Though he brandishes it high in the air like a trophy and the sun even co-operates by suddenly shining past the breaking clouds and glowing through the fog, none of the reporters offers the intake of breath he hoped for, so he goes on.

"It reads . . .

Lord Rathbone:

I have captured your daughter. She is breathing
. . . but perhaps not for long. You may save her
life by preparing a quarter-million pounds in
small bank notes immediately, and placing said
sum at my command when and where I say. You
shall be notified of the details of this exchange
within three days. Failure to comply will result
in your daughter's execution before the sun sets
that day. Be assured that I shall not be made a
fool of . . . though I may make a fool of you.

I remain,

The Enemy"

As the reporters write furiously, Lestrade begins to exhort
them to publish this "evil" note verbatim, to encourage their
readers to search its contents for clues, and to report anything they know to the Force.

But Sherlock Holmes is ignoring the detective's drivel.
He is focused on a series of distinctive points he's heard and
an enormous one he's seen. First, there is the fact that this
ransom note comes after more than two and a half months
of absolutely no communication, but then suddenly puts a
very short deadline on its target; secondly, since the note
insinuates that there is just one fiend at work, there's a high
probability of there being several; thirdly, the money asked
for is gargantuan (making it almost impossible for Rathbone
to comply on time), and fourthly, the abductors seem to

want to taunt the rich man, again making it difficult for such a man as he to accede to their demands. But the most important clue is the visual one. It is so good that it scares the boy – it is almost irresistible.

As Inspector Lestrade holds the paper high in the air for the reporters to observe and the noon-hour sun begins to dominate the day, Sherlock glimpses something . . . a very faint watermark. It is the barely detectable outline of two faces.

"I knew you would be here."

That sweet smell of soap.

Instinctively, Sherlock's hands go to his perfectly-combed, raven-black hair, intent on making sure it is in place. He had spent a good deal of time attending to it this morning, gazing into the cracked little mirror he has attached to the inside of his wardrobe door. He straightens his poor frock coat, adjusts his necktie, and smoothes out the frayed waistcoat.

Irene Doyle is standing directly behind him, and likely has been for a while.

"It is a case of some interest."

"Turn around and look at me, Sherlock Holmes. I won't bite you."

She is radiant in the sun-drenched fog, dressed beautifully in a buttoned-up white coat with high collar, holding a parasol delicately above her bonneted blonde hair. He hasn't spoken to her for months, though he's seen her once or twice, when he just happened to pass by her home. He could swear that he's also noticed her at least three times on Denmark Street, glancing toward the shop as she walked by on the foot pavement across the road.

Irene has a way of looking at him, examining, almost caressing his features. It is different from other girls. But today there is a grim intensity in her expression, as if she is deeply worried about something.

"It isn't that, Irene."

"Then what is it? Because I have never been certain why we can't be friends. It doesn't make sense to me."

"I . . . I must be going."

The parasol comes down violently on his head.

"So must I."

Sherlock rubs his scalp.

"I am acquainted with the victim," says Irene as she turns and starts moving rapidly away from him.

"You *know* her?"

"Now you are interested." She keeps walking.

"Irene!" He runs after her. "You are *acquainted* with Victoria Rathbone?"

She stops and smiles. "Why else do you think I came here? To see *you*?"

Sherlock would never admit that he had ever thought such a thing, had hoped that it might be true.

"Yes, I know her." She pauses and her voice drops. "She will be murdered, won't she?"

The boy is surprised to see her eyes moistening.

"Not necessarily," he says.

"But her father will *never* pay."

"Perhaps she can be found."

"By whom? Inspector Lestrade? He of the *remarkable* Whitechapel and Crystal Palace solutions?"

"He is a professional of long standing."

"Sherlock, you hate him. And what about you? I can't believe you are *simply* here to watch?"

"I was fortunate before: in the right place at the right time. My day will come."

"Yes, you are correct. You would fail at this one."

"I didn't say that."

"You are just a boy and one who works *alone*. This case would be much more difficult than the others. You would begin it without a single clue and no inside knowledge of the incident or the people involved."

"There may be a starting point."

She smiles.

"Sherlock, you've noticed something! You *are* interested. You are going to look into this, aren't you?"

"I didn't say that, either."

"You would need assistance this time."

"Not necessar –"

"You would need to know something about Victoria and her family, what her life is like, who she really is in person, who her father's enemies might be. Does she know her abductors? Was it an inside job? Is she delicate? Did the kidnapping kill her? . . . Is that why there has been silence?"

"There are ways to –"

"How could you, working class and a boy, know anything about her and her world?"

"I –"

"But *I* know her. I know a great deal about her . . . and I understand *girls* too, and how they think. In case you haven't noticed, I am one."

The boy wraps his frock coat tighter around his thin frame in the bright, cold air. *Inside job?* It disturbs him to think of where Irene is picking up talk like that.

"If you were to try to investigate this, you would need someone with such information on your side. I want her found too, and not just because I know her. We could help each other, Sherlock. The police are the most proficient at this, you're right, but who knows how we might contribute? It's worth trying."

The people who committed this crime must be desperate fiends – he does *not* want Irene anywhere near them.

"You are under the illusion that I want to do this."

She gives him a sly smile.

Sherlock wonders if Irene knows as much as she claims. She is a girl, that's true. He will admit that. But he doesn't believe that she could help him with this case simply for that reason. *How different can girls be, anyway?* He's not sure about that smile though. Is she toying with him? Usually he can take the measure of anyone; but this young lady has always been puzzling. Does she indeed know things about Victoria Rathbone that might be useful?

"Tell me what you know, Irene."

"It's my father and I who want her back . . . for reasons I cannot say. We *need* to find her. I will do whatever I have to do to help solve this. If you won't lend a hand, then I have a friend who will."

He knows who that is.

"I should tell you that the life of a little boy hangs in the balance, too."

"What do you mean?"

"He lives in a workhouse. I saw him yesterday. He is going blind and the Rathbones are the only people who can help him. But they aren't speaking with anyone now."

"There are thousands of little boys like that, Irene. You know that better than I. Why do you care about this one? And why is Miss Rathbone *so* important to you?"

Her eyes moisten again; then she looks angry.

"I knew you wouldn't care about the boy. I don't know why I told you. He's a child, Sherlock, with even less in his life than you have! I thought that might mean something to you, but I guess I was wrong."

"Tell me what you know first, then maybe we can talk about what we might do."

Irene pauses.

"Before I give you *any* information, you must promise me that we will share everything we find. This will be you and me . . . or my *other* friend and me. What is your answer?"

"Irene, let's just . . . maybe . . ." he hesitates.

"Whoever solves this will have my father's eternal gratitude. If someone were to lay the solution at his feet, he would provide that person with anything that is within his power to give."

Sherlock feels a surge of excitement. *Anything?* He thinks of school – which he must continue to pay for with the meager income that Bell has started paying him – of university after that, of A.C. Doyle's influence at such institutions and at Scotland Yard.

"I . . ."

"Yes?"

If Sherlock agrees, it would mean that he would have to include Irene, put her in danger, and share the credit. She thinks she has him right where she wants him. But does she? Surely her father wouldn't want her involved. In fact, he might very well thank the boy for keeping her out of it.

"Such a case . . . could be very dangerous."

This time, when she turns, she keeps moving. She steams east toward central London.

Irene wouldn't work with Malefactor, would she?

Still rubbing his head, trying to resist watching her walk away, Sherlock turns back toward Scotland Yard. He tells himself that her attractiveness has nothing to do with her golden hair, the sweet sound of her voice, or those beguiling smiles that disarm him. . . . It's simply that she may have a tantalizing connection to the kidnap victim, which would indeed be helpful to anyone investigating this case. *What does she really know?* He turns back to watch her. She is far away now, nearing the ornate stone arch that connects The Mall to Trafalgar Square. *I must get her to talk to me.* He wants to run after her. But then several short figures and a tall one appear in the shadows near her. Irene pauses, looks back at Sherlock, and vanishes into the darkness under the arch.

He moves toward the Yard again, thinking about what he's seen and heard this morning. He has a clue, a good one that he doubts the police have noticed. And if he doesn't hesitate, looks into the case while he has this advantage, there is an opportunity before him that can change his life. Can he let this chance go?

At that instant, there is a commotion a few hundred feet in front of him.

Inspector Lestrade and his son are attempting to walk out from police headquarters onto wide White Hall Street, where a black four-wheeler awaits them, but the veteran plainclothesman is being hectored by a dozen newspapermen, among them Mr. Hobbs. They surround him like a swarm of bees buzzing with questions. He isn't answering and looks angry.

This case has been a monstrous public failure for the senior inspector. Sherlock smiles and scoots over. He wants to hear this. It will do his heart good.

"How is it possible, Inspector, to have *no* clues for three months?"

"Do you think she is already dead?"

"Has anything like this ever happened before?"

"Is your job in jeopardy?"

Even that question cannot draw a comment from Lestrade, but the next one does. And not simply because of its content, though that is bad enough. It comes from Sherlock Holmes. With his lust for vengeance growing as he watches the inspector get what he deserves, the boy shouts at him from behind the mob.

"Are you not ashamed?"

There is silence. All the reporters turn to look at the audacious working-class boy who has just insulted the senior inspector at Scotland Yard.

"What was that you said, you young blackguard?" shouts Lestrade. "Step forward!"

The reporters part and Sherlock walks through them like Moses, unafraid, his big nose lifted high and proud. *This* is for his mother.

"I said . . . are you not ashamed?"

Lestrade reaches out with one hand for the boy, the other balled in a fist, but his son pulls him back.

"I ought to thrash you here in public!"

"Desperate men often resort to violence."

The newsmen are speechless for an instant. Then *The Times* reporter recognizes the boy.

"Say, aren't you the lad who –"

"Shut your gob, Mr. Hobbs!" hisses Lestrade. "This child is a loiterer and if he does not move along I shall call a constable."

"But he isn't –"

"SHUT UP, Hobbs!"

"I have a clue in the Rathbone case," says Sherlock calmly.

Several reporters laugh.

"You what?" asks Lestrade Junior.

Aha, thinks Sherlock, *they have none*.

"And I am the Duke of Wellington come back to life," smirks the inspector. He puts his hands on his lapels, as if to commence a speech. "This boy is a lunatic. A Jew who wanders the streets, does bit work for an impoverished quack, and several times has pretended to know things about certain well-known crimes. He consorts with young ruffians and has been in jail. We are well aware of him. His parents' reckless marriage made him a half-breed."

"Father, I don't think it is kind to –"

"If you choose to work with me, sir, then you shall be silent."

The older boy looks at his feet.

"As I was saying, he has delusions and deserves our pity more than anything else. Let me demonstrate. I ask you, Master Holmes, did you not solve both the Whitechapel and Crystal Palace crimes?"

"Yes, I did."

The reporters roar with laughter.

"Father, we shouldn't –"

"Silence, boy! I shan't speak to you again."

Lestrade is hitting his stride now. He sees Sherlock Holmes shrinking in front of his very eyes and smells blood. It feels so good to get the upper hand for once during this black time. At least he can put an end to this meddler.

"The truth is that his mother was murdered in cold blood by the Whitechapel villain, poisoned like a rat . . . and *he*, gentleman, was the cause!"

With that, Lestrade steps up into his carriage, pulling his astonished son with him.

The reporters walk off, mimicking the boy in the threadbare dress clothes. "I have a clue," snorts one in a child-like voice. They all laugh again, except Hobbs, who gazes at the boy.

♥

With eyes as red as blood, Sherlock Holmes stumbles into an alley off White Hall. He boots over a rotting rain barrel and lets the water in it drain. Then he picks it up and flings it against a wall. When it doesn't smash, he kicks it, again and again and again . . . until it splinters into pieces.

"You insult me!" he shouts, "You insult my MOTHER!"

If he were a man, he would challenge Lestrade to fight him in a public place. He doesn't really give a farthing for the life of that upper-class girl, nor does he know anything of that wretched child in the workhouse, but if he has ever been certain of *anything* in his life, it is this: he will find Victoria Rathbone! No matter what it takes. He will gain the keys to his future . . . and announce his solution for all to hear, right in front of that ferret from Scotland Yard. No one and nothing, not Malefactor, not even his own inexperience, will stop him.

"I challenge you, Lestrade! I cannot fight you with pistols at twenty paces, but *this* will be a duel. I will put a bullet in you!"

He leaves the alley and walks toward Denmark Street, at war with himself.

"Be calm," he says out loud, grinding his teeth. "Be rational. That is the only way to proceed."

His mind turns to Irene for an instant. *Don't think*

about her. You don't need her. He can't believe she would work with Malefactor. *Pay attention to what you must do. You have a clue. Pursue it and pursue it now.*

The watermark.

He is nearing the apothecary's shop. *Watermarks aren't made by stationers, but by the papermakers themselves*: he's learned that in school. This was a faint one, very faint, apparently not even seen by the police, only visible when held at just the right position in the noon-hour sun.

The ransom note was sent yesterday and had a three-day deadline. Rathbone *won't* pay, there is no doubt. There are just forty-eight hours left before they kill his daughter . . . before opportunity vanishes.

Sigerson Bell is hard at work in the chemical laboratory when his apprentice arrives with a smile pasted on his face, ready to pick the alchemist's big brain. At first, things don't seem promising. The old man's eyes look slightly wild and cloudy, likely from some sort of solution he's administered to himself. But, as usual, there is a file inside his skull that promises to be of considerable help. They dip into it.

"Yes, I once had a papermaker as a patient," says Bell. "Something wrong with his bowel, if I recall correctly. Not enough water in the gut was producing a hard stool that smelled like —"

"Uh, sir?"

"Yes, my boy?"

"I'm not certain I need to know about the odor of his stool."

"Quite. A very good point! More pertinent for your purposes is the question of the watermark."

"Yes, sir."

"Well, let's see. . . . This patient was a foreman at one of those new-fangled mills about a forenoon's walk from central London, out Surrey way to the south where they use wood pulp to make the paper and steam-powered machines to process it. In his earlier day he had toiled at a smaller operation where they used rags, so he was conversant with all aspects of the making of paper. A loquacious sort, he was, though what man in England who has risen above semi-literacy cannot talk your ear right off when given a chance? We are a chatty race. Had terrible halitosis, as I recall, his breath smelled like a dog's behind after it rolled in . . ."

"Uh . . . watermarks, sir?"

"Keep me on the trail, my boy, my nose right to it. Excellent! . . . What was the trail again?"

"Watermarks."

"Watermarks! Right you are! Let me see. This gentleman used to speak of the fact that not long ago there were nearly a thousand paper mills in England, but just a hundred or so now, much bigger and more efficient at the art. I recollect him speaking of watermarks indeed, saying they have become much simpler. Just a single letter often suffices now, the sign of the mill. That wasn't the way in the old days."

It isn't much, but it's a start for Sherlock. The watermark is an old one.

There's no sense in going to school now: it is early afternoon. It would be impossible to concentrate anyway. The boy works for several hours in the shop, cleaning up around the laboratory, his mind focused on what he should do next. The big clock in the lab seems to be ticking faster and faster. His thoughts wander back to Irene. Her possible contributions remain tantalizing. *Does she really know something valuable?* But it wouldn't matter if she did. He simply *cannot* share the credit for the solution to this crime.

He grows anxious – he *needs* to come up with something. But he reminds himself to be as emotionless as possible. He sets jars of oozing liquid, containers of severed limbs, mysterious cans of powder that make his nose tingle, all in their proper places. He dusts the many leaning towers of books that make up Bell's teetering library, and polishes the three precious statues of Hermes.

Trying to construct a theory, he focuses on how he might learn more about old watermarks. Just as he does, he notices an old copy of the *Telegraph* on a stool, and an idea comes to him. When Bell goes off on a mid-afternoon call, he slips out the door. His next stop is Trafalgar Square to speak to the cripple, Dupin, who will be setting up to sell his evening publications. Nothing in the newspaper business escapes the legless man, and Sherlock is betting he'll know something about the material his sheets are printed upon. An old watermark should be his cup of tea – Dupin adores the history of everything.

"Paper? Don't know much about it Master 'olmes."

The boy's heart sinks.

"But I do have the acquaintance of a stationer, one of the best in London, been in that line for many generations. He buys his dailies from me. Loves to talk about our glorious past, 'e does. Just like me, Master 'olmes." Dupin's twisted lips smile. "Two faces, you say? I'll inquire of 'im. 'e'll be 'round in about an hour."

Sherlock can hardly wait. He doesn't want to pause more than a minute, let alone an hour – he may be about to make progress on the *only* clue to the kidnapping. He stands near the newspaper kiosk, examining every customer, sure he will be able to guess which one is the stationer. For a while, deciphering the occupations, ages, and habits of the many men and women who buy Dupin's papers is interesting. Then his interest wanes. But after Big Ben chimes the next hour, the game becomes more tantalizing: the stationer should be here soon. Which customer will he be? Finally, the perfect candidate appears: a middle-aged chap with an intellectual look on his bespectacled face, a certain historic flair in the cut of his suit, and great height to his hat; he takes the paper from Dupin with long fingers tipped with the black-smudged nails of someone who often works with ink.

Sherlock can't stand it any longer. He approaches to eavesdrop. The two men are engrossed in their conversation.

"Two faces, you say?"

"Yes, sir."

"That *is* interesting."

"'ow so, sir?"

"Why, it's the mark of the Fourdrinier Brothers, pioneers in our line, stationers here in London long ago. They used some of the first modern papermaking machines very early in the century, but you can't get that material now."

"Why not, sir?" Sherlock pipes up.

The two men turn. Dupin regards him with a look that says "Shoo!"

"Who is this?" inquires the stationer, raising his head and looking down his nose and through his spectacles at the boy in the worn-out frock coat.

"No one," says Dupin, glaring at Sherlock.

"Be that as it may, he has an excellent question," smiles the man.

Dupin looks relieved.

"You can't get that paper these days, my son, because it isn't manufactured anymore."

"But where was it made in its day?"

"The town of St. Neots, well north of the city, not far from Cambridge, but . . ."

The boy doesn't wait to hear the whole answer.

4

RASH DECISIONS

King's Cross Station serves those passengers taking the Great Northern Railway to and from London. Though Sherlock isn't exactly sure where St. Neots is, he certainly knows all about Cambridge, forty or fifty miles north of here, dominated by its famous university. He's guessing this rail line will take him close to where he needs to go – he'll find out at the terminus. He rushes through the city, not even stopping at the apothecary's to tell the old man he is leaving London. All his work responsibilities have fled his mind. So impetuous is he that he barely considers what awaits him at his destination, if it might all be for naught, how long he might be gone, or if he can even get onto a train. He is simply filled with a desire to go.

He has to pass through Bloomsbury, and decides to slip up Montague Street where Irene lives, not to see her, mind . . . just . . . he isn't sure why.

A leg wearing a big dirty boot sticks out as he turns the corner onto Montague, knocking him to the hard foot pavement.

Grimsby.

He is Malefactor's most vicious lieutenant: dark, wiry, and sadistic. Beside him stands the silent Crew: big, blond, and blue-eyed. Grimsby steps over Sherlock, arms folded, one foot on either side of his torso.

Their boss materializes from behind. Dark-haired and gray-eyed like Sherlock, he sports his black top hat and fading, long tailcoat, and carries a walking stick, which he twirls in the air. His head protrudes as he talks, as if examining others suspiciously.

"Sherlock Holmes, I perceive."

There was a time when Sherlock was almost pleased to see Malefactor. They have a strange sort of connection, similar pasts: both were destined for more than fate gave them. But Sherlock hates him now. The young criminal befriended Irene through him and has taken to deceiving her, pretending that he will allow her to reform him. And this summer, Sherlock is sure, Malefactor tried to kill him. He will never trust the rogue again.

Holmes doesn't feel particularly threatened as he lies there on the footpath: they are in public, in daylight, and he knows the young boss won't unleash his thugs where the full force of their brutality can be observed. All the same, when he gets to his feet, he will be careful not to turn his back.

"Anything I should know?" asks the criminal.

"Go away, rat."

Grimsby accidentally kicks Holmes in the ribs.

"You aren't in a position to say such things, Jew-boy. Anything I should know?"

There is nothing he wants to tell Malefactor. They have nothing in common now. Sherlock is a crusader for justice, the other a thief; they are natural enemies and shall be forever. That's why Malefactor wants him dead.

"You are onto a case, I can see by the look in your eye," smiles the master crook, examining his fingernails, not even glancing down at his opponent. "I am guessing . . . the Rathbone kidnapping."

Sherlock says nothing. If Malefactor truly guessed his cause by a look, that means that Irene hasn't spoken to him yet. *Or does it?*

"It is perfect for you. It would gain you the fame you seek, in the cause of . . . *justice*."

Grimsby giggles.

"Stay away from it. I am warning you. We do not need more detectives about. Let them wallow in their incompetence. This little career you are considering is a fantasy."

Sherlock isn't listening. He's thinking of Sigerson Bell and his oriental art of Bellitsu. *How does one defeat an opponent while lying on the ground, when he is standing over you? Ah!*

The boy makes a quick move, rolling to his side, forcing Grimsby downward by driving his shoulder into the other's calf and seizing the outside of his leg with his arm. In an instant, the young tough is on the ground, groaning, Sherlock looming above him.

There are indeed too many passersby here for the other two to respond with noticeable violence. Sherlock backs up, his eyes on his opponents.

"The child is learning," says Malefactor.

Sherlock nods.

"I did not try to kill you, you know. Believe me. I am still interested in your progress. I hold out hope that you will come over to our side some day, where the realists are. Your methods are sinister enough. Let me offer some advice as a show of friendship. If you indeed ill-advisedly pursue the Rathbone situation, do so quietly; do it like a thief in the night. Never seek notoriety!"

But Sherlock is running now, up Montague Street toward King's Cross, his rival's raised voice fading in the distance. He doesn't care a fig for Malefactor's advice anymore. He is sure that that nasty piece of work will try to eliminate him again the instant he gets the chance. *Never seek notoriety? The rascal revels in it.*

It was his father who first taught him to be scientific, never rash, never a guesser. And that's what he has been trying to be over the last few months. But this watermark clue is just too enticing. The only approach now is a bold one. He won't be deterred or slowed down, not by Malefactor, not even by common sense. He is heading north to St. Neots . . . where he has no idea what he will find.

He spots the huge railway station a long way off, on the north side of Euston Road, an imposing building made of yellow-brown bricks. The clock on its tower tells him that London's busiest hours are nearing: the crowds are growing.

That is good, because it will allow him to lose himself in the flow of people and steal onto a train – there isn't a farthing in his pocket. He rushes inside through one of the big archways. The noise here, contained and echoing in the great hall, is making it difficult for travelers to even hear themselves speak. He observes the many Bobbies walking in the throngs under the arched ceiling, watching for miscreants.

Just past the front doors he finds a map on a wall, showing the route of The Great Northern. Following its black line up the illustration, he almost cries out when he sees where it goes: just west of Cambridge, right through the little town of St. Neots.

It leaves from Platform 8, the 4:10 to York. He glances at the clock. *He has two minutes!* He runs. Ticket offices, a dispatch office, and little shops selling newspapers and sweets ring the interior of the station. A brick wall extends its full length to his left, cut with interior archways, separating it from the platforms and their glass-covered ceiling. *Where is number 8?* His heart sinks as he glances toward the first doorway – PLATFORMS 1 & 2, reads the sign above it. He keeps running, past 3 & 4, then 5 & 6, aware now that his train will leave from the last platform in the building, way down at the far end. He has no ticket, no plan to get through without one, and he's desperately late! His future may depend on making this train. Racing through the crowd, darting in and around ladies and gentlemen and children dressed like little adults, he finally sees the number 8 archway, a single cut in the wall, narrower than all the others. Through it, he spots the mighty black steam locomotive on the track, hissing away, belching filthy smoke out its stack, making deafening noises . . . about to pull out. There may not be another train until tomorrow. In two days Victoria Rathbone will be murdered. He *must* make it.

He sprints toward the ticket inspector at the gate, who is dressed in a navy-blue uniform, pillbox cap tipped lazily back on his head. That's whom the boy *has* to get past. He eyes his surroundings as he runs: passengers are swirling around him, rushing in different directions toward their trains, fares evident in a few hands. *Can he knock into them like a cricket ball into a wicket, like one of Malefactor's ruffians, and snatch a ticket in the confusion? Can he show it to the inspector with his fingers obscuring its surface? How closely do they check? What —*

The inspector raises the palm of his hand toward Sherlock.

"This gate is closed, lad. The 4:10 is on 'er run."

The locomotive's shrill whistle makes the boy jump.

"But . . ."

"Best be on your way."

Sherlock looks past him and sees that the train is beginning to move.

Shove the inspector, leap over the gate, and make a run for it.

"I asked you to move, lad. What are you lookin' at?"

The man's eyes are following Sherlock's.

"Not a thing, sir."

As the boy walks away, the official's gaze follows him with interest. Holmes slips into the crowd.

He has missed the train.

"Hurry, Constance!" an old, rail-thin gentleman in a chimney-pot hat exclaims beside him in the din. He's begging his poor wife to get moving. "The train departs in a quarter hour." She is as plump and prickly as a porcupine, and almost as smelly. She natters at him, huffing and puffing as she waddles forth in layers of heavy clothing, sweating profusely in the cool station.

"Might I be of assistance?" says a porter in an impeccable uniform, who has spotted them from a distance. He is pushing a wooden wheelchair.

"Ah! Yes, my good man. We are bound to Peterborough, on the 4:25, Platform 1. The slow train it is, but our pace of life. These steam horses are fast enough at any speed!"

"Well, just sets yourself down 'ere in this wheeled chair, madam, and we shall fly to the gate on time."

The old lady drops with a sigh into the wheelchair. It shudders, and instantly they are off.

Peterborough.

It is *directly* north of St. Neots. And the 4:25 is the slow train: that means it stops at nearly *every* village. Sherlock is desperate to be on it. Platform 1 is all the way back down the hall near where he entered. He follows the porter pushing the fat old lady and the skeletal husband who is hustling to keep up. Having to return the entire distance across the station is a good thing for Sherlock – he needs time to figure out how to get past Platform 1's inspector.

The boy arrives with ten minutes to spare. Observing from fifty feet away, he concocts a plan. The inspector is turned sideways, examining tickets, a brick wall facing him, an iron gate stretched across most of the gap behind him, leaving just a narrow passageway for travelers to squeeze through to the platforms. There is nothing for it. Sherlock will have to rush past in a crowd. He has something to work with already: the two men with the lady in the wheelchair will be a perfect diversion.

He surveys the crowd and looks for more. He spots a family approaching the gate. *They will do.* They are a good twenty feet in front of the wheelchair group. There are six of them. *Time to move.* Sherlock darts toward them and cuts in front of the father. Then he stops without warning, forcing the whole family to come to a sudden halt: they almost pile into him. He looks down to check if he's stepped in something and as he does, the wheelchair group catches up to the family. Now there are nine people, ten including Sherlock, bunched up near the gate. The father gives Holmes a stern look.

"Oh, my goodness!" says the boy. "Apologies, I am sure."

He bows, slides behind both groups . . . and immediately wonders if he's stepped in something else. So concerned is he that this time he bends down to examine a shoe as the others all turn to the inspector. Staying low, the boy slips through the opening, nine people and a wheelchair blocking the railway employee's view. It happens in a second.

Once he is safe on the other side, Sherlock can't resist a quick glance back. A round-faced child in a sailor suit, no more than five, the littlest member of the family and about the boy's height when he bent low, is glaring right at him. Holmes turns his head quickly and marches away.

He moves on the double, way down the train toward the third-class carriages, the only kind he can board. Otherwise, he would stick out like a pauper on Rotten Row.

The first-class coaches have compartments, each with its own door. The carriage he will ride has rows of wooden benches divided by a narrow aisle, and only two doors all told, one near each end. Both are open, awaiting boarding. He steps up into the train. It is almost full. And it's loud. He can smell body odor, horse manure, and the animal fats used to grease this long iron horse. He walks to the far end, finds an empty bench, dirty like all the others, and slides in. He moves over to the window and lowers his head, keeping a hand in his pocket as if he were holding his ticket.

It is such a relief to be safely onboard. It is incredible, really: he will succeed in getting from London to St. Neots, fifty miles, without paying. But as he sits breathing heavily, the magnitude of the chance he is taking begins to dawn on him. *What do they do to people who get caught without a fare?* Turn them over to the Peelers? He was put in a jail once, several months ago, after he became a suspect in the Whitechapel case. He can't let that happen now. His plans, his chance to save Victoria Rathbone, his hopes for the future, would all disappear. And then Sigerson Bell would likely throw him into the streets. He knows he should have thought of that before he acted so rashly; maybe he should have thought of many things. The old man will be waiting for him back at the shop as the sun descends, deeply concerned.

But the chance to get to St. Neots quickly is too alluring for Sherlock Holmes. He will deal with things as they come. Maybe he can return before morning.

The carriage sighs as a line of people enter: the family of six. The last is the round-faced child. He settles onto a bench next to his mother, on the aisle. As he does, he looks down the carriage . . . and spots Sherlock Holmes.

As the train eases out and heads north through the city and into the suburbs, the child doesn't take his eyes off the older boy, who scrunches down as low as he can in his seat and turns his head toward the window. But he can feel the little one's glare. All the way to Highbury, it follows him like the beam from a bull's-eye lantern. Sherlock turns his head farther, so he is almost looking backwards, and watches the many neighborhoods on the north side of London fade one after the other into the distance. They are packed with soot-stained brick warehouses, gray homes with black smoke spreading into the cool, foggy air, vanishing as quickly as they appear.

The train makes a stop. Sherlock holds his breath. He rubs his face and peeks through his fingers down the carriage toward his tiny enemy. The child is talking to his mother, tugging on her sleeve, pointing up the aisle . . . *right at him*. But she is engrossed in a conversation with her eldest daughter and angrily shushes him.

The child seems to give up. They chug out again. The dense population begins to ease. Soon Sherlock spots the construction site of the mighty new entertainment building in Alexandra Park, the Crystal Palace's new twin on the big hill at Muswell. That means they are truly out of the city. As an image of the Sydenham Palace flits through his thoughts, so does his poor father's face. Sadness engulfs him. *Focus on the task at hand.*

The locomotive whistles and groans; grime billows from it. They shoot through Cockfosters and in an instant, it seems, are in the countryside passing villages at breathtaking speed. This is just the second time Sherlock has been on a locomotive. They are likely exceeding forty-five miles an hour! He gapes out the window.

But his mind never leaves the other danger, standing now on his seat at the far end of the carriage, dressed in that sailor suit, with a finger up to the knuckle in his nose. The little boy leans forward, to dig even deeper. When he does, Sherlock sees something that makes his blood run cold.

Directly behind the child, a railway guard sits calmly reading a paper. *He must have boarded at the last stop.* Sherlock had been too busy looking away. All he can do now is pray that the boy never turns around, that the family is going past St. Neots and so is the railway employee, who perhaps lives farther north.

But then the little devil drops his sweet – a putrid-purple cane of hard sugar he'd worried a few times before turning to mine the contents of his nose. It drops to the floor. He looks at it, aghast, falls to his knees on the chugging wooden surface and seizes it in a pudgy fist. When he gets to his feet, he turns around, facing the guard.

No!

It is as if the child has expression in the back of his head . . . and that expression says "YES!" In an instant, he is tugging at the blue sleeve of the crisp uniform and pointing up the aisle again toward Sherlock Holmes.

Lip-reading is a skill that any detective must learn.

"He has no ticket, sir."

Chug-chug. Chug-chug. Chug-chug.

"Who?"

"Him, sir. That one with the black hair who is peeking at us. The one in the dirty suitcoat."

"Him?" The railway guard points.

"Yes, him."

Up gets the guard.

The train is still steaming forward at high speed.

The man pats the child on the head, as if to say "I'm sure you are incorrect, young passenger, but I will ask on your behalf, as a Great Northern Railway employee should." He fixes his eyes on Sherlock and steadies himself. Then he staggers down the aisle toward him.

No!

They are in a sealed rocket. There is no way out. But getting caught is unthinkable. The door at Sherlock's end of the carriage is several steps up the aisle from where he sits. Glancing around, he notices the opening to a round ventilation can in the ceiling, just slightly narrower than his shoulders. They line the roof every five feet or so.

Sherlock stands up.

The sign for Potter's Bar village flashes by.

There is no good reason to be on his feet. There is no water closet on this third-class carriage, no place to go for food. It gives away his crime. But he has to do something. What, he isn't sure. He edges along the bench toward the aisle.

The locomotive gives a heave and decelerates rapidly. The guard almost falls on his face. Sherlock slips into the aisle and races for the door. *Can someone actually survive a leap from a moving train?*

"You! Young lad!" shouts the guard, so loudly that everyone hears him above the engine chugs and clacking iron wheels.

Arriving at the door, Sherlock seizes the belt on the window and pulls it. The window falls open. He feels the cold air on his face.

"Don't do it, lad!" shouts the guard. He stops no more than six feet away.

The train rocks violently as its brakes squeal.

Sherlock looks outside. The ground is still a blur. He doubts he can struggle through the opening without the guard seizing him.

They must be about to enter Potters Bar. That's why they are slowing. It is still countryside out there. As Holmes hesitates, the guard takes a step toward him. The boy looks out again. He *can't* be caught.

He puts his hand through the open window, draws the bolt on the outside, and snaps the door open. Now the freezing air hits him like a gale.

The guard lunges.

Sherlock jumps.

❦

Ten minutes later he is still lying where he landed, but alive. He wouldn't be, if the train had not slowed before he leapt. Still, he's feeling sore all over as he lies in the tall grass, reluctant to move in case someone spots him. But he *must* get up. He rises and staggers about for a moment and then gets control of his legs. He knocks the dirt off his frock coat and carefully fixes his hair. There don't appear to be any broken bones. He can see Potters Bar just up ahead. No one is approaching. When he thinks of it, he figures that such a passenger as he isn't worth an investigation. The train will just move on from the village. He will simply be in the guard's report. He starts to walk. It is still many, many miles to St. Neots.

Sherlock avoids Potters Bar, makes a wide detour through a field, and then returns to the rail line on the village's north side. *Stick to the tracks*, he tells himself, *that's how to find your way*. He wonders if there is any chance there's another train on the Great Northern line this evening. Not likely. He shivers and wraps his coat tighter. He can see his breath in the dimming light.

He passes many farms and a village but it takes about an hour before he sees the lights of a substantial place in the oncoming dusk.

"Finally," he sighs as he slows his pace and steps up

onto the slippery black tracks. He holds his arms out from his sides to walk the rails like Blondin balances high above the crowds. But then he hears something in the distance behind him, growing louder. It is blowing and puffing, sounding its horn.

Another train. And it's coming right at him.

He jumps off the rails and starts to run. *This has to be the last locomotive going north tonight.* In seconds it is upon him, then flying past just yards away, screaming, fouling the air, the wind of its wake almost knocking him down.

He is pumping his arms now, running with everything he has. He *must* make it to the town before the train leaves – he cannot waste more precious time – the last carriage grows smaller out in front of him, and for an instant he feels like stopping.

Then the train begins slowing to enter the station.

Sherlock picks up his pace again, his long legs advancing as fast as he can make them go. He runs past the rear of the first buildings – a green grocer shop, a tobacconist's – his eyes never leaving the train coming to a halt in the station up ahead. He can see a few passengers disembarking, others heading for their carriages, a porter hastily pushing a barrow heaped with luggage. On he goes, his breathing growing heavier. The porter deposits his load; the passengers sit; two guards close the doors. The train will pull out immediately. He notices the guards signaling the conductor, turning their backs, returning to the stationmaster's office. Sherlock is straining with all he has, his arms whipping the crisp, coal-contaminated air.

He draws within one hundred yards . . . fifty. Iron fences line both sides of the tracks and the rails descend below the platforms. As he enters the station, the platforms are above his head. No one will look for someone running up the tracks to illegally board the train. Not at this last moment.

One of the guards turns to take a final look at the engine. A fireman is stoking it with coal. Smoke puffs out in rancid clouds and the locomotive begins to move, easing out of the station.

Sherlock sprints . . . and leaps up onto the platform in a single bound. He races past the rumbling luggage carriages and seizes a door in third class. The train jerks and speeds up. He hangs on, fumbles for the latch, and shoves out the bolt. The door swings open and he with it, clinging for dear life.

The guard turns back again, as if he senses that something has happened. He looks along the platform and through the windows of the receding carriages, but doesn't see anything. Then he notices that a door appears slightly open. *How is that possible?* It slams shut. He shakes his head, shrugs, and the train whistles away. When he gets to the office he sends a telegraph up the line, just in case.

Every face in the third-class carriage turns when the boy suddenly smashes through the door and lands inside on the fly. Sherlock offers his audience a weak smile. He pulls the belt and drops the door window down, reaches out, locks the bolt on the outside, and shoves the window back up. But when he turns again, all eyes are still on him.

"Stopped for tea," he says.

There are no seats available near the door, so he makes his way down the aisle until he comes to an empty bench. He slides in and slouches even lower this time. The train speeds up. Outside, the countryside is becoming black, lit dimly by occasional candles glowing in farmhouses.

A lady in a flower-patterned bonnet in the seat in front of him is talking to her young daughter.

"I will warn you here, child, don't look out when we passes St. Neots."

"Why, Mamma?"

"There's bad luck there, I've heard tell. We'll talk no more of it."

Sherlock also wants to ask why, but he must keep to himself. Really no need to know anyway: superstition is rife in the working classes.

A short distance farther up the line, at the Stevenage stop, the train idles for an extended period. They weren't this long at other places. There appears to be some activity in the supervisor's office too, which is in plain view through windows. Several train employees are conversing. Sherlock's foot thrums on the floor. *How will he get past the ticket inspector at the little St. Neots station?* He drops his gaze down and concentrates. It's just moments later that he feels the carriage moving.

Several passengers have boarded. Once the locomotive is moving at high speed again, he is curious to see who they may be. When he looks, it makes his heart pound. The railway guard, the *very* one who had tried to stop him from jumping off the first train, is standing in the aisle holding a telegram, examining the door at the other end of the carriage! The man must have disembarked at the Stevenage station, perhaps had some business there, and for some reason, has been asked to check the doors.

Sherlock sits bolt upright, actually lifts slightly out of his seat, staring at the guard in disbelief. He realizes his mistake too late, for the man turns to look down the carriage in the direction of the other door, and sees him. The guard's eyes bulge. Sherlock reads his lips clearly.

"You!"

This time the railway employee comes at him with great speed, stumbling forward, falling into passengers and benches, apologizing as he goes. If Sherlock is caught for *twice* illegally boarding a train, they will surely jail him.

That's where he'll be when the kidnappers murder Victoria Rathbone.

Holmes jumps to his feet.

He can't make it to the door this time. It is too far away. And besides, they can't be near a village yet. A leap will kill him. He glances up and notices the round opening to the ventilation can again, one of many that provide air to the stifling, smoky carriages on hot days. It is a good four feet up, a small circle narrower than his shoulders. Even Pierce, the little "snakesman" whom Malefactor employs for cracking houses, would have problems wriggling up through there. Certainly no grown man could make it. The boy recalls Pierce giving a demonstration to the Irregulars once, which he observed from a distance. "Sherlock," his mother used to laugh as she watched him get ready for bed, "you are the thinnest thing in London!"

The guard is within a few strides.

Sherlock jumps up onto the bench, then onto its back, his frame so long that his shoulders reach the ceiling. He shoves his hands up through the vent and slams open the steel cover. It rattles on the roof of the train.

"You can't go up there, lad!"

Passengers scream.

Sherlock grips the sharp rim of the ventilation can and pulls himself up. He can feel it cutting into his fingers. This will take not only arm strength but abdominal muscles.

"One! Two! Three! Four! . . ." Sigerson Bell often counts off their calisthenics in the laboratory. The old man does the exercises with the same verve that he insists the boy utilize. Sometimes with too much: flasks go smashing on the floor, pickled human organs end up hanging from their crude chandelier. "This shall be useful to you some day, my boy!"

Sherlock gets his head through the opening and the blast of air is alarming. In fact, it feels as though it will pull him out of the train and pitch him overboard. But he keeps drawing himself up, folding his shoulders inward, just like Pierce. Blood is trickling down his hands onto his wrists, but he ignores it. He sucks in his breath and yanks his torso upwards. The vent feels as though it will squeeze the life out of him, pressing on his ribcage as he holds his breath as deeply as he can. But he pulls hard and his torso literally pops out of the opening. He bends over the top of the rim onto the roof.

Then he feels the guard's hands gripping his ankles, pulling him downward! His thighs are held tightly together by the narrow opening, but Sherlock kicks a foot as hard as he can, feels it connect, hears a groan, and the man's hands release him.

Holmes gets his slim hips out, his legs, his boots . . . and lies flat on the curved roof, holding onto the ventilation can for dear life. The wind is incredible. It feels as though God himself is using all his strength to sweep him off the train. The skin on his face is rippling like putty. Sherlock looks down through the vent and sees the guard lying on top of a middle-aged widow, dressed in black. She is smiling; he isn't: he's glaring through the opening at the boy.

Holmes slams down the lid. The train rocks from side to side, jerking back and forth. He imagines what would happen if he were to fall off. Fractured bones from head to toes: a broken neck, a crushed skull. They would find his corpse limp some distance away. And if he were to be swept under the wheels, he would be severed in half.

The train chugs and he tries to keep his grip on the vent, wound into the tightest ball he can create, eyes protected from the cinders floating in the locomotive smoke by pressing his forehead to the roof. His arms are tiring, his fingers want to release. He wonders if the railway guard will open the door and try to climb up the ladder at the end of the carriage. Probably not. He will think the boy is done for . . . either in a gruesome fall or arrest at the next station.

The boy hangs on for what seems like an eternity. Just as he feels he cannot last any longer, the train starts to slow. *The next station!* It gives him an idea. The train heaves and slows again. The whistle sounds.

Sherlock lets go of the ventilation can.

The wind blows him down the slope of the roof toward the edge. Crying out, he spreads his fingers and flattens himself to the surface like a spider – and stops sliding. Then, ever so slowly, he inches his way toward the end of the carriage. Thank goodness it isn't far. The train keeps decelerating. He gets to the end, finds the top of the ladder with a foot, and descends.

When he reaches the bottom, he hears something to his right . . . and sees the railway guard coming around the corner, his boot tentatively groping out for a rung, his face contorted with fear as he tries to negotiate his way onto the same ladder. The train is still moving at a mighty speed. Holmes steps off the bottom rung and onto a ridge low on the carriage, cricks his neck around to see the passing countryside, spots a grassy field . . . and jumps.

Sherlock's arm is screaming. And it is pitch-black. He struck a rock soon after hitting the ground and then whirled around countless times until he came to a stop. Fortunately, he had kept his head tucked into his chest.

He is near Biggleswade village, the last stop before St. Neots. There is no need to hide here. Though the railway guard will be livid and the local constable may be called from his home for a search, that will likely be the extent of the inquiry on this cold, dark night. Sherlock can't see more than a few feet in front of his face; just a scattering of lights show dimly in the distance.

He crawls to his feet and begins to walk, clutching his throbbing arm, which aches at the elbow joint. St. Neots can't be more than an hour away. He takes a big detour around Biggleswade and keeps going. When he feels something dripping from his hands, he remembers the rim of the steel vent slicing into his fingers. He opens his coat and wipes little streaks of drying blood onto his waistcoat, then buttons up again. Later, he stumbles into a stream and cleans his hands as best he can.

But Sherlock stops before he's certain he is at his destination. He can't go on: the pain in his arm bothers him too much, and he doesn't want to be seen coming into the town in the middle of the night. Besides, fatigue is consuming him.

He steps over a stone fence within a football pitch or two of the first lights of the town. Shivering, he curls up and gets as close to the fence as he can. Lying there, he surveys the dark, starlit sky.

This harrowing trip will be worth it, he tells himself, if it saves a human being's life, if it secures his own future . . . if he gets to see defeat on Lestrade's face.

But it is dawning on him just how rash he's been. When he left London he was enraged and full of thoughts of vengeance, trying to do something very adult. Perhaps his actions today have proven his immaturity.

Why did he come here with so little evidence? It is against everything he believes a scientific detective should do. Where will he search in the morning? Will anyone speak to someone like him? Will the parish constable be called in to collar him and take him away? Even if the paper is made here, the culprits could have purchased it somewhere else. He was *far* too impetuous. It isn't smart to be so driven.

Sherlock examines himself. He is a mess. He had preened himself early this morning, like a monotoned peacock. Now, he isn't even presentable.

He twists around on the cold, damp ground like a stirring child in the womb. But finally, sleep begins to descend upon him, so he isn't sure whether it is a dream or not when he sees something eerie on a hill in the distance. It is a manor house, big, dark, and spooky on the horizon. Only a single, weak light shines from one part of its innards. He hears the frightened calls of animals, exotic beasts, crying and growling way off on its grounds. Or is it the wind? Then a shadow lurks up above it all, like a gigantic phantom against the moonlight, rising in the glow of a lamp that is being carried across the grounds, the light swinging back and forth as if someone were walking with it in the middle of the night. The phantom seems to snarl.

"A dream," he whispers to himself.

Then he drifts off.

Sherlock Holmes is surrounded when he awakes. A circle of little people are looking down at him. The sun is bright directly behind them in the cold, early morning and he can barely make them out. Their faceless heads are ringed with black lines, and their breaths hang in clouds.

"Is it real?" asks one.

"Course it's real, donkey-face, but it 'as a costume on, it does."

One of them pokes Sherlock with a stick. The boy decides he's had enough. He jumps to his feet, feeling pain in his arm and surprised to find his whole body aching. They all step back, five farm boys and a girl, all dirty, all wrapped in layers of heavy clothing, every one in bare feet. The fear in their faces betrays their readiness to run.

But Sherlock doesn't want that. Fortune has smiled upon him: this is the perfect greeting party. Adults would be a much bigger problem for a stranger. He straightens his clothes and combs down his hair with the palms of his hands.

"My name is Sherlock Holmes," he says with a winning smile.

"Told you 'e weren't real."

"And I am pleased to make your acquaintance."

"Why you wearin' them duds?" asks the girl, who is in a stained linen dress. Her greasy red curls escape from her soiled bonnet.

"I am from London."

"That explains it," whispers one boy.

"That's brilliant!" cries another.

"And I am lost. I would wager a bob that you lot are intelligent individuals and can point me in the direction I need to go."

"Where is it?"

"I beg your pardon?"

"The bob."

Sherlock needs to change his tactics. "What if I box your ears?" He takes a step forward and his coat falls open. They all backpeddle.

"To where do you need to find your way, sir?" asks the girl quickly.

"The paper mill at St. Neots."

"That ain't where it's at, sir, it's five miles on the other side o' town, in Little Paxton on the Great Ouse River. Just follow the banks. It flows right through the town."

"I wasn't really going to cuff any of you. You do know that, don't you?"

Sherlock doesn't want the local adults thinking that a London child-beater has entered the parish and needs to be pursued.

The little people stand still and don't respond. Most are staring at his open coat. There is silence for a moment. Finally, Sherlock turns and walks away. They watch him.

"What about that bob, you layabout?" inquires one of them after Sherlock has stepped over the fence and moved toward the road.

When he looks back, they are all running, laughing as they go. But one pivots and unloads a rotten apple at him. Well bowled, it passes within an inch of his face. *As bad as the Trafalgar Square Irregulars*, thinks Sherlock with a smile. He starts walking again, fixing his hair, working on making his clothes more presentable. That's when he notices that his jacket is undone and sees the blood stains on the dark waistcoat inside.

❦

St. Neots is the market town for the area, sitting in a gentle green valley through which the beautiful blue-silver river winds. Sherlock wants to be inconspicuous so he approaches the town cautiously and stops when he spots the first few clusters of buildings ahead, just over an old stone bridge. Beyond that, the road leads to a main square where the spire of an imposing old church with a clock tower looms above it. A few folks are moving about just where the narrow road, lined with shops, opens into the square. St. Neots is half deserted at this hour, and eerie.

Sherlock makes a wide turn and heads for the countryside. There, he marches quickly along a narrow, dirt road lined with a stump fence, a minute's walk to the west. Red and yellow leaves fall around him and others cling to the trees that hang out over this little artery. The valley rises far away on either side of him, and nearer, the river appears off to his right, flowing, just as the children said, through the center of town.

Soon he is past St. Neots and about a mile later comes to the small gathering that makes up the village of Little Paxton – a few humble homes, stables, and a church. The paper mill isn't hard to find. It is the only place of any size, evident farther up the river just beyond the buildings, its tall chimney of red brick pointing like a mighty lance high into the sky. Clouds are gathering, some dark and threatening.

Sherlock keeps moving at a good pace in the tall grass beside the river, but falters when he nears his target. It is long and intimidating, with several grimy mills stretching along the water, the biggest one a sort of warehouse three or four storeys high, above which that chimney ascends. He can actually hear the giant complex, rumbling as it makes paper, like some monster with a grumbling stomach.

The boy begins talking to himself.

I am obviously a stranger. I can't just walk into the mill and ask a detailed question about its products. I must have a convincing reason to be there.

He sits in the grass and hangs his worn leather boots over the riverbank, nearly dangling them into the water. Almost immediately, his eyelids descend and his mind drifts off. It's a bad habit, this ability to instantly slip away – sometimes he appears almost unconscious when he's deep in thought; "Dead to the world," his mother used to say. Such powers of concentration are only good if they bring results.

There is a sound behind him; something approaching on the run, brushing the tall grass. Sherlock bounds to his feet, setting them wide in a perfect Bellitsu stance.

But the approaching figure means him no harm. In fact, it is startled and cries out. She is terrified.

About forty-five, a mother of either six or seven, works with her hands, a papermaker, late for her job, beaten by her husband, loving eyes, susceptible to kindness.

He has examined the direction and speed she is going, her thick, rough hands, the number of dirty little ribbons with names pinned to her dress. One of them is black and larger than the others.

"My apologies," he says, offering a slight bow.

She looks into the distance toward the mill as if trying to decide if it is wiser to stay or flee. One of her eyes has been blackened. She shivers under a ragged woolen shawl on a cotton dress and strands of her auburn hair sweep across a once-pretty face.

"You are a stranger."

"And you, I am grieved to notice, are late."

She almost smiles, but then looks at him with concern.

"Are you a runaway?"

He cannot have this.

"No, mum," he blurts out. "I am . . . representing a stationer, from London . . . here to speak to your owner about his paper. . . . That's all."

"This ain't the usual way they do it."

Sherlock blanches.

"My . . . My governor is not a usual sort. . . . We are looking for a new papermaker. Will you take me into the mill? I have long legs and can walk quickly. Perhaps I might say it was I who delayed you?"

She smiles fully this time. But it doesn't last. "Had a spot of trouble at home," she says, touching her eye. Then she takes a longer look at him.

"My eldest wasn't much older than you. She is gone now."

"I'm sorry, mum."

"Thank you – that is kind of you to say. You are certain you have not run away? Your mother would be powerfully worried."

He feels an ache in his chest. But he dismisses that soft emotion the instant it arises. There is too much to do to waste time on it. Not sure that this woman believes him, he holds out his good arm to her to see if she will take it. To his relief, she does.

"I am certain," he says.

The noise from the water-powered turbines inside the mill fills the big building and makes it almost impossible to be heard. Long sheets of paper, looking like wide white ribbons, are forming between horizontal spools on huge iron machines that rise almost up to the ceiling. Dirty, burly men and several industrious women are at work. Somehow, despite the whirring clamor, they all look up when Sherlock and his companion enter. He is eyed suspiciously.

His companion, looking nervous, motions for the boy to follow her and they move toward an office with rows of glazed windows caked with grime, revealing only shadows within. She opens the door and they enter: the sounds from the mill are immediately muffled.

"Penny Hunt! Past seven, wench!" growls the fat foreman who whirls around in his chair, "I won't keep you on if – Who is this?"

"Sherrinford Bell," says Sherlock quickly, extending his hand. "I am a messenger from a stationer in London, and I am afraid that I have kept this lady from her duties. In short, her tardiness is entirely my fault."

The man's mouth is slightly open. Had his cigar not been sticking to his thick lower lip, it likely would have dropped on his greasy desk. He sits there, looking out of his moon-shaped face, the three rolls of fat under his chin matching in number the rolls pressing against the inside of his stained shirt. He has never seen or heard anything quite like this boy: dressed in a dirty frock coat and waistcoat, as tattered as a street Arab, yet speaking like a Cambridge University professor. He also thinks he saw a spot of blood on the boy's waistcoat when he extended his hand.

Not much past thirty, thinks Sherlock, *hands pudgy and soft, never worked with the paper machines.*

The foreman won't take the boy's hand. "What do you want?"

Penny slinks out the door.

"I would like to be the agent of the purchase of a large order of paper."

"Who do you represent?"

Sherlock has the name of Dupin's friend and gives it. The foreman offers no recognition.

"I hain't the boss anyways, can't make that decision."

"Then perhaps you can simply tell me something about your paper."

The foreman says nothing.

"We are looking for a certain kind which I believe you manufacture. It has a watermark with two faces upon it."

"All our watermarks is but three letters – large *S*, small *t*, large *N*. You are awfully young to come all this way representing a London stationer. How did you hurt your arm?"

Sherlock had winced when he raised it in greeting.

"Uh . . . I carry our materials every day, sir. Sometimes they are quite heavy. This arm takes the brunt of it . . . chronic aches."

"Is that a fact? Well, we hain't got the paper you want. . . . Perhaps I should send a man out to get the constable in town so you could explain your needs to him?"

The foreman stands, opens the door, and shouts a name.

Sherlock tries to get to the entrance, but the fat man blocks the way. Looking out into the mill, the boy can see who the foreman is calling: a big man with a dirty face, near-bald head, and blacksmith's arms; Penny stops him for a moment and whispers into his ear.

Moments later, the big man is ushering the boy along the river toward the town.

"I'm not takin' you to Constable Bradstreet," he says, "Penny 'unt says you is a good lad and you should just get on back to where you come from. I will figure an answer for Rumpleside. Mind, it isn't smart for low-dressed strangers to ask unusual questions in a small town."

Sherlock has failed miserably. And he has wasted a precious hour.

He examines the man. He's past fifty, has thin strands of white hair and big hands curled into the shape they assume as he works with the paper.

I wonder.

"Have you been at this job long, sir?"

"Since I were younger 'an you."

Sherlock is thinking about what Sigerson Bell said: that paper mills used to have more complicated watermarks than they do now. The flabby foreman was a young man, perhaps handed his job due to family connections – he hasn't been employed there for long.

"Have you ever seen a watermark bearing two faces at the mill?"

The man stops.

"'ow do you know that?"

"My employer . . . is a paper historian . . . knows all about the St. Neots mill and its famous past."

The man starts walking again.

"Well, 'e is absolutely correct."

Sherlock's heart leaps.

"There was a day when all our paper used to bear the

mark of the Fourdrinier Brothers. Pioneers in papermaking, they was."

"But all that paper is gone now?"

"Afraid it is, just three letters we 'ave these days, that's all you'll find on a St. Neot's sheet of paper. . . . 'old on, that ain't exactly right."

This time Sherlock stops.

"Used to be a man by the name of Muddle in Little Barford just south of town, who bought several dog carts full of our paper on the last day we made that watermark. I remember it well because it was such an unusual thing to do. 'e owned a little tobacconist shop on the main road. Said that paper was the best ever made and wouldn't 'ave any of the new. Stupid goat, it was the same. I wonder if that old crate is still alive."

Within an hour, Sherlock Holmes is at the tobacconist's shop in Little Barford. The old man is indeed very much in the land of the living. And more importantly, he appears harmless.

Inside, the shop looks like no one has purchased a thing since Shakespeare's days. The cracks in the plank floors are lined with dirt, cobwebs hang from much of the merchandise.

"You want WHAT?" shouts the wizened little owner in the long orange garment from behind his dusty counter. He places his tin hearing horn, which looks like a silver petunia, into an ear that is flowering with a mass of thick white hair. "Speak into the machine!"

Sherlock puts his lips right into the spout and loudly repeats his request for paper with a two-headed watermark.

"Fourdrinier brothers?" asks Muddle.

"The very one."

"Or two!" exclaims the old man, almost collapsing into a paroxysm of laughter. "You see, there are two Fourdrinier brothers!" He holds onto the counter in order to keep himself from falling backwards with mirth.

"Yes, I am aware of the source of the humor," says Sherlock.

"Speak! Into! The! Machine!"

The boy firmly grips the hearing aid again.

"Much call for it lately?"

"You haul for it bladely? That doesn't make any sense, my boy."

"MUCH . . . CALL . . . FOR . . . IT . . . LATELY!"

"You don't need to shout!"

Sherlock steps back from the counter, awaiting the answer.

"As a matter of fact, yes, I have had, as you say, call for it lately; but just lately. Had one sale of this marvelous paper in the past thirteen years. It came about two months ago. I believe the folks who bought it lived up there."

He motions over his shoulder and upwards with his thumb.

Sherlock's pulse quickens.

"Up where?" he asks.

But the old man can't hear. He has set down his hearing aid. The boy seizes it to bellow, but the owner snatches it back and waves him off.

"I am tired. My nap was to begin at precisely . . ." he fiddles around in his faded red waistcoat under the orange garment, searching six pockets until he finds his watch, ". . . three minutes and thirteen seconds ago. I never miss my forty winks, you know. Good day, sir. You may come back tomorrow."

He drops his hearing horn into a drawer in the counter and swiftly locks it.

At the very point of a sale, old Muddle walks away, heading for a door at the rear of the shop. It seems incredible. He trudges through the door and closes it behind him. The latch clicks. Still standing at the counter, the boy is frantic. The man was about to tell him who purchased the old paper: the *only* customers to buy it at the *only* place it has been available for the last thirteen years.

Sherlock considers following the old man and getting it out of him. But Muddle is in a locked room and his hearing aid is secured in the drawer.

The boy walks outside. He *cannot* wait until tomorrow.

Then he notices something up on the hill and thinks of where Muddle was standing at the counter, which direction his thumb pointed when he said, ". . . from those folks *up* there."

The shop owner had been motioning up the hill. Sherlock turns to it. Sitting there in the distance, looking down on the town like an enormous watchdog, is the manor house he had seen just as he fell asleep last night: the one with the lamplight swinging on its grounds, the one with the looming phantom shadow, with the eerie sounds rising in the darkness, the ghostly place he thought he had dreamed. He looks at again. It is real indeed. It appears bleak and abandoned: a haunted house on a hill.

Sherlock turns toward St. Neots and starts walking, careful not to allow anyone near, especially vigilant for the local constable. He has a dangerous day in front of him. Word will be out that a stranger is about. That foreman will be talking and saying he lied, that he seemed injured. Even worse, those children saw the blood on his waistcoat. The stains are fading into the graying black material now, but he buttons up his coat anyway. His stomach grumbles and he's cold. He must steal food, perhaps from the back of the baker's shop he's noticed at the edge of town, and drink from the river. It isn't right to steal, he knows, but murder is much worse. No matter what, he has to survive . . . until nightfall.

GRIMWOOD

I t is getting dark when Sherlock touches Penny's dress as she glides past on her way home from the mill. He's been hiding in the long grass by the river. Thankfully, she is alone, and the little cry she utters doesn't travel far. He is betting that he can trust her.

"I need some information."

"Master Bell, I must be off. My husband owns a pocket watch. I am expected home within ten minutes. I've promised the children a bonfire for Guy Fawkes Night, too. I *really* must be rushing. Rumpleside wouldn't give us the day off." She pauses. "I know you are a runaway. You need not play games with me; mothers know. You should get back home."

"My mother is dead."

Penny gently puts a hand on his shoulder. "I am grieved to hear that. But you must go home anyway, to your father or your siblings, whoever you can be with. I know about family troubles. . . . My daughter, the one your age I told you about . . . when I said she was gone what I meant was . . . she run off, too."

"I haven't run away, Mrs. Hunt, I promise you. Could we walk together? That wouldn't slow you down."

"I don't think that would be wise."

"Then please tell me what I need to know quickly."

"You sound desperate, Master Bell. What is this about? Truly."

Sherlock pauses. "I am not employed by a stationer, I will admit that. But I assure you I have good reason to be here."

"What reason is that then?"

"I am looking for someone."

She regards the anxious boy for a moment. "Someone from your family? Your father?"

"Yes. . . . My father."

"And you think he is here somewhere?"

"Who lives in the place on the hill?"

A flash of fear crosses her face. "The manor house? You shouldn't go there."

"Why?"

"It doesn't matter who or what you are after."

"Why shouldn't I go there?"

She looks around, then drops beside him in the tall grass. Sherlock recognizes the expression on her face, the one his mother used to give him whenever he came to her with a problem.

"Grimwood Hall has a history. No one from these parts ever darkens its grounds, let alone the buildings. Except them folks who is in it now."

"And who are they?"

"None of them is old enough to be who you are looking for."

"Who are they?"

"It's a young couple and the gentleman's brother. It cost little to rent, I suppose, maybe that was the attraction, maybe it was because they weren't from these parts, or perhaps they just don't care."

"About what?"

Penny glances fearfully up the valley in the direction of Grimwood Hall. When she speaks again, her voice is low.

"It was built long ago, only God knows how long. It housed many lords and ladies. Henry VIII stayed there shortly after one of his wives went to the chopping block. An early owner is said to have put holes in the walls and secret passageways everywhere, to spy on his guests. Then, two generations ago, a lord murdered his lady. Her headless body was found one night on the grounds. A horrific scream had been heard not long before. He was never even brought before the magistrates because he had friends here and in London. But his friends abandoned him afterwards. He lived alone up there for many years, had no visitors, and was kept company only by the strange animals he brought back from India in his earlier years. One night during a terrible thunderstorm, another scream was heard and the lord was never seen again, eaten, many think, by one of his beasts. People claim the animals still live on the grounds, behind those walls with the iron fence on top."

"No one knows that for sure?"

"No one goes near, Master Bell."

"But what about the three who live there now?"

"They came maybe three or four months ago, spent time in town at the outset, heard about Grimwood and made inquires, and then paid for their lodgings in cash. At least that's what's said. For the first few weeks they was often seen in town: at the public houses, the greengrocers, the tobacconist's in Little Barford, but then they started keeping to themselves. Those who dare to look for long up that way, say that the lights were only on in one part of the house for the first while, but then one began showing upstairs too."

The boy swallows.

"Thank you," he murmurs.

"They've only ever had one visitor that folks know of. The same man come three, maybe four times: reasonably well-to-do . . . stood very upright when he walked, some say he had a military bearing . . . but he wasn't dark-haired like you."

"Not who I am looking for, you think?"

She takes his hand. "You mustn't go there."

"Of course not."

"It's haunted if ever a house was."

"I am not superstitious . . ."

"If your father really is one of them, then find another way. Hide in the countryside near the village and see if they come down. They do go out on occasion, one at a time."

"I won't go there. I promise."

She has a mother's nose for a liar.

"What is your name? The truth, this time."

"Sherlock Holmes, my lady."

"Master Holmes, my daughter was a free spirit like you. She liked to play up near the manor as a youngster, though her father whipped her when she did. The day she disappeared, the blacksmith said he saw her walking up the hill toward Grimwood. It is my hope . . . that she just ran away."

"I am sure she will return."

"May God be with you, my child."

The distance to Grimwood from the town is much farther than he'd assumed. In fact, it seems like he walks for an hour and the mansion keeps moving away. Only a few minutes into his journey everything grows black; the terrain is wet and marshy, then rocky for a stretch, like a moor. Far below, down near the town, the citizens of St. Neots are setting bonfires to celebrate that day, long ago, when England was saved from the villainy of the rebel, Guy Fawkes. Ghoulish faces watch the flames, like sinister little circles sitting atop devils warming themselves in the underworld. The town is alight. But up here, Sherlock fumbles his way forward in nearly complete darkness, almost blind, starting each time he hears a distant shriek or a Roman candle explode with a crack in the night. He struggles forward and the sounds fade. Finally, he arrives. Soft lights from a few windows cast lambent beams into the darkness, giving him a dim sense of what is before him. A tall granite wall with a short iron fence on top surrounds the expansive lawns. Though it is difficult to be certain, when he stands on tiptoe and looks through the bars, he sees what appears to be a labyrinth of hedges, unkempt bushes, long grass, and forests of copper beeches and weeping willow trees, hanging down their manes like distressed giants on the sloping land. Sherlock cups his sore hands and blows on them.

Something roars inside the walls and the boy feels as if every little hair on his neck and down his spine stands up straight.

What, in God's name, was that?

It sounds exotic indeed, but before he can identify it, he hears other animals respond: growling like a pack of dogs, or even wolves. *Can that be the wind?*

Sherlock looks up at the bleak house stretching along the top of the hill. Webs of ivy grow across its surface.

Has he lost every last one of his marbles? Is he a lunatic? *Why doesn't he just turn around, sleep in a field near St. Neots, and steal back onto a train for London in the morning?*

But then the opportunity to change his life would vanish, Lestrade would win, and the girl would die. There is a solution to every crime, and he can pursue this one on these spooky grounds. He must find whatever courage he needs.

Looking up at the house, he sees something that makes him want to go on.

There are lights on the bottom floor, around to the south end of the building, but there, *right there*, a very dim one glows on an upper floor. *What* is up there? *The people living in this mansion rented a place that no one would dare near, bought the rare stationery that was used for the ransom*

note, and have kept to themselves the last few months. What . . .
or who . . . do they have up there?

He has to get into Grimwood Hall, whatever the cost.

He should have brought a weapon. The hand-to-hand combat of pugilism or Bellitsu wouldn't work against powerful beasts with fangs, against a lion or a tiger or whatever it is that is on the loose on the other side of this wall, but Sigerson Bell has been teaching him how to use a horsewhip in a lethal manner, and the Swiss art of stick-fighting too. The old apothecary has a large collection of heavy hickory poles and he and his protegé have shattered many windows and taken down numerous skeletons while practicing. Sherlock wishes he had one of those long weapons with him now. But he has no choice. He must go in unarmed.

At least he will have the advantage of being unexpected. No one in the house or on the grounds, either animal or human, is apt to be looking for an intruder. Grimwood Hall is protected by its gruesome legends and by what may lurk in the night.

And so he boldly scales the damp, mossy wall and the fence atop it, directly in front of the part of the manor where the lights are glowing. He drops onto the other side as silently as a panther, and moves forward on his hands and knees. It is like being in a jungle. He hears crows cawing and answering, making their mysterious sounds, deeper voices like ravens', and the jungle talk of parrots. There are whistles and shrieks from bigger voices. He begins to sweat despite the cold air. Twigs snap, leaves rustle, something snake-like slithers by and a creature laughs, the way a hyena might. Scurrying as fast as he can, Sherlock moves along the hedges, into the bushy labyrinth, under copper beeches and weeping willows, and finally, gets up and sprints through the twisting avenues of the maze. Instantly, he hears something following him, charging forward, gaining on him with every stride!

He doesn't dare look back as he moves in the direction of the house, racing through the green tunnels, getting closer. The dark, granite building has three storeys. The lights on the ground floor, now visible just above the hedges, appear to illuminate several rooms. The small, single glow above is two floors up: the highest storey, where the castle-like turrets loom. There is darkness in between.

Sherlock emerges from the labyrinth. Now only a stretch of tall grass separates him from the house. There's an entrance in the darkness to this side of the ground-floor lights. It's under an alcove with an ironwork fence in front.

He makes for it.

But he seems like a goner when he's still ten feet away. Summoning extra energy, he takes three bounds, of Spring-Heeled-Jack proportions, and leaps up onto the top of the fence. He scrambles over, but loses his grip and falls hard onto the cobblestones on the other side, right on his sore arm.

He doesn't care. He's inside the gate. *Safe.*

Sherlock looks back into the jungle. All is silent. Only the cold breeze wafts through the mist. He thinks he sees movement up in a tree, the glint of yellow eyes, but he isn't sure. In a blink they are gone.

Then there's a rustling in the undergrowth right near

the fence. A beast is about to appear, just a few feet in front of him!

"Meow," it says in a tiny voice.

A kitten, as white as snow, steps out of the jungle and marches through the fence. It walks up to his face, regards him, and licks his hawk nose. Then it turns and disappears into the tall grass again.

Before Sherlock can smile, something else attracts his attention. The sound of human voices: *inside*.

He gets to his feet and tiptoes over to the door. It is wooden and rounded at the top, thick as a chopping block, exactly like the castle entrances Sherlock always imagines when he reads the romantic tales of Sir Walter Scott. A big iron latch holds it shut. He tries the handle. *The door opens.*

Inside, a tall vestibule widens into a grand hall. Far away, on the other side of that long room, through an open door, Sherlock can see figures moving about in a smaller space. They are laughing and talking loudly: two men and a young woman.

"Tomorrow is our Lord's day . . . Lord Rathbone's day!"

"The day his daughter dies."

"Or . . . comes back to life!"

Their laughter bursts through the door and echoes in the great hall.

Sherlock feels a thrill go through him. He has to get closer. He slides from the vestibule into the hall, glides along the wood-paneled wall . . . and slams into something. The collision is loud. At least it seems so to him. But the conversation and laughter continue. Sherlock has caught what he ran into, which he now sees is a full suit of armor, with a helmet, sword, and spiked ball and chain.

He gently repositions the armor and moves cautiously toward the open door at the far end of the hall. On his way, he comes to an entrance on his left. It is an opening into a corridor that leads to the central part of the house. Way down at the far end of the passage, a staircase is dimly evident.

"A quarter-million pounds!"

"A mere trifle."

"All mine," cracks the young woman.

Though Sherlock is anxious to see their faces, he doesn't dare stick his head out from the wall. He can hear the clink of glasses; words sound slurred.

"Not quite all!"

"But in a sense . . ."

"Yes, in a sense . . . child."

Sherlock is hearing everything he needs to hear. Or is he? When he considers it, he realizes that they haven't actually said anything incriminating. Perhaps they are simply making light of what is on everyone's lips at the moment – the famous kidnapping. It is the biggest news in the land, on the front page of every paper. It is true that he also has the evidence provided by the watermarked paper, but that is not nearly enough. *Where is Victoria Rathbone?* That is what matters.

He keeps glancing down the corridor that leads away from the hall toward the staircase. Should he try to get closer to these three people or . . .

That staircase would take him one floor nearer to where the soft light is glowing from the upper-storey window. He is here ahead of Lestrade and Irene and Malefactor. He must be bold.

Sherlock slips from the hall and into the corridor. It grows dimmer as he nears the end and enters a big room where the staircase sits. It is magnificent: made of wood, its banisters elaborately carved, and wide like a platform at the bottom. He recognizes the images in its surface: they are all of Narcissus, a character from Greek mythology. Each one depicts an identical scene: a face staring at its own reflection in a pool. Sherlock looks up the staircase. It ascends into total darkness.

The trio of voices is still echoing in the house, but has become indistinct.

Up he goes, treading carefully on the creaking steps. When he reaches the next floor he can't see more than a few inches in front of his face. There is silence – the downstairs voices have entirely faded. He inches around on a landing until his foot bangs up against another step: the next staircase, leading up.

Sherlock ascends again and comes to a hallway. It seems to him that he is on the correct floor now and that the glow he'd seen outdoors came from a room off to his right. He turns that way, though there isn't any illumination down the passage. Feeling his way along, his heart begins to pound. This is a massive building. He could get lost in here. It may soon be difficult to find his way back; perhaps he should turn around.

No. It is time to strike.

He must walk blindly on until he finds that room.

But something else disturbs him. His mind has been so riveted on the presence of the three people downstairs and the upstairs light, that he has pushed the manor's eerie history to the back of his mind.

"It is haunted if ever a house was." That's what Penny said. Despite her class, she is a well-spoken woman and doesn't seem like the sort who is given to wild superstitions. Sherlock feels his stomach burning. *Such tales are nonsense,* he tells himself. In the end, she is just a poorly educated country woman. *Be like steel; use cold reason.*

He feels a sudden breeze blow across his face and through his clothes. The hallway is in the center of the house . . . without a single window.

A breeze?

Sherlock freezes. He is ashamed of himself, but he freezes. Then he thinks he might faint. He sticks out his arms to feel for the walls, to at least hold on to something. An object comes into in his hands. It is cold and round and severed from its base.

A human head.

Sherlock does everything he can to keep his scream inside his throat and releases the skull. It shatters on the floor.

A bust – likely made of porcelain. It must have been sitting on a pedestal.

There is silence again. The boy pushes the shards off to the side so they settle against the wall. He doubts the crash could have been heard two floors below in this huge house, but if anyone comes up here with a lantern, he wants the pieces well out of the way.

On he goes, feeling embarrassed, adamant about removing all those ridiculous haunted house ideas from his mind.

He proceeds in total darkness, edging along corridors, finding nothing. Finally, when he steps into another wall and realizes that he has come to the next *T* in the halls, he notices something that gives him hope.

He can see the passageway to his right. It is dim, but he can make out the walls, the outlines of dusty paintings, and a little hall table. There's light in this direction!

Sherlock moves quickly down that corridor. He can see the next *T* too, and the light is slightly brighter around that corner. He rushes to it, looks along the next hall and . . . spots a glowing line on the floor.

A door to a lighted room!

He treads silently up to it and puts his ear against its surface.

Nothing.

Then . . . the faint sound of someone sobbing . . . a girl.

He tries the latch, but it's locked. The girl gasps.

There aren't any knobs with keyholes to look through on these old doors, but as Sherlock had crept closer, he'd noticed two very slight vertical lines of light rising from the brighter one on the floor – the entrance isn't perfectly sealed. He presses his forehead against a crack and tries to peer into the room. At first he can't discern anything, so narrow is the sliver of light. But then he sees her. She is sitting at a table straight ahead, near a dark window, looking toward the door with what appears to be fear in her eyes. Behind her, through the window, little bits of light from the distant bonfires flicker like tiny sparks and then go out. Her strawberry blonde hair is done up, a necklace glows around her delicate neck – she looks weary and disheveled but high-born: the skin across her high cheekbones is as white as precious china. Sherlock remembers what the newspapers said Victoria Rathbone was wearing on the day of her abduction . . . the girl in the room is clothed in a fine scarlet dress.

He has solved it! He has solved this impenetrable mystery in a mere two days. The crime that all of Scotland Yard, all of England, is talking about, has been unlocked by his brilliant deductions. And *only* he, squatting at this door in this frightening manor house fifty miles north of the city, knows it.

Sherlock sits still for a moment, smiling. Andrew Doyle will give him whatever he wants, he can put his bullet into Lestrade, and he's saved two lives as well. Irene will think him a genius and have no need of Malefactor.

Then he hears a sound in the distance, yet within the building. It is growing louder with every second. *Someone is coming up the staircase.*

Sherlock springs to his feet. He has everything he needs. Now he must get out.

But the approaching person is already on his floor, moving rapidly, and will arrive in no time at all. Sherlock has lost his bearings. It is impossible to know which way to go to get back: he will be lost if he blindly stumbles away.

An idea comes to him. *Go in the direction of whoever is approaching. It will be the way out.* It is a reckless thought, but it makes sense.

The boy is shaking as he starts to move.

"I am doing the right thing. I am doing the right thing," he whispers. "Hide when the fiend nears."

The footsteps approach. The boy can see the corridor up ahead getting lighter. Whoever is out there has to have a lantern. Sherlock must calculate this perfectly: he must get as close as he can without giving himself away, then duck out of sight and let the villain pass.

He walks down the hallway and turns at the *T*. The light appears at the end of the passage and shoots straight toward him. Whoever is coming this way has arrived even sooner than he imagined, *too* soon! Sherlock has made a big mistake – and there is no time to retreat. The light is glowing on the floor a few yards in front of him and advancing rapidly.

He drops onto his stomach and rolls against a wall in the wide hallway.

The footsteps fall heavily on the old wooden floor. The boy hears a bass voice. It is a man, talking to himself. Sherlock peeks up. What he sees nearly makes him black out. *The advancing figure has no head.*

But when the man takes a few more steps and lowers the lantern a little so it isn't blocking Sherlock's view toward his upper torso, the boy realizes that a cranium is indeed appropriately fastened to his shoulders.

The man carries a scarf in his hand.

"One more day. Leave tonight. Get there by dawn. Captain's orders."

Sherlock tries to make himself part of the wall and flattens almost into it. He can hear rats scurrying inside the floor boards. He holds his breath.

The man comes closer. Three steps away . . . two . . . one . . . and walks past, still talking to himself. His light, and apparently his gaze, are cast straight ahead – he hadn't expected to see anyone on the floor in the hallway.

The boy sighs.

The man stops.

Sherlock doesn't know if the crook is looking around because he doesn't dare move, not even his eyeballs. The man sighs too.

"Ah, the headless woman again," he says with a chuckle and resumes his walk, down the corridor and around the corner in the direction of Victoria Rathbone.

Sherlock waits a long time before he gets to his feet. He hears the man come to the door, hears it open, and the distraught young girl say something.

Only then does he move, walking as quickly as he can without making a sound. He knows the way out now, follows the direction the man came from, descends the first staircase, the second, and then comes to the ground floor. As he slips through the great hall and heads back to the outside door, the voices of the other two kidnappers are clear in the far room.

"Rambunctious rebel rogues rule rotting royals from Rotten Row," says the woman. She is imitating the sound of an upper-class lady, rolling her *R*s. She sounds younger than she did when he last heard her speak.

Sherlock doesn't have time to listen. The evidence he has is sufficient, and he is beside himself with excitement.

But then he realizes that he's forgotten something.

He still has to get off the grounds.

Sherlock stands inside the barred gates at the alcove at Grimwood Hall, looking out into the jungle, wondering where the beast with the yellow eyes is, and *what* it is. Gifted with the sort of memory that can photograph things it has seen, he casts his mind back to his first passage across the grounds and considers his most direct route out.

A mist lies heavily over the dark lawns now. There's no sound or sign of the devil-animal. There is nothing to do but get on with it.

Sherlock scales the gate and drops noiselessly onto the overgrown grass. He crouches low and moves, slowly at first, across this first stretch toward the labyrinth, looking from side to side into the darkness, then entering the maze and going faster and faster. Soon he is sprinting, twisting and turning along the hedge-lined passages. He tells himself that he knows the route, moves by instinct, and when he emerges on the other side near a particularly large weeping willow, he thinks he has reached his destination . . . but there's no sign of the granite wall. In fact, he can barely see anything: it is too dark and murky.

But there *is* a sign of the beast.

That horrible growl; the shriek of a gargantuan cat in the night. It cuts the silence and actually drops him to his knees.

He must run. But to where? *Where?*

He rises and picks a direction: into the mist directly ahead. *The wall must be there.*

The instant he begins moving, the beast is after him again. It glides swiftly, but silently – a formless phantom. He can sense it gaining ground. In seconds it will be on him!

The wall materializes. It rises up so suddenly in the mist that he nearly runs into it. In a flash he is scaling it, clutching the ivy and moss, miraculously holding on and climbing to the top. When he gets over the iron rods, he pauses to look back. He can't see anything but mist. He peers into it. For an instant, he thinks he sees two glowing yellow eyes again, low to the ground, moving away, in the direction of the manor house.

It doesn't take him long to get down the hill and draw close to St. Neots. The bonfires have been put out – he passes mounds of burning embers, smoldering as if some terrible thing took place in the night. He crosses the old stone bridge this time, walks right into the town, and moves through the deserted square. The railway station isn't hard to find. He is trying to contain his excitement. What he experienced at Grimwood Hall seems like a dream. *Did he really see Victoria*

Rathbone, the girl all of England seeks, in that locked room?
He finds a wooden bench outside the station entrance where
he can try to sleep until the first train going south to London
arrives. The air is frigid, but Sherlock snuggles up, happily
hugging himself, and doesn't feel the cold.

The train will come soon after the morning light.
Sherlock has carefully considered how he will get onto it.
He has no choice but to travel by locomotive. Walking to
London would take him all day . . . by then the villains will
have murdered the girl. He is certain they will do it: there
was malice in their ransom note, almost as if they were
daring the wealthy lord to resist them so they could find
an excuse to commit their evil deed and show the nation's
most vigorous opponent of crime the power that the dangerous classes possess. Sherlock remembers their nefarious
conversation at Grimwood Hall, their excited talk of
tomorrow being a special day. Terror is as much their game
as kidnapping.

His plan for getting onto a carriage is simple, but
effective. At least, that's what he thinks.

With his mind racing, he takes a while to fall asleep
and then wakes at the first sound of activity in St. Neots:
shop owners moving about, opening shuttered windows,
setting out their wares. He makes himself scarce. There are
three old oak trees with thick trunks about a hundred yards
away, where the tracks run into the station. He slips among
them, thankful to be dressed in dark clothes.

Just as he hoped, the station is soon crowded – even
here in little St. Neot's, there are a great many folks preparing

to make their way into the city. This is their busiest time of day. Sherlock plans to enter the station in a crowd of passengers while the ticket inspector is busy, almost the same trick he tried at King's Cross Station: the boy knows it's a crude ruse and wishes he had a squad like the Irregulars to work with, so he could create what they call a fakement, a diversion, to turn the inspector's head away at just the right moment. But he is alone and doesn't have their skill. He pulls his collar up around his face and slips out from the trees. Instantly he knows he is in trouble. Unlike Londoners, the villagers have queued up in a neat line. Anyone trying to steal inside is going to be easy to spot. He needs a clump of passengers, bunched up, rushing, jostling, being *im*polite. Or . . . his *own* diversion.

The inspector is watching every approaching person, as if he were counting them. Is he on the lookout for a boy in a tattered black frock coat, streaks of blood on the waistcoat?

There is a lady in front of Sherlock and he can see a bulge in her pocket on the right side of her dress. He waits until the line is near the entrance. He racks his brains to remember all the subtleties of Malefactor's art of "dipping." But this will be more complicated than a simple pluck. He won't really take her coin purse, but has to make it seem that she has been robbed, and then slip through the line and past the inspector as she raises a hue and cry, as everyone turns to her. He either tries this, or all is lost. He slowly extends his hand toward her pocket.

Someone seizes him by the arm.

He turns in horror. He will be jailed, his life destroyed. He won't make it to London – the fiends at Grimwood Hall will do their sinister deed. No one here will believe a word a pickpocket says.

It's Penny Hunt . . . and a policeman.

"This is the boy, Constable Bradstreet."

"My . . . my arm still hurts, Mrs. Hunt. I was giving it a stretch."

It's all he can think of. But thankfully, they haven't noticed his intent.

"He wants getting home."

"Well, the sooner he's at it, the better."

"Master Holmes, I went to see this gentleman last night and told him that you had run away from your London family. It is best that you be moved along. He agreed to see you off."

"None of your tricks either, boy. Penny Hunt is a good woman. I watch out for her when I can. If she says you are a good lad, then I will believe it, though I have my suspicions. The children about these parts have encountered you, they have, and don't like the look of you. I shan't examine the inside of your frock coat, I just want you gone from St. Neots forthwith. The inspector will let you pass. You can disembark at Hornsey Station, north of the city. We knows the ticket man there. Word is being sent and he will let you by. Be off with you. And if I ever see you in these parts again, I shall place you in the stir and put you before the magistrates."

Bradstreet turns on his heels and walks away.

Penny stays with Sherlock while the line moves toward the entrance. She speaks softly and looks about.

"I'll tell you why I asked the constable to move you along: other police was here last night."

"Other police?"

"From London. And do you know where they made their visit? To the paper mill, not long after I left. Must have almost passed you and me by the river. A friend rapped on our door after supper and told me. It was the Force themselves at the mill, Master Holmes: three constables and a detective named Lestrade."

Sherlock is stunned. The old inspector isn't as dull as he looks. It took him a while, but he must have traced the paper, too.

"My friend heard them talking as they left, mumbling about bad clues and returning to London."

"They didn't go to Grimwood Hall . . . or Little Barford?"

"I don't know why you would ask that, Master Holmes, but no, they didn't. The foreman spoke to them himself, didn't allow any worker to even near them."

Sherlock smiles. Lestrade's trail is cold. It died in the paper mill.

"I don't like your smiling. Did you lie to me about your father, too?"

The boy wipes the look from his face.

"I came here for good reason, Mrs. Hunt, I promise you. I was looking for someone. And I think I found . . ."

"Who?" The color has risen in her cheeks.

Sherlock's voice drops to a whisper.

"I can't say anything more."

"Promise me it isn't you that the London police is after."

"No, Mrs. Hunt, it isn't. I promise you on my mother's grave. I only lied to you to do good."

"That is a queer idea, lad."

"I know."

"It is my understanding that the police didn't ask after you. But I thought it best that the constable move you out. He doesn't seem to have any interest in you – I counted on him just wanting a loiterer gone."

"I . . ."

"But I surely don't like you asking about Grimwood Hall, Master Holmes. I don't know why you wanted to go to there, or if you went, or how you got out alive if you did. It is fortunate for you that you reminds me of my eldest . . . who left us . . . stood up to her father, she did. . . . You have her look, Master Holmes, her stubborn look. Your mother, God bless her, would want me to get you away from here."

"Thank you."

As he starts to step away, she pulls him back.

"I know there is bad happenings about. And I know that you are mixed up in them. Let whatever your concern is be, child. Don't ever come back here. I pray the curse of Grimwood Hall hasn't touched you . . . like I fear it has touched my own."

The Hornsey Railway Station in North London is more than an hour's walk from Scotland Yard. Sherlock must speak to the police as soon as possible. The ransom note said the kidnappers would kill Victoria Rathbone before the sun sets today. Every minute that passes puts her in mortal danger. He will barely make it on time to save her, and that's if there are no delays.

He sits upright this time on his bench in the third-class carriage. There are so many things running through his mind. Not only does he need to get to the police on time, but he must find a way to immediately draw them out to Grimwood Hall without giving everything away. He simply can't tell them what he knows because Lestrade would leave him out of it, just as he did twice before. And he must bring witnesses other than the police who will acknowledge that he, Sherlock Holmes, solved this crime. That way, Mr. Doyle will know as well. Could Sherlock do what he did when he found the Brixton gang last summer? Insist that Scotland Yard bring the reporter from *The Times*? What if Hobbs is not available? And St. Neots is so far away.

More than three-quarters of an hour later, after steaming along without delays, the train pulls into the Hornsey Station. He still hasn't come up with a solution.

He has no choice but to disembark here. He cannot attempt to stay on the train, or leave and sneak back on, use any of the tricks he employed on the way north – the inspector here would be alert to him.

He is standing at the carriage door when the train stops. He steps down and races away, smelling the burning locomotive coal as he thuds along the wooden platform, past the inspector who gives him a nod, out of the iron-roofed station, making a beeline for Scotland Yard far away near the Thames. He is still trying to figure out what he should do when he gets there.

This race will be mostly downhill. North London is on a higher elevation than the city itself. He can see the metropolis spread out below and spots the river, the tiny dome of St. Paul's Cathedral, the smoke and fog lying in clouds. The population is in pockets in these suburbs, so Sherlock isn't being slowed by crowds. He can full-out sprint. His breathing grows louder and more labored as he rushes downward on a new foot pavement along a wide road on the edge of Hornsey Wood near an open area where a public park is being built, a beautiful place for Londoners to escape the stench and noise of urban life. But Sherlock doesn't even glance at it. He comes to the famous Seven Sisters Road, an artery he has never seen, but often read about – it has always sounded to him like a spooky spot where witches live, and it's true that people were once taken here and burned at the stake. Today it is nearly deserted.

By the time he sees the yellow-brown stone tower atop King's Cross Station, he is moving through heavy crowds. But he does well, gets past the busy area quickly, and heads farther south, through the narrower roadways in north-central London.

Bloomsbury nears.

That's when the boy makes his mistake.

The Doyles' house. It isn't time to talk to the philanthropist – he wouldn't be home at this hour anyway. It isn't that. It's Irene. *She wants Victoria Rathbone back, too. She has a stake in this.* He wonders if he should stop at her house and tell her everything, get her to help. She will be amazed at what he's done. Her Stepney boy can be saved.

Sherlock smiles. *Yes, this is the solution.* He should tell her. He can use her. Given that she is the daughter of a particularly respected gentleman, Lestrade would likely believe whatever she says. Her influence might be just what he needs to draw the Force to Grimwood Hall on the double. And *she* can get word to a newspaperman. She will be pleased to be involved. Irene Doyle may be the answer once again.

He reaches Montague Street and hurries along until he comes to her residence across from the British Museum. The Doyle place is three-and-a-half storeys high with a cream-colored ground floor and brown brick on the upper levels. Bright red flowers still bloom in the window boxes despite the increasingly cold nights.

Sherlock comes to a halt at the passageway that runs off the street to the little backyard. He knows it so well. His breathing begins to slow. He had lived in that yard in great fear in a dog's kennel after Irene helped him escape from jail during the Whitechapel investigation. He smiles for an instant when he thinks of John Stuart Mill, her gassy little dog. But sadness soon sweeps over him. In those days he and Irene had been friends . . . and his mother had been alive.

He hesitates. *Does this really make sense?* He vowed to exclude Irene from all of his endeavors, to thrust her from his life and thereby keep her safe. The correct way to proceed is emotionless: cold and calculating. *Find another way.* Perhaps he can simply shout his evidence in front of the policemen and any members of the public who might be at the station. There would then be many witnesses knowing that he, not Lestrade, had found Victoria Rathbone.

But what if there are only policemen there and every last crusher closes ranks like they've done before, saying that it was their boss and no one else who solved this complicated crime.

Irene is a better option. He would only need her for a brief time and then he could distance himself from her again. Perhaps her name can be kept out of this? The villains need never know that she was involved.

He walks down the alleyway, the argument in his head. Is he deceiving himself? Is he weakening? Will he put her in danger again? Does he merely want his friend back?

Happy voices come from behind the house.

He stops and peers around the corner.

Malefactor is in the Doyles' backyard. Irene is with him, sitting on a stone bench near the dog kennel, looking into the rogue's eyes, appearing charmed.

"I am thrilled," he hears her say.

John Stuart Mill barks and the instant he does, Sherlock is lying face-first on the cobblestones at the entrance to the yard, Grimsby sitting on top of him, Crew looming over them.

"Caught a bad guy, boss."

Irene and Malefactor get to their feet. She colors; he smiles. John Stuart Mill advances, whimpers, and smells Sherlock's face.

"Bring him here."

Sherlock thinks his bones may snap, so tight and nasty is the expert grip Grimsby puts him in, twisting his arms behind his back. But Holmes won't satisfy them with a grimace. He relaxes his face and smiles.

"Sherlock Holmes, I perceive."

"Irene, I want –"

She looks away.

"What you want isn't germane," growls his rival. "What you were doing sniveling around here is. You were spying on us."

Sherlock is in deep trouble. He can't talk to Irene now, knows it was ridiculous to come – he was being weak.

"Speak!"

Malefactor, to say nothing of his two idiot lieutenants, has appeared at precisely the wrong time. If Sherlock isn't out of here in minutes, doesn't devise a plan on his way to the Yard and get back to St. Neots this same day, Victoria Rathbone is dead.

"Maybe we should let him go," says Irene.

We?

"Not yet. Something you want to share with us, Holmes?"

An idea occurs to Sherlock. *Maybe there is*, he thinks. *Yes.* He should tell Irene whether Malefactor hears it or not. It's his only option if he wants to get to the Yard on time. Maybe telling his enemy what he's found isn't a bad idea after all. Perhaps it will impress him, somehow make him back off. And if Malefactor is intrigued, wants to show off, he might even be helpful – he knows the police like no one else.

Sherlock yanks himself away from Grimsby.

"I know where Victoria Rathbone is."

"But . . ." begins Irene.

"Please, Miss Doyle, let Master Holmes continue."

The young crime lord's expression is disturbing: he doesn't look angry; something more like amusement comes over his face. Off to the side, Grimsby and even Crew are laughing. Sherlock can't figure it out, but he goes on.

"I can convey the exact location to the police. I know where her kidnappers can be found and how many there are. There is no time to be lost."

Irene wants to speak, but Malefactor holds up his hand.

"A most intriguing tale. You have triumphed again."

Grimsby laughs out loud.

"Shut your gob, you boor."

Malefactor menaces the little goon with his walking stick and then turns to Sherlock with a smile. "You are in luck, sir. Lestrade, that moron, is about to speak to the journalists at this very hour. You shall have the entire press of London as your audience. I must admit that I have under-estimated you, Holmes. This will be an extraordinarily shameful moment for the Force and I shall enjoy it. Here is what I suggest: all five of us should make our way with alacrity to Scotland Yard. We shall even pay your way upon the omnibus, our lady here, of course, ensconced comfortably inside. At the police headquarters, we three shall make ourselves scarce. Miss Doyle's presence will ensure that you are not evicted from the crowd by the Force: no one can resist the desires of the fair daughter of Andrew C. Doyle. You can then speak up, Holmes, shout your solution for all to hear, loud and clear."

Irene has a pleading expression on her face as she glances at Malefactor. But he won't look back.

Sherlock is flabbergasted. Malefactor has come up with a similar, yet more effective plan than his own. The young villain has the means to execute it, too. *Why is he being so helpful? Just to shame the police?*

They find an omnibus on bustling Oxford Street, the four boys on the knifeboards up top, Irene in more genteel confines below. She won't look at Sherlock. He tries not to think of her and readies himself for the thrilling task ahead.

The scene at Scotland Yard is not what he expected.

Yes, a crowd is gathering in the square in the center of the Yard, dominated by men bearing pads and pencils, and standing in the same spot they gathered two days ago, but Lestrade is looking alarmingly pleased and so is his son. *How can that be?* They are running out of time. Lord Rathbone is there too . . . with a glow on his face. His perfectly groomed, graying whiskers are veritably shining.

What is going on?

Malefactor and his thugs spread out and vanish into the crowd. Irene stands next to Holmes, her head down, not even making a motion to escort him to the front.

The boy is growing uneasy, not sure if he wants to raise his voice to interrupt once Lestrade begins.

"Sherlock, I must tell you something. You know that Malefactor has ways of finding out things, people who can bring him news from even inside Scotland Yard. . . . Well, he came to see me this morning because . . . he had just found out that –"

"I am here this fine day," announces the senior detective loudly, "to revel with you in the solution of the case of the vanishing girl!"

"What?" gasps Sherlock out loud.

"Here she is! Safe and sound!"

An apparition appears before them on the little platform. *Victoria Rathbone!* She steps forward, smiling, tightly gripping her father's arm, leaning her pretty head on his shoulder.

"I'm sorry," says Irene, keeping her head down.

Sherlock scans the crowd. He spots three laughing young thugs in three different places. When he looks up to the podium again, he sees that Lestrade has noticed him, and is beaming.

"We have confounded the fiends," proclaims Rathbone to a cheer. "We have proved once and for all that one must never give way to villainy. When we find them, I shall have their heads!" The crowd roars.

When they find them? The kidnappers haven't been found? How can that be?

Lestrade steps forward again and puffs out his chest.

"Our tactics worked perfectly. After we consulted the public about this case, we received several helpful tips. A note came to us early this morning and through it we traced this dear child to the culprits' lair just hours ago. The cads, having somehow been warned of our approach, had only just vacated the premises. But we shall catch them! I assure you that we are on their trail!"

Another cheer goes up.

"As to the location, she was found . . ."

"In St. Neots," says Sherlock under his breath, "at Grimwood Hall."

". . . on our southern coast."

The boy nearly drops.

"A perfect place to keep her, mind," continues Lestrade, "where a sea-going getaway would be simple. But our knowledge of the workings of the criminal brain had caused us to suspect the region beforehand, and we already had elements of the Force in that area. The time between our gaining knowledge of her whereabouts and our arrival on the scene was barely more than an hour. A special locomotive has never moved so quickly!"

"Can you tell us where on the coast?" shouts Hobbs.

"The continuing pursuit of the villains prohibits that, sir. All shall be revealed when we have them in chains." Lestrade fixes another smile on Sherlock down in the crowd.

But Holmes has stopped watching. His shoulders droop as he moves out through the reporters. Irene follows.

"Sherlock, I'm . . ."

He picks up his pace and leaves her behind. A tear streaks down her cheek as he walks away from her.

"About my acquaintance with Victoria . . . I . . ." she says to herself.

He has failed; failed miserably. There can be no doubt. Lestrade has once again put the bullet into *him*.

He wonders for a moment if the police are lying about where they found her. But it wouldn't matter if they were. *They have her.* And why would they lie anyway? He thinks of his "evidence," considers it coolly and rationally for the first time, and it all begins to seem ridiculous. It shatters like that bust dropped on the hard floor at Grimwood Hall.

Old Muddle had merely said he *believed* the residents of the manor house purchased the stationery – and he was deaf and barely of sound mind. Even if they did purchase it, what did that really prove? And the locked door upstairs at Grimwood? He remembers now that he didn't locate the bolt. It was almost certainly locked from the *inside* . . . which means no one was keeping that girl captive – he had made absolutely unfounded deductions. She had obviously locked herself in and was crying about something else, maybe an argument with the other three. No one in their right mind should have assumed that *she* was the Rathbone heiress. He had been far too rash. The girl was barely visible in the dimness through that crack in the door and was sitting at the far end of a room. She likely didn't have the color of hair he thought or the dress or anything – he had *wanted* her to be his catch. Whomever he saw at St. Neots wasn't who he assumed she was.

Perhaps he saw a ghost in that haunted house . . . because he had just observed Victoria Rathbone in London. She was standing there in full public view, in the flesh, right beside her own father and a gloating Inspector Lestrade.

PART TWO

ROBBERY

Feeling ashamed and weak, Sherlock wants to go home. All his plans seem pie-in-the-sky now, far too adult for a boy his age. A detective? Sherlock Holmes? What he really needs, as Penny Hunt said, is his family. But where is home now? Is it the apothecary shop from which he has been away without permission for nearly two days? Will Sigerson Bell take him back? His dear mother is dead, his little sister too, his much older brother employed and distant, and his father . . . could Sherlock go south to the Crystal Palace and talk to Wilberforce Holmes? He needs his wisdom and love. But it is difficult for his father to even look at him now. Wilber will always be reminded of the death of his wife when he sees his son. Sherlock doesn't want to put his father through that. The boy knows he has done all of this to himself: this is where his selfish pursuit of glory, his pride, has taken him.

He holds back his tears as he trudges toward Denmark Street. He can't see Irene, he's wary of Malefactor and his gang . . . he is all alone.

Or is he?

The apothecary has been like a father to him before. Perhaps, if he is contrite, the old man will accept his apology. Baring his soul, telling Bell exactly what happened would be difficult, but maybe it is what he has to do. He approaches the latticed bow windows of the little shop with his mind made up.

There's an awful sound coming from the laboratory at the back when he arrives. But it isn't one of those terrible explosions he has often heard, the result of Bell's inventive and reckless mixing and heating of chemicals, that have variously: shaken the building, left slime on the walls, shattered glass, and singed the septuagenarian's bushy white eyebrows clean off. Neither is it a gunshot, which the boy has occasionally heard in the shop too. . . . The alchemist sometimes empties his firearms indoors, picking off various ribs or even the eye sockets of his hanging skeletons.

No, it is music . . . or so Bell thinks.

He is sitting in his favorite basket chair holding his old Stradivarius violin in that awkward, gypsy-styled manner of his: low on a knee. His face is red, sweat pours down his substantial dome onto his forehead, and he is humming at the top of his lungs. Every now and then he stops playing and conducts, flailing his bow through the air. It isn't that the music is being played so badly: Bell is as strangely gifted a violinist as he is at many other eccentric pursuits. But his sense of invention on the instrument, which goads him into experimenting with all sorts of pieces, new and old, results in admixtures of music at least as bizarre as his dangerous chemical concoctions. It is an alchemy of sounds, resulting in a jarring alloy.

Sherlock doesn't mind. This is his mother's favorite instrument.

Sigerson Bell doesn't hear the boy enter, so when he looks up and sees him, he is so startled that he flings the bow across the room.

"Excuse me, Master Holmes," he apologizes, scurrying, bent-over in his question-mark shape, to retrieve the implement from the porcelain sink where it has landed.

Then he stops in his tracks.

"YOU!" he says loudly, pivoting with stunning quickness and pointing a crooked finger at the boy, "You are two days late for your work! Where have you been?"

He has never sounded so angry. Has the ancient apothecary run out of patience after all? Is the apprentice about to be sent back to the streets? While Sherlock was away, he had barely given a thought to the fact that he hadn't told his old friend where he'd gone and that he'd missed school. All he had considered were his own goals.

"My deepest apologies, sir," says the boy. And he means it.

Sigerson Bell has a heart as soft as a marshmallow. It is especially squishy when it comes to Sherlock Holmes. He admires the boy's brains and integrity, though he worries about his inwardness and the sadness he doesn't seem able to shake.

"Solipsistic, that's you," says the apothecary, clearing his high-pitched voice. "Look up that word in Dr. Johnson's dictionary some day, my boy. *Solipsistic!*"

"Mr. Bell, I will understand if you –"

"Well, well," declares the old man, "no need to wallow in past disappointments, get right down into the mud, the . . . cow dung of regrets . . . are you well, young man?"

"I have something to tell you."

Bell smiles in spite of himself. He motions for Sherlock to take a stool at the long lab table and sits on one by his side. He is "all ears" at this moment, bending one of his elephantine lugs in the boy's direction.

Sherlock tells him almost everything. He includes the way he feels: how, against his better judgment, he tried to investigate the Rathbone kidnapping, what Inspector Lestrade said about him in public, and how desperately he wanted to defeat and shame him; how he hoped to blunt the plans of the devious criminals who did this, members of a class of humanity he hates. He doesn't mention what Mr. Doyle might have done for him because that dream is gone, and he forgets about the little boy in the workhouse.

"Well, first of all, one must pursue things for the right reasons," says the old man after a lengthy pause. "And secondly . . . you know, you know very well, that I am an alchemist as well as an apothecary. That doesn't simply mean that I embrace the ancient dark arts of the sciences, that I believe I shall one day make gold from another substance. It also means that I am a disciple of the philosophy of the alchemist, which is to say that I believe one can turn *life* into gold."

Sherlock smiles.

"I embrace, I veritably hug and cuddle, the concept of optimism. It is at the core of my approach to my existence. I shall give you an example. Fetch me my stick."

Sherlock retrieves the Swiss fighting stick, a long, thick pole with the belting power of a stallion's kick, one of two leaning against a wall beside the water closet, resting where it was left after Bell's last lesson in clubbing an opponent.

"Strike me!!"

Sherlock doesn't hesitate. The apothecary has taught him the importance of the tactic of surprise: get off a blow when least expected. He has also taught him to never hold back. The boy expects Bell to show him some sort of unanticipated defensive move, something that will act as a metaphor for his ideas about optimism.

But the old man just stands there and Sherlock's strike, delivered smartly, makes a cracking sound like a pistol going off as the stick connects with Bell's forehead. It echoes all the way out to the shop's front room . . . and likely into the street. The ancient apothecary goes down like he has been axed.

For an instant, Sherlock can't see Sigerson Bell. Then he hears a weak voice on the floor.

"I shall be better shortly."

Though it takes the boy several hours to truly bring the old man around (a shot of laudanum is found to be most helpful), he is, indeed, eventually better. "One can rise from any blow," he finally squeaks. That, in short, was his message, built upon a sacrifice he offered up for his apprentice.

❦

With the old man moaning in his room upstairs, Sherlock goes to his little bed in the laboratory wardrobe thinking about this lesson in the school of hard knocks. The boy knows that Bell has more to say to him and looks forward to the encouragement he will offer. He hopes it is enough.

Holmes has come to understand that his is a moody disposition. The occasions when he drops into terrible bouts of sadness – recalling his mother and how he caused her death, or thinking about everyday activities and wondering where stimulation will come from next – seem to be increasing in frequency. For some reason, much of life bores him. Most of it is what he remembers the writer Shakespeare calling *diurnal*, just day-to-day, humdrum existence. Sherlock can't abide that, never could. His big brain, his big ambition, needs constant excitement. Life must either be filled with challenges and thrills or . . . he doesn't want to participate at all.

But tonight, a glorious dream comes to him. At least it is wonderful when it begins.

He is twenty-seven years old. He has found a way to achieve his plans. He is a detective unlike any the world has ever known, and everyone is aware of it. He is impeccably dressed, well groomed, and brilliant; a black-and-white peacock that London admires. The city is at his feet, Lestrade Junior his devoted supporter, the police are his begrudging acolytes. No problem is beyond his considerable gifts of deduction and he thirsts every day for more; his methods are unique and irregular. Criminals fear his very name; justice results from his intercessions; Malefactor has been vanquished; Irene is . . . barely visible. She appears every now and then, looking beautiful, but much different. He can never see her clearly. He realizes too, with a start, that he is still unhappy, and wakes in a sweat.

🐻

"I am fully recovered, my boy," croaks Bell in the morning, as the flames in the fireplace struggle to catch. The two friends huddle over their breakfast of asparagus and brown sugar spread on a thick slice of bread. The old man sports a goose egg the size of a small orange on his forehead. But there is a smile on his lips.

"This is what you must do, Master Sherlock Holmes. You must move forward immediately. You must return to your studies, fighting lessons, our chemical investigations, your work around the shop . . . and perhaps some violin lessons?"

Sherlock smiles and nods.

"And we shall continue to read, read, read, read, read." The old man nods toward the teetering books that surround them and then winces.

"That shall not only take your mind from your brief stumble, but increase your powers. You must always be increasing your powers . . . looking for gold, doing it for the right reasons. That attitude shall get you where you want to go. Life is about growth. Let's remind ourselves again to be patient, my boy, never rash: meticulously build yourself into what you want to be."

They eat silently for a few moments, Sherlock vowing to himself that he will work with even more dedication than before. He will do all that the apothecary says, attend school every day, too, and make sure his grades keep heading all the forms.

"And we will continue to scan the papers!" shouts the old man, smiling like he has a secret. He says nothing again for a while and eats in his characteristic way: with his maw gaping wide open, the green-brown oily goop of the asparagus and sugar evident on his darting tongue and hanging in drips inside his mouth. But he can't keep quiet for long: the twinkle in his eye is betraying something. "And I . . . I shall have you ask a news agent this morning," he finally blurts out, "to arrange for both *The Illustrated Police News* and *The News of the World* to be delivered to my door, or you may pick them up from Dupin himself at Trafalgar Square!"

Sherlock's heart soars. His scandal sheets! He is back on the job. He can at least search for another case, a perfect one. He is ready, again, for anything.

But the crime he will soon discover stuns even him.

Three days later, in the East End, the windowless exterior of the Stepney Workhouse looks darker than usual in the cold rain. It towers, like the wall of a fortress, over the hansom cab that pulls up to its front doors, the hooves of the black horse clapping on the cobblestones. Inside the two-wheeler sits a large, well-dressed man and his beautiful daughter. He takes his hat from the rack and rises to back out, so he will be in a position to help the girl down after he lands.

"Wait," says Irene, pulling him back to her side. "I can't go in."

Andrew Doyle sighs and eases back onto the cushioned seat. "I doubt I can face him, either."

"I don't understand why Miss Rathbone won't see me. It's been three days. You would think she would be overjoyed to be home and safe, and anxious to speak to others. Instead, she seems to be in seclusion!"

"She is just overwhelmed, I'm sure. I will seek an interview with her father again tomorrow."

"He saw you the moment you sent your card last time."

"Let us see what tomorrow brings."

"I fear more of the same. . . . little Paul can't go on if he is blind."

"Be strong, my son."

Doyle's error is out before he can stop it. He grimaces – he's made this slip before. "My dear sweet *girl*," he adds quickly.

Irene forces a smile, and then takes her father's walking stick and raps it against the roof.

"Driver! Home to Montague Street," she says sharply.

Inside the workhouse at that moment, Paul is making a mistake. He steps from his little room into the hallway to meet the folks who are to see him. He is clutching his most prized (his *only*) possession under his arm. Usually, he hides it in the thin blanket on his bed. But he wants it near him today for good luck. Two dirty, burly boys approach, their gray, sack-cloth uniforms adorned by greasy chokers tied in similar bows at their necks and tattered caps cocked at devilish angles on their heads.

"Why if it ain't Captain Paul out for a stroll. A rare thing it is! Down to Rotten Row?" cracks one.

"Paul . . . Dimly!"

The little one doesn't look up. He can barely see them anyway. He edges forward.

"What's that you got, Captain?"

He ignores them.

"I do believe I knows what it is. Let's 'ave a look at it."

The bigger of the two kicks the little boy in the stomach, making him release the hat, which the other expertly snatches. As Paul drops to the floor, trying to get his breath, they toss it back and forth.

"Paul Dimly's dad 'ad military might."

"But 'e dumped 'is son without a fight!"

Paul rises. His face is beet red.

"Come and get it, dwarf."

"Dimly dimly dimly dimly dimly."

Paul lowers his head and charges, intending to butt the other boy's midsection like a battering ram. But the bigger one simply reaches out and seizes him by the hair. The little bull then becomes a tiger. Reaching up, he digs his filthy nails into a cheek and rakes them across the skin, drawing blood and a curdling howl. The hat drops to the floor.

There are footsteps coming up the stairs. They fall faster and a young man in a clean but modest suit appears, rushing onto the floor.

"Paul?"

The three boys turn and the man instantly understands what has happened. He's seen this before.

The bullies run off.

"You mustn't let them get your goat," says the young medical student. "Now we see through a glass, darkly; but then, face-to-face. . . . God will look after you."

The little boy says nothing. He simply picks up his hat and holds it tightly to his thin chest. He keeps looking down.

"I am sorry to say that the Doyles don't seem to be coming. They must have a pressing engagement elsewhere. But you and I shall have a visit, just the two of us again. I shall have you in my school next year, you know, whether those peepers are working well or not. I promise. . . . May I see your hat today?"

The boy holds it tighter to his chest.

"It is a captain's hat, is it not? A fine one, I must say."

"My father," says the boy.

"Yes. Yes, I know. Your father's."

"My father."

"I believe you, Paul. . . . Now, we must take your pulse and check those eyes."

When the news comes on another cold morning three weeks later, Sherlock doesn't have to search the papers. It is there on the front page of each and every one. Friday, November 29, 1867:

LORD RATHBONE ROBBED!

And it wasn't a little job. The thieves didn't take a vase or two, or even a stack of bank notes from a safe. They cleaned him out. The Rathbones' fashionable home in Belgravia was stripped of *all* its greatest valuables.

The *Daily Telegraph*:

> Police estimate that the nobleman may have been relieved of precious items, paintings, and assets numbering close to a quarter-million pounds, perhaps the most lucrative getaway in the annals of English crime. Inspector Lestrade was not available for comment.

"Take my hand, lad!" shouts Sigerson Bell, and he and Sherlock Holmes dance around the lab, performing a sort of Highland fling in duet, the old man kicking his legs clean above his head.

"I dance not due to the misfortunes of the eminent Rathbone family, for whom I am sorely grieved. One cannot but feel distraught for snobs who are rich beyond their merit . . . and are relieved of their baubles!" Bell performs a little jig. "I dance for *you*, my knight. You, who can entertain your brain with this!"

The news is indeed a stunning turn of events. What are the chances that one man could suffer such indignities twice in the same year? Perhaps the crime world has had enough of Lord Rathbone and is fighting back. Perhaps these two crimes are connected. Sherlock unlocks himself from Bell's grip and sits down to read on, buoyed by the possibility of having a second opportunity at a crime attached to the Rathbone family. It almost feels like a reprieve. He couldn't solve the first case, but perhaps he can shed some light on the second. What if he could beat Lestrade just when the detective thinks he has him down? What if he could steal back the thunder Scotland Yard gained just weeks ago . . . and humiliate his persecutor?

He turns to *The News of the World*:

The thieves struck at precisely the opportune moment. The Rathbones, overjoyed at the recovery of their child, had retired to their country home and taken almost every servant with them. Even the groom and footmen had been withdrawn. The hooded villains bound and gagged

the two housemaids who had been left behind
and went through the home, making quick work
of their job. Only Lady Rathbone's bedroom was
left untouched. Carriages or carts of an undeter-
mined kind and number were loaded near the
stables at the rear of the home. It wasn't until the
following day that a passerby noticed one of the
maids banging her head against a window and
notified the Force. Inspector Lestrade was not
available for comment.

Sherlock wants to get up and dance again, but a voice
inside nails him to his stool. *What is he thinking?* Has he
learned nothing? He is entertaining ideas he has no right to
consider. This is what caused him to make a fool of himself
at St. Neots, got him captured by the Brixton gang, put
Irene in danger, and killed his mother. It isn't for him to
solve this crime.

But . . . can't he just investigate a little from a distance?
Discover a few points the police might not observe? Make a
few deductions to see if they turn out to be accurate? Across
the burn-streaked, chemical-stained lab table, the old
apothecary, still breathing hard, is holding up his copy of the
Telegraph and pretending to be engrossed in another section.

"Were I a medium upon the stage reading the synapses
of your brain, I would divine that you shall be requesting the
morning off," he says into the pages. "It is a Friday anyway.
Look into this, *mon garçon*! Just keep your distance!"

Moments later, Bell is pacing like an aging robin on a

worm-filled ground as Sherlock fixes himself in the mirror and puts on his tattered frock coat.

"Anything in particular stand out for you in the reports, my boy?"

"Lady Rathbone's room was left untouched."

"Precisely! Ah, this is like the beginning of a diagnosis!" The apothecary takes several more bobs. "And where do you start?"

"At the crime scene."

Sherlock turns to go. Bell is given to talking to himself even when others are in a room. Before Sherlock reaches the out-of-doors, he hears the old wizard say in a voice chocked with emotion:

"I cannot wait to find out who did it! Go to it, my boy! For England!" Then there is a pause. "Calm yourself, Sigerson. Calm yourself!"

Holmes doesn't see Irene Doyle standing near the door as he walks out. She is wearing a heavy pink coat and bonnet, but is shivering, and trying to decide whether or not to enter.

"Sherlock!"

Every time he sees her, he feels as though he will immediately give in to her and allow her back into his life. Today, it is tempting indeed. It isn't just the way she looks – the milk-white skin pinched with red by the cold air, the magnificent blonde hair cascading out from her hat, and the style with which she holds her rose-colored umbrella over her slim shoulder. The expression in her large brown eyes draws him too – she looks distraught.

"*Let us be friends again,*" he says to her . . . but only inside his head.

His silence makes her tentative.

"Have you read the papers?" she asks.

"Yes."

"What do you make of it?"

Be like steel.

"What you or I make of it doesn't matter. This is for the police to sort out. There are heinous fiends about in this city, doing terrible things every day. It is best we stay clear of them. *All* of them. This is a new case and Victoria Rathbone is not part of it, so it is no longer your worry. She is as safe as houses. I am sure the family has done what they can for your workhouse boy."

He is expecting Irene's umbrella to come down on his head again and has measured the distance he must keep from her. But she surprises him. She doesn't become angry. Her eyes are filling with tears.

"The Rathbones won't speak to us. And this crime will make things worse. We are powerless: we still can't help my bro . . . that little boy."

She is so upset that Sherlock is again in grave danger of giving in. He straightens himself.

"My father feels strongly about this," she says.

"As strongly as he did before?"

"Yes."

Holmes does all he can to hide the thrill that goes through him.

"You could gain as much as before," she says, and reaches out to take his hand. But he steps back. Her expression turns to a glare and she wipes her cheeks.

"Perhaps I *will* join forces with my *other* friend then. I didn't when Miss Rathbone was kidnapped. I held off. But I doubt I can wait this time. He may know who did this, and might tell me . . . so I can deliver the news to Inspector Lestrade. At the very least, I am guessing that my friend would consider helping me."

The words are spit out.

"Should you be referring to a certain blackguard who roams the streets at night with a group of ne'er-do-wells who prey upon the London populace, I would advise against it. I could produce these villains before he or Lestrade were even on their trail."

"I am helping Master Malefactor to . . ."

"He is a thug and he shall remain one."

"I can change him."

"And we shall all fly to the moon one day."

"He understands misery. He knows the sort of pain people endure in the workhouses."

"Really?"

"You don't know him, Sherlock. His life fell apart when he was small. His father's railway investments collapsed after they left Ireland and came to England – they lost everything. His family went to an almshouse in Liverpool.

His education ended. His parents died . . . and so did his little sister. She'd held them together through everything. All he has left is his father's coat . . . and his memories of her. He's angry and bitter about life, but he can change."

"A story meant for the pages of the agony columns, I'm sure. I prefer Samuel Smiles and instructive novels . . . where folks rise from their troubles, where they choose the right path, not evil. He is a *rat*. And he tried to kill me." He turns from her and marches away.

"I shall show you!" she shouts after him. But she looks undecided.

Sherlock dodges tradesmen on narrow Denmark Street, his jaw set tightly.

❦

Andrew Doyle will still give me what I need. The instant she told him that, his mind sped up. By the time he nears Trafalgar Square, it is racing. And he can't slow it down. The game is afoot!

Scotland Yard first, he figures, *then to the scene.* He needs more than facts now.

It isn't a police file that he wants to investigate – it's something inside a particular detective's brain, in the skull cavity of a chap named Lestrade. He plans to march right up to him and ask directly.

At Trafalgar Square he glances west toward The Mall, the beautiful, tree-lined pedestrian lanes that border St. James's

Park and lead to Buckingham Palace. Ladies and gentlemen are strolling on the grass avenues and governesses walk with children, all pursued, from time to time, by street vendors. He has read in the papers that the queen is in London – the flag is out atop the palace in the distance. The green squares and beautiful residences of Belgravia are on the other side of her magnificent home. He'll speak to Lestrade and then make his way there to the Rathbone mansion, even if it is watched by a hundred policemen.

White Hall Street runs south from Trafalgar Square. He turns onto it. Wide and impressive, it is lined with regal government buildings. Soldiers in spotless red tunics ride horses outside the Roman columns of the Admiralty directly across from the Yard. Sherlock slips down a passageway between the police buildings and finds the black, stone exterior of the detectives' office.

The same sour-faced, grandly mustached sergeant he'd encountered in the summer when he rushed in here flushed and on the trail of the Brixton gang, is standing behind the desk in the damp stone office. When he looks up to see the boy, there are no signs of recognition. "Observation is the elementary skill of the scientist and the primary talent of life," his father used to say. Obviously, the rank and file of the London Metropolitan Police were never taught such things.

"I would like to speak with Mr. G. Lestrade."

"*G?*"

"Yes, the junior."

"I shall see if he is present."

A bored looking Peeler sitting on a worn wooden bench that creaks each time he adjusts his position is coaxed into rising and dispatched. Moments later the younger Lestrade approaches from the hallway.

Sherlock has been observing this boy for several months: beady-eyed and not very tall, fuzz on his face, brown tweed suits of a distinctly adult cut, anxious to be a man and follow in his father's footsteps . . . but of a kinder, more curious disposition. It is those last characteristics that Sherlock is counting on. He has noticed that when they talk there is often a trace of empathy in the older boy's face, even admiration, and a touch of pity for the way Sherlock has been treated. It is time to use these things.

"You?" says Lestrade. He looks unsure, glancing back down the hallway.

"Is your father here?"

"Yes."

Sherlock lowers his voice.

"Might I have a word with you . . . outside?"

The budding young inspector hesitates before he consents.

Rain has started to gently fall, another pre-winter drizzle. They stand under the awnings close to the buildings.

"This is highly irregular."

"That is often what is needed. I won't mince words. Do you know anything about the Rathbone robbery, anything that hasn't been in the papers that I might employ? I need more to go on than what I have read."

Lestrade is taken aback by his boldness.

"Even if I did, I wouldn't tell you, Master Holmes. It wouldn't be right. I am sorry."

Not all bad . . . the last three words are promising.

"This doesn't concern you," adds the older boy.

"I understand your position. But perhaps you can accompany me?"

"Accompany you?"

"WHAT IS THE MEANING OF THIS?"

Both boys turn to see Inspector Lestrade in the doorway. Sherlock can hardly believe it is the same man he saw just a few weeks ago. On that glorious day, he had noticed Lestrade preparing to speak, licking his fingers and using the saliva to preen his hair and slick his mustache; he had stood very erect and bellowed proud words to the masses about the recovery of Victoria Rathbone; and then beamed down on Sherlock. Now the senior detective looks as though he has aged ten years – his eyes are red and heavily bagged, his shoulders slumped, and it seems to take a mighty effort to simply hold up his receding chin. He obviously didn't sleep a wink last night. He's escaped one nightmare . . . and plunged into another.

"I was . . . asking him to leave," says his son. The look on his face says "Run!"

Sherlock does. He takes to his heels and flies out the passageway between the buildings and onto White Hall. The constable whom Lestrade sets upon him gives up a short distance down the street.

The boy isn't deterred. He heads west along the queen's beautiful park with its many flowers and swan-filled lakes, toward the palace and Belgravia. Walking briskly, he soon passes Buckingham and stares up, imagining himself a prince, though a much more respectable one than Victoria's reckless first son and heir, Albert Edward, the Prince of Wales. He slows at the beautiful Royal Mews, trying to get a glimpse of the horses and the gleaming four-ton Gold State Carriage used for coronations. Oh, to be transported in that vehicle, watched by adoring crowds. But he doesn't allow himself more than a moment's pause. Belgravia beckons.

●

Though there aren't a hundred policemen outside the Rathbone home, it seems like it. They don't speak to the brightly dressed gentlemen and ladies who stop on the foot pavements and stare, but regular folk are gently disbursed. The milkmaids, hawkers, and the street children looking to make a farthing by picking a pocket or offering to run an errand, are instantly sent away, with rude comments and rough encouragement.

Sherlock spots the house long before he reaches Belgrave Square, and not simply because of the Force and the gawkers. Everyone in London knows where Lord Rathbone lives and his place stands out even in this posh neighborhood. Its Georgian, yellow-stone exterior, five storeys with red-curtained bay windows, large grounds, and majestic columns on its wide front portico mark it as a home of distinction. This is a relatively new residential area, built for the rich just a few generations ago, and its pale homes are even taller and more "perfect" than the mansions of nearby Mayfair. Mozart and Chopin once lived here, and Mary Shelley, who wrote that frightening book about the monster named Frankenstein. People often come to Belgravia simply to catch glimpses of luminaries.

Though Sherlock himself is often distracted by famous faces, that will not happen today. He is looking for no one and seeking to be invisible. What he wants is an indisputable fact or two about the robbery – a clue, a starting point like the watermark, which he will then investigate with much more care. Pulling his collar up around his neck against the cold air, he sneaks into the fading green confines of the park across the street and stands behind a tree, sizing up the building and how to get nearer without being shooed away. He is hoping that the police haven't disturbed the scene any more than is necessary. He knows he can't get inside the house, but it may be possible to sneak onto the grounds. There he might find something that would at least help him build a profile of the thieves.

Belgrave Square has some unusual corners where its big houses almost seem to jut out into the street at sharp angles. The huge Rathbone mansion is one such home. It also has a little lane with stables at the rear. Sherlock observes closely: there are policemen on duty near the street at the front of the house and a few evident through the windows inside, but there seem to be an inordinate number down the passageway and at the rear. The boy thinks of what he read in the papers. The getaway vehicles must have been stationed at the back and . . .

"You were saying?"

Lestrade Junior is standing right next to Sherlock, who nearly jumps into a tree at the sound of his voice.

Holmes gathers himself, adjusts his coat, and fixes his necktie.

"I asked you to accompany me."

"And here I am. I knew you were coming this way."

"How perspicacious of you."

"Uh . . . yes, well, I guessed, knowing what I know about you, if that's what you mean, that you would be bold enough to come right to the scene of the crime."

"*Guessing*, my good fellow, should be left to the horse-racing crowd. It is not a tool for the detective."

Sherlock can see the color rising in the other boy's face.

"You are no detective, sir. My father is."

"Absolutely, I stand corrected, and a fine one he is, the best in London."

"You are just a boy whom circumstances have favored in a couple of matters."

"Yes, I have been fortunate."

"Well, he hasn't treated you the way he should, perhaps."

Perhaps? He is a cad and a fool. And one day I shall make him acknowledge me as his superior.

"Nonsense," says Sherlock. "He does what he must. Who are we young people to question such a man? Do you have a moment?"

"If I am gone long, my father will ask where I have

been. I came because I feel he and I are somewhat in your debt, though he need not acknowledge that. It wasn't right to say what he said to you in public a few weeks ago, nor to simply send you away today. He could have at least heard you out."

And you came to learn from me too, you imbecile.

Sherlock glances across the street at the house.

"I would like to investigate the crime scene . . . very briefly."

Young Lestrade glances toward the Rathbone home and then back at the boy.

"How briefly?"

"Just a few moments in the laneway and at the back of the house. That is all. Can you arrange it?"

This was why Sherlock had gone to see Lestrade Junior in the first place.

But the detective's son is torn. Should he be loyal to his father and deny this request from the disturbingly ingenious half-Jew who seems to somehow always be one step ahead of the great Scotland Yard? Or should he do what he knows is right, by aiding someone his father has mistreated and who, in the end, might actually help lead the police to the thieves. If by some wild chance this charmed boy should somehow be successful again, there will be time to decide whether or not he should be allowed any credit – it can be given to him or swiped away, by the hand of the law.

"I can arrange it. Follow me."

They cross the street and stroll to the gate at the walkway that leads to the front door of the house. A constable immediately turns in their direction, hand out, palm toward them, in a stern signal to halt.

"That is far enough!"

"Constable Gregory?"

The policeman examines his questioner.

"Lestrade's boy, aren't you?"

"Yes, sir."

"Seen you about with him."

"I am apprenticing. I thought I'd take a look around, report back to him."

"And who is *this*?"

Gregory lifts his nose and looks down it at the poor boy with the hawkish nose.

"A pickpocket who frequents Trafalgar Square and has been giving me information of late. I intend to reform him."

"The best of luck to you then, mate."

"Shall I go through?"

"You have five minutes. If you want more, I shall need a signed note from your father. Do not touch anything."

"Thank you, sir. Best not to tell my father I've been. I hope to find something I might surprise him with."

Constable Gregory laughs. "Genius in training, I see. If you can find anything here in five minutes that Scotland Yard hasn't found these past hours, you are welcome to observe it."

The two young investigators head down the passageway.

"Impressive, Master Lestrade," says Sherlock under his breath.

He knows the other policemen are giving him disapproving looks, but doesn't pay them heed. It is time to concentrate.

"Your lens, please."

Lestrade is surprised by Holmes's tone. Suddenly it isn't friendly anymore – he sounds strangely adult and business-like. The older boy's father doesn't carry a magnifying glass, but he himself has taken to the practice . . . ever since he realized that Sherlock Holmes had employed one in the great Whitechapel murder solution. But he is reluctant to admit that he bears one, let alone to hand it over.

"You shall find it concealed in the interior of your clothing, left side, coat pocket," says Sherlock.

"I don't . . ."

"You want to keep its existence from your father. You are right-handed, so placing it on the left side makes it easier for you to reach it, and you carry it high, in your coat, in order to seize it in an instant."

"You astound me." Lestrade didn't intend to say that. It just came out.

"It was elementary. The lens makes a slight bulge when you walk."

The second the other boy hands over the glass, Sherlock is moving away from him, gripping it tightly in a palm, that hawk's nose pointed at the ground like a blood hound sniffing for a scent. The door at the rear is a wide one. It's a perfectly placed entry point for the thieves. In fact, everything about this area suits the villains' purpose – the wide, rear door, the secluded passageway – he paces off the ground – space to park exactly *two* carriages or carts so that both are unobservable from the street.

In addition to knowing that the Rathbones were away and left but two housemaids at home, it is becoming quickly evident to Sherlock that the scoundrels knew exactly where things were both inside and outside, almost as if they had a plan of the house and its contents. The boy is now aware that he is searching for someone well acquainted with the Rathbone residence. *Perhaps friends? Or employees, past or present? Someone somehow connected to the family.*

All his senses are tuned as he moves about. Nearby, two constables are chatting.

"Are you on duty tomorrow?"

"What, at the ball? Not so privileged, no."

"Well I is; there's a whole army of us. Their excellencies is having it despite their cleaning out – word is it's been scheduled ever since they got her back. A celebration, it was to be. Not such a happy occasion now, is it? But I heard our Lady R. wouldn't hear of canceling it, or of having it in . . . an empty little house."

They both laugh.

"What, need glitter for superior folks to look at?"

"They'll bring in the glitter, mate, rent some props and grovelers."

Sherlock is glancing at the ground. The fool policemen have been tramping about; but a Peeler's boot is a unique piece of footwear, thank goodness. The boy also sees the slight prints of the carriage ruts: indeed there were two. *Four-wheelers, narrow gauge, but not too narrow, front wheels smaller.* Sherlock has been making it his business lately to learn all he can about prints, whether made by boots or carriage wheels: identifying them will be, he is sure, a central skill in his occupation. He thinks of what carriage type this might be. *A phaeton of some sort? A High Flyer? Fast and nimble, one horse or two. A Tilbury? No, more than likely a Mail phaeton or a Demi-Mail, lots of space onboard, covered to hide the thieves' treasures, but still, very speedy. Phaetons . . . named after the son of a Greek god who rode chariots across the skies.* The horses' hoofprints are evident as well: *two for each carriage, for added speed,* narrow prints like the feet of thoroughbreds.

Sherlock glances toward the end of the lane to see which direction the wheel prints go once they head out. But they fade as they run toward the street. Strapped for time and anxious to get to the heart of the investigation, he turns back to the footprints and the identity of the thieves themselves.

The crooks walked right here. Who were they? How many were there? Sherlock sees faint shoe prints near the door. They lead just a few steps away and then stop at the point where the carriages must have been. *They don't seem like the markings of police boots. The villains would have drawn the phaetons up close to the door and loaded them as quickly as possible. So quickly! These few prints must belong to the thieves.* He drops to his knees. *This will have to be done fast.* He lowers his face close to the ground, the lens trained on them. *Yes, these marks are different.* And from what Sherlock can tell, they betray that there were just two . . .

"You there! What are you doin'?"

A big constable, dressed in a black coxcomb helmet and one of those long blue coats with the brass buttons, is yelling at Sherlock.

Lestrade reacts instantly.

"Hand it over!" he shouts, reaching down and wrenching the magnifying glass from Sherlock. He turns to the angry constable who is approaching on the hop. "Don't know how he did that, officer. Must have plucked me. Pickpocket, you know."

"Remove him from the premises. Now!"

"Yes. Quite right. We were just leaving."

♥

Young Lestrade isn't pleased and leaves Sherlock standing on the street. But it doesn't matter: the boy has learned some important things. Two four-wheeled phaeton carriages were used in this robbery, drawn by a pair of horses each, with a single thief in each conveyance; by the size of their boots and the length of their strides, it is apparent that they were adult males and that one of them was game-legged – his gait was irregular. That is a start. But he has *so* much further to go.

He sits on a park bench in Belgrave Square, thinking, gently tapping his fingers together. *What else is there to work with?* It comes to him.

Something he heard back in the driveway gives him a daring idea.

THE SETUP

T hat night, Sherlock is asleep in the wardrobe in the shop, curled up on his narrow feather bed and wearing Bell's old deerstalker hat to keep his head warm, dreaming of his daring plan when . . . he hears a frightening sound. *Someone is tinkering with the lock on the front door.*

He is particularly exhausted tonight – it had been an exciting day, and then he had spent time with his studies before bed. He is adamant that he will keep them up. When he was doing his sums, he had thought for a moment of a certain schoolgirl who has had (it seems) all sorts of trouble with her ciphering lately and many long questions for him. Not a day goes by that she doesn't approach. She appears to hold him in high regard. He had been pleased to be back at his school desk these last few weeks and yesterday had been a red-letter day. After arriving late in the morning from Belgravia, a forged note from Bell in hand, he had eagerly climbed the creaking flights of stairs in his cramped little National School on Snowfields Road south of London Bridge, ascended past the children's room on the first floor, the girls' on the second (where the student in question –

Beatrice, the dark-haired, dark-eyed hatter's daughter from his old neighborhood in Southwark – was standing outside her door in her blue bonnet, smiling at him), all the way up to the boys' room at the top. Soon after he entered, the headmaster addressed the classes.

"I am perhaps grieved, perhaps pleased, to announce to you all that Mudlark, one of our two remaining thirteen-year-old boys, has taken up an apprentice position with a Lambeth bootmaker. That leaves Sherlock Holmes as our eldest boy."

It is hard to believe. The near-homeless half-Jew has outlasted them all. A few years ago, no one would have guessed that such a thing was possible. Sherlock certainly wouldn't have – he would have been appalled to even think it. But now he is the school's pupil teacher and intends to stay a few more years, probably a record at the grimy little school. He is pleased to be the boy who earns the best grades, too. No one bullies him anymore, no one calls him Judas. The application of some violent Bellitsu on the last boy who tried (Mudlark himself) has taken care of that.

"Congratulations," said a glowing Beatrice when she saw him descend the stairs at the end of the day. Sherlock had to admit that she wasn't a bad sort, rather pretty actually, and much less complicated than Irene.

Lying in bed that night, he is only half asleep, despite his fatigue. He has been teaching himself to be alert at all times, even in the small hours, practicing the art of snoozing lightly like a soldier alert for an attack. Sigerson Bell, of course, was once an expert at this and has shown the boy several approaches . . . though when the old man teaches the art, he unfailingly falls asleep and then commences to belt out the most ungodly, trombone-like snoring one can imagine.

Sherlock's mind is razor sharp and at the top of such techniques because of his hard work at school and the intriguing case he is contemplating. So he manages to stay half awake tonight. And his alertness pays off.

The sound at the front door awakens him fully. He listens intently. *Someone is trying to force the latch!* The tinkering stops. Then the door creaks open.

Sherlock sits up.

He hears Bell's trumpeting snores coming from his upstairs bedroom . . . *and soft footsteps moving stealthily across the front room*. They edge toward the laboratory!

The boy silently pushes the wardrobe door slightly ajar and peers through the crack. It is pitch dark and he can barely make out the form now advancing through the lab entrance. It seems to know where it is going, avoiding the skeletons, formaldehyde jars on the floor, the stools . . . and comes directly toward the wardrobe!

The shop is in a bad neighborhood and it is part of Sherlock's job to guard it. He has taken to sleeping with the horse whip Bell gave him earlier this summer, the weapon the old man deems supreme in the art of self-defense. Either its decisive employment, or a scientific maneuver selected from the Bellitsu repertoire will do nicely against this fiend, then he will shout at the top of his lungs and wake Bell for assistance. But as the figure comes closer, it occurs to Sherlock that there may be another more brutal and direct way to respond. After all, his opponent looks slight, perhaps a youth.

As the shadow nears to within a foot of the wardrobe, as it reaches out to grasp the latch, the boy presses his back to the interior wall and drives both his feet against the doors, crashing them into the figure. The intruder falls backward like a dead weight and gives a small, curiously girlish shriek.

Instantly, Sherlock is out the wardrobe and on his feet. As the villain rises, Holmes seizes him.

But it isn't a *him*.

Irene Doyle is in his arms. Their faces are inches apart. A series of alarming feelings courses through Sherlock's body and he notes them: he feels strangely at home in this position and excited – and terrified. He releases her.

She is dressed in a plain black dress without crinoline, and a matching black bonnet into which she now tucks a hatpin. *That was how she picked the lock. . . . Malefactor!* She looks afraid and yet she has come here in the night, all alone through the London streets; a remarkable girl . . . *learning how to make like a thief.*

The trombone upstairs had stopped for a note or two when Sherlock sent Irene reeling to the floor. Now it resumes.

"Miss Doyle, my sincere apologies," whispers Sherlock. "But what are you *doing*?"

"I have something to tell you."

The boy feels a waft of fear float into his chest. He takes her lightly by the arm and begins walking her out to the front room.

"And speaking to me in a civilized manner when the sun is out would not do?"

"Malefactor has me watched during the days."

"I'm not surprised."

"I understand why."

"You do?"

"I am learning about his kind. He doesn't trust people. He needs to know all about anyone who tries to be close to him. I didn't want him to know that I had come to see you."

"He is a rat. And you should stay away from him."

Their faces are close together in the darkness. She examines his strong jawline and prominent chin.

"I have some things to tell you that I would prefer to say in private, things I don't want him to know."

Sherlock had been about to tell her that she should leave. They are near the outer door. He stops in his tracks. *Irene hasn't been able to bring herself to involve Malefactor after all*, he thinks. She knows valuable things about Victoria Rathbone. *Is she about to reveal them?*

"All Malefactor knows is that solving this crime is important to me. I didn't tell him – he figured it out. He's like that, as you know. But he doesn't know exactly why I'm *so* interested."

"Well, that makes us even."

"I'm going to tell you."

Sherlock motions to two chairs near the crude display counter. They sit, their knees almost touching.

"What are your conditions?"

"There are none."

"Truly?"

"Other than that you try to solve this crime," she smiles.

Sherlock smiles back. He can't remember when he last did that with her. Inside, he is glowing. If she really means this, then perhaps their friendship can resume.

"Let me start at the beginning."

"Always a smart –"

"Lady Rathbone is my father's cousin."

Holmes sits up.

"What?"

"You can see the resemblance in their eyes and the color of their hair. It is rather striking, when you look. Observation, Sherlock, is the elementary skill of the scientist and the primary talent of life." She says this in a deeper voice, imitating him, and then grinning.

"You are very wise, Miss Doyle."

"Lady Rathbone's mother and my grandmother are first cousins. That makes her and Father second relations, and Victoria and me third. Lady R. is a Shaw, Irish like the Doyles."

She gathers herself.

"About three or four months ago, in the late summer, I visited a Ragged School for Father in Stepney, set up by a young medical student named Thomas Barnardo. He told me about a pitiable boy in the Ratcliff Workhouse nearby, who was the adopted child of two elderly people in the East End who had died suddenly from the cholera epidemic about a year ago. A beadle who took the boy to the workhouse told him all about it. Mr. Barnardo said the child was lonely, distraught, and ill, and asked if I would visit him. But when I went to see him it upset me . . . *very* much."

"Because he is going blind? Irene, I said this before, there are so many –"

"No, not because of that."

"Then why?"

". . . He looks like someone. *Exactly* like someone."

"Who?"

"I can't tell you. I shouldn't. It is a very personal matter. It isn't something you need to know, anyway. But it matters to my father . . . and to me. We can't let him go blind . . . because it will kill him."

"Why are the Rathbones the only ones who can help him?"

"Paul, that's the boy's name, has a rare infection. Good and well-placed people who help the unfortunate have sent him to doctors and they all say his sight cannot be saved. But Lord Rathbone's personal physician is the best in London for eye infections, the best in Europe, a miracle worker, it is said. You must know what he did for Lady Rathbone."

"I have heard."

"The doctors say Paul's problem is similar to hers."

"Then just go directly to the physician. Ask him to help."

"He only treats Lord Rathbone and his circle and makes no exceptions. Half an hour after seeing Paul, my father sent his card to Belgravia by carriage. The lord is aware of our work and of our relation to his wife, so he saw us the next day. He said that he felt saddened by the child's plight, but that if he interceded on his behalf, he would have to do the same for every such boy in London."

"That's ridiculous," says Sherlock loudly. He lowers his voice. "How many London children need that kind of special help?"

"The lord also offered a few opinions. He said that God has a plan for us all, and only helps those who help themselves."

"I hope God has a plan for Lord Rathbone . . . at the end of his boot."

Irene takes Sherlock's hand and he doesn't pull back.

"But that wasn't the end of our visit to Belgravia."

"Our?"

"I accompanied father. Victoria was there. She had visitors, a few friends our age. She seemed anxious to appear fashionably interested in her inferiors, especially someone connected to my father and the work he does – she has her father's political instincts. So we girls talked. Then . . . she showed me her home."

"She what?"

"She showed –"

"How much of it?"

"Everything."

"Everything? You have seen every last room in the Rathbone mansion . . . the one that was just robbed?"

"Correct."

"Tell me. Don't leave anything out."

As Sherlock listens to her detailed account of the kitchens, the drawing room, the dining rooms, the observatory, the ballroom, the servants' quarters on the upper storeys, and even the bedrooms – their exact locations, points of entry, and their size – he clearly remembers what he so admires about this girl. Yes, she is attractive in her own way, with that shining blonde hair and those big brown eyes . . . but her brain, *oh what a brain*. Were she a boy, what a detective she would make!

Finally, her account draws to a close.

"Thank –"

"I am not finished, Sherlock. You should know about the servants, too." And off she goes again, describing all nineteen of them, from scullery maid to butler: how they are dressed, their ages, and their appearance. One in particular stands out for the boy: a young dark-haired footman, tall and very thin, only employed there on busy days.

"And what of Lady Rathbone?" asks Sherlock.

"She spoke to us when we arrived. I noticed the resemblance to Father immediately. Folks always say to me that I shall want to marry a handsome man because my father is good looking. That is true, by the way – I will. But I must say that Lady Rathbone received a remarkable amount of the family comeliness indeed. She really is breathtakingly beautiful and so much younger than her husband. Her eyes are still a little cloudy, but striking nevertheless. We didn't see her for long. She barely said hello. Father says her snobbery has to do with her upbringing. She feels the need to play at being the upper-class lady in every way. She married above her station, you know, beauty for money and position."

"Always convenient."

"There are rumors though."

"Rumors? About what?"

"Father said she was rather wild when she was young. Not a crime, in my mind. It is said she loved a man, a dashing sort, but a drinker and not of her social standing. She was from country squire people and he was barely middle class. It is said she had more lovers than just him, and he had more than her. But they accepted that in each other. Then Rathbone saw her at a ball and was smitten. He had to have her and had the means to get her. She went without complaint, and he had her vision healed, of course."

"So the rumors are just about her past?"

"No. It's more than that. These days, she still disappears from time to time. She was gone once, about five years ago, for six months or more. On a vacation, it was said. But I'm not sure Lord Rathbone cares, as long as she returns. She lives her life . . . and he lives his."

"And what about the lord? What sort of chap did he appear to be?"

"Exactly as he seems in public, as far as I can tell. He is big and brash, without a tender bone in him."

"And Victoria?"

"She had just returned from school in India. In fact, she had been abroad for several years and hadn't been home for more than a few days. She said her parents told her that they felt she'd changed so much that they barely recognized her. She laughed at that, said her parents hardly ever saw her all the years she lived with them from birth in London anyway, that she was raised to be 'seen and not heard, and barely even seen,' that her mother, often away, was 'still half blind,' and her father hadn't spoken to her from closer than the far end of their 'mile-long dining room table' more than five times in her whole life. But she said that had its advantages. . . . That was when I played a card."

"You what?"

"Well . . . the advantages she spoke of had to do with her father giving her anything she wanted whenever she wanted, whether she asked him from India or sent a servant down the hall. That was his way of loving her, if it can be called that. A stable of horses? A dozen new dresses? Such things have always been hers for the asking. My father had just come out from seeing her father when she was telling me this, and he looked terrible. I knew what had happened. So, I played my card . . . I told her about little Paul and about what we were asking Lord Rathbone to do for him. And she, trying to impress me and my father, did what I hoped she would do."

"Which was?"

"She said she would speak to Lord Rathbone for me. And she said not to worry about it for another minute: all she had to do was ask and he would comply. He had never refused her before, didn't dare. She said she would say she wanted it as a present. When we were going out, just to be sure, I asked a stable boy in the drive about Victoria and her father. He grinned and said: 'Whatever Miss Rathbone wants, our Lord provides.'"

"So, why didn't she do it?"

"Because the moment we left their home, she went to her room to dress, to take her carriage to Rotten Row. And within an hour –"

"She was kidnapped."

As Irene lowers her head, Holmes thinks he should hug her. But he can't. He needs to say something that shows he cares. "How is Paul?"

"He is getting worse." Her voice cracks. "He is *so* small and helpless. He is going to die just like my – When I visit him and hold his hand, it is limp. You know, he had a full and proper name when he came to the workhouse, but the other boys took to sneering at him, calling him Dimly. And as if to spite them, spite them all, he will only respond to that name. Call him Paul Dimly, and he will look at you with those swollen, fading eyes. Anything else and he just stares down."

Irene looks like she is about to sob. Sherlock doesn't know what to do again. Putting his arms around her would indeed be best. But he can't. Better to seek a solution.

"Victoria Rathbone has been home for three weeks now, Irene. Why isn't she responding to you?"

"I don't know. She just won't see me. Her father won't see my father, either. Sherlock, they tell me Paul can barely find his gruel bowl when he eats now. Mr. Barnardo thinks his sight won't be recoverable soon . . . he thinks he has about two weeks."

Two weeks left.

"Help us help the Rathbones, Sherlock. Help me. Time is running out. If the thieves are found, everything will go back to normal. Lord Rathbone will see Father and Victoria will speak up for us."

She leans closer to the boy.

"If you could actually solve this, Sherlock . . . and let it be known that we were supporting you, the Rathbones would be *truly* indebted to us . . . and my father would be the same to you."

"I will try," he says tenderly.

She beams at him. "What if we did this together?"

I thought as much.

"No," he says firmly and stands up. "You said there were no conditions."

An expression comes over her face that he has never seen before. It isn't anger or sorrow. It has ambition in it: her jaw is set. She rises to her feet and walks toward the door.

"I don't *really* believe you can solve this, Sherlock. As you once said – you are just a boy. You are very much . . . a boy. I just need as many irons in the fire as possible. I need you fully baited. There was a time when I cared about being your friend, but that's gone now. You have seen to that."

Sherlock is taken aback.

"No, there aren't any conditions, Master Holmes. I just thought I'd ask one last time. Here is the situation as it stands at this moment. I have you hooked. You will do any-thing you can to solve this crime now. . . . Next I will visit Malefactor and tell him every last thing I have just told you."

"What? You wouldn't."

"I would and I shall. We have a little competition afoot now and if you two lads are worth your salt, my father and I shall benefit from it. I am guessing that Malefactor will best you. He knows the sort he seeks. Imagine if it is he who defeats you, Sherlock, on the *very* case you must win, the one that holds the key to your future. He, of course, can't take the credit . . . that will go to Inspector Lestrade. Good luck. May the best boy win."

And with that she pivots, pulls open the door and slams it behind her.

Sherlock is so stunned that he stands stock still for a moment. Then he opens the door and calls after her.

"Irene! You don't need to be involved in these things. You are a lady, not a *man*, some desperate boy. I keep you away for your own good – your safety."

She is still within earshot.

"It is about more than that, Sherlock Holmes," she says without turning around. Then she pulls a thick stick out of her dress, which had obviously been concealed in her lining, looks around like an expert in the art of avoiding a trailer, picks up her pace, and disappears into the darkness.

What was really so awful about having her work with him? Perhaps he has been making a mistake.

"Irene!"

But she is gone.

THE RATHBONE BALL

H e can't go to sleep after that and tosses about on his bed, trying to get Irene out of his mind. Every now and then he thinks he hears Bell upstairs, as if the old man were listening to his nocturnal tribulations. But when the boy lies still, all is silent throughout the shop.

He knows he must master his feelings, so by an effort of will, he stops thinking about Irene and concentrates on what he needs to do: immediately follow through on the daring plan he began to consider after he investigated the crime scene. Sherlock thought it a good (though certainly reckless) idea when he conceived it, but now, given the information Irene has provided, it has become unquestionably the best way to proceed.

His plan is informed by two singular points.

The first is the most important. It is the key fact of the crime, much more telling than his discovery that the robbery was committed by two thieves with two fast carriages who knew the house inside and out. It is this, *Lady Rathbone's room was left untouched.* It doesn't make sense, and when something doesn't make sense about a crime, strict attention must be paid to it. Any thief would have certain obvious targets in a great house: the safe, the silverware, the art, and . . . the jewelry in the lady's bedroom. The thieves had attended to all but the latter, and it, when robbing a home with such a pampered mistress, should perhaps have been their primary concern. Why did they avoid it? What about Lady Rathbone or her bedroom kept them from fleecing her?

The second point is really a couple of things that go together: according to the two constables conversing outside the mansion, the Rathbones have a fancy-dress ball planned for some time this evening, *and* according to Irene, the family employs an extra footman on busy occasions, one who is young, dark-haired, tall, and thin.

Sherlock also considers this: Malefactor is about to pursue the case. He will do everything he can to solve it and do it immediately. He may even already know who the villains are. There is no time to waste. That snake has the means to destroy his future. Sherlock must get into Lady Rathbone's bedroom and do it today.

But he needs a particular weapon at his disposal. It has already occurred to him where he can find it. A certain fact has informed him. . . . *Sigerson Bell can knock human beings unconscious in several different ways.*

❦

Just a fortnight past, the old man had held forth on the subject. He and his apprentice were in the tight confines of the laboratory (trying not to smash too many vials and bottles), stripped to the waist, perspiring, and wearing muf-flers on their hands – those over-sized, stuffed leather gloves worn by pugilists when training in clubs and gymnasia. Real, skin-and-bone fists are used in actual matches, and Bell had seen many of those, had been asked to be present numerous times: to help revive an array of famed members of the fighting fancy who had been pummeled nearly to death. He had once stood within a few yards of the leg-endary little gamecock Tom Sayers during his thirty-seven round battle for the bare-knuckle heavyweight champi-onship of the world upon Farnborough Field, when the scrappy Brit was matched against the big American, John C. Heenan. In the twenty-ninth round, the Yankee's blood had even splashed across the apothecary's shirt, giving the appearance that he had been sliced with a rapier.

Sherlock wore his dark trousers that day in the lab, Bell a pair of pugilist's tights with Sayers' colors wrapped around his waist. The old man's leggings, unfortunately, displayed every nuance, even the hairs, of his scrawny legs. But despite being hunched over in his question-mark shape and the flesh on his chest hanging from him like the udders of a cow, he was lightning-quick and supremely skilled, showing great power and never once letting up on Sherlock. "It is all technique!" he bellowed. Fisticuffs was a truly manly art and he intended to teach the boy to do it right, so he would fear no foe.

Bell puffed as he instructed, punctuating his thoughts with strikes.

"One must turn one's hips when mixing, my boy. This will allow you to deliver your blow with tremendous force. The destination of the strike is equally important. There are certain points upon the jaw, the chin really, where, if a cross, left hook, or jab is landed, the brain shall be immediately concussed. Let me show you."

Sherlock instantly put up his dukes in a defensive posture and stopped him. The apothecary had knocked him unconscious once before. Poor old Bell had labored for an hour bringing the boy around, and then spent the following week apologizing to him . . . every time he rose in the morning, when he came in at night, and several times during meals. So, Sherlock peeked between his guard and directed Bell to a skeleton.

"Quite right, my son," said the old man with a grin, "I shan't strike you in that manner again." Then he shattered the skull in a hundred pieces. Sherlock made a mental note to visit Bell's favorite grave-robber and request another specimen.

"I recall Sayers vanquishing The Tipton Slasher, as brutal a member of the fancy as England has ever seen and almost as large as Heenan. It is not the hound in the fight that matters, but the fight in the hound! Technique, my boy! Thin and young as you are, I can make you the most feared man in the Empire!"

But it wasn't such advice, nor even the actual fistic encounter that was in the boy's mind as he lay there making plans in bed – it was something the apothecary said, rather casually, right afterward.

"Of course, there are more ways to skin a rat than one can imagine. One may concuss one's opponent with a technically sound blow, take him down with a walking stick in an alley, or send him to fairyland with a little Bellitsu if attacked from behind. But those are the *physical* arts of rendering an opponent unconscious. There are also more subtle, scientific ones."

Sigerson Trismegistus Bell is a good man, there is no doubt about that, but from time to time a slightly nefarious look comes across his face and when it does, it is often accompanied by a twinkle in the eye.

"A little powdered opium, spread upon a strong meal that won't betray its flavor . . . would knock a villain out as surely as Sayers floored the Slasher," he smiled.

Sherlock is waiting with breakfast already prepared (onion and parsnip sandwiches) when Bell descends in the morning.

"You have risen early, my boy! Is there an occasion? Is it not a Saturday?"

"Yes, sir, and I am ready to work."

"Ah! Nothing planned on the Rathbone front?"

"No, sir."

Though it pains him to be so patient, Sherlock doesn't even broach the subject he dearly wants to pursue while they eat, or even for the first hour afterward. He waits for the opportune moment. The old man has been reading Dickens' latest novel, *Our Mutual Friend*, and begins his day, much to Sherlock's chagrin, by holding forth on its message.

"We are all connected, my boy, in a complicated web of humanity, we are all in a sense friends. We look more alike than we realize we do, act more alike, think more alike. We are all motivated by the same things . . . like money. Money is our mutual friend too! We are all very, very, very selfish. The more aware we are of this and try to put a stop to it, the better off we are."

Finally, Bell puts the book down and turns to what Sherlock hoped all along he would do: continue the boy's chemical education in the properties of various alkaloids and narcotics. Holmes is depending on the old man coming around to the subject of the poppy plant, so opium can be discussed. But for what seems like an interminable amount of time, likely only about ten minutes, he sticks to much more benign extracts. Finally, Sherlock forces the issue.

"What about the poppy, sir?"

Bell is a bit taken aback.

"The seeds of the poppy? The solidified latex of its pods? That isn't for today. We will get to that in a fortnight. Now let me show you what –"

"I find it of particular interest."

"You do? Why is that?"

"Because it is so . . . because its effects on the human being can be so extreme."

Bell looks suspicious. "Yes, well, that is true. After all, opium, morphine, laudanum, and heroin are its by-products. None of them trifles."

"And opium can render one unconscious, can it not? I believe you told me that once."

"I did."

"And yet one may purchase it from any chemist . . . or apothecary."

"Yes, I keep it here, a great deal of it. I have often had occasion to prescribe it, in small, carefully measured amounts, mind you."

"You once told me that if one were to powder it and mix it liberally with a meal, it would have serious side effects on anyone who consumed it."

"I did?"

"What, exactly, would occur . . . in biological terms, that is?"

"Anyone who ingested it would slip into a stupor from which he would not awake for perhaps four or five hours, depending on the amount. But that isn't something you need to know."

"Quite right."

"May we return to the garlic onion and its properties? It is a plant not well understood upon our shores."

"Yes, sir, I am sorry to have diverted you."

"Not at all."

But Sigerson Bell seems to find it difficult to concentrate after that. He speaks for a while and then eyes the boy as if trying to read his mind. Finally, he calls things to a halt.

"Master Holmes, you aren't planning to do anything, shall we say, sinister, with powdered opium, are you?"

"Why would I do that, sir?"

"It escapes me. But the powers of chemical elements are to be used by professionals for the maintenance of the human body, to heal others, not to injure. Fighting, likewise, is either a test of human skill in a freely-agreed-upon match between apparent equals, or simply a matter of self defense against a fiend. You cannot do evil to someone in order to do good. Your methods must always be of the highest standard. Do you understand me?"

"Yes, sir."

But Sigerson Bell has his doubts. He knows that justice is an enormous concern in the boy's life and that he believes it is acceptable to use any means to achieve it. That is a fact that both disturbs and thrills the old man, though he wishes it were merely the former.

❦

Sherlock acts the instant Bell leaves to attend to a Southwark lion tamer in the early afternoon. He is up on a stool in a flash, examining the contents of the apothecary's glass cabinets. Everything has been meticulously labeled. He reads: Cocaine, Deadly Nightshade (the very name frightens him), Laudanum, Morphine . . . and Opium.

He takes the big jar down, sets it on the lab table and retrieves a mortar and pestle. *Just a bit, enough to do the job, but little enough so the old man won't notice a pinch is gone.* He cuts a small piece off with a scalpel and drops the bit of hard brown material into the cup-sized stone dish and begins to grind it. Dust rises and some wafts up his nose.

It tickles and makes him smile. Life can be so boring, but sometimes . . .

There's a noise near the entrance to the shop.

Sherlock hesitates. Should he put everything back? Or just cover it up? He throws a cloth over it and goes out into the front room of the shop. It's someone rapping at the latticed bow window, knocking clouds of dust down onto the wide sill inside. The shadowy figure, seen through the dirty translucent glass, seems tall and dark. Then it moves toward the door.

What should he do? Should he answer? Rush back to the poppy plant extract and put it away? What if it's Bell? *No, he wouldn't be knocking.* Or what if it's . . . then the boy notices that the figure is only a head, or rather just wings and a very small feathered skull. It's a black bird, a crow or a raven, smacking its wings against the glass and then flying off.

Stay calm, don't be thrown by such trifles, or you won't be able to do this.

His heart still beating fast, but under control now, he returns to his job, finishes, and pours the powder into a tiny vial. It will carry well in his pocket. When the opium is put back in the jar and set up on the shelf and the cabinet is closed, it looks just as before. At least that's what he tells himself.

Next is the daily paper. Some days he goes out to get the shop's copies in the morning. Other times, like today, they wait for the news agent to deliver in the afternoon. Theirs come from Dupin at Trafalgar Square. Sherlock hides the vial and slips out to find him.

The cripple is always glad to see Sherlock, though he notices something different today.

"Your face is lit up like a tallow candle, Master 'olmes."

"I am onto a scent, Mr. Dupin."

"Looks like more 'an that. Looks like you is ready to kill someone."

"Nonsense."

He finds the society pages and reads while he walks, unable to wait until he gets back to the shop. He needs to check something.

"THE BALL WILL GO ON

Word is that Lord and Lady Rathbone's private Celebration Ball to toast the return of their daughter, Victoria, shall go on as intended. The best of society shall be gathering this evening, no doubt to attempt a cheering-up of our tenacious, leather-skinned Lord, he whose pocketbook and home have suddenly become distinctly lighter. Art works and silverware have been brought in to make those in attendance feel at home. Guests shall be arriving at seven."

Bell isn't supposed to return for another hour, so when Sherlock returns to the shop he takes his time getting ready. He drops the paper onto the lab table where the old man will see it and retrieves his small vial of opium from under the blanket on his bed in the wardrobe. But just as he is about to open the outside door to the street, it opens on its own.

Sigerson Bell. He has come home early and he's eyeing Sherlock suspiciously.

"My boy."

"Yes, sir."

"I observe a reddening of your face."

"Calisthenics."

"Ah! Shall I join you?"

"I have just finished. I was going out."

Sherlock isn't sure, but it seems to him that the old man's eyes wander to his coat pocket, where the boy's hand has slipped inside to guard the vial.

"Well, if you must, I shan't stand in your way. I trust your work is done."

He steps aside and the boy begins to pass through the doorway.

"Sherlock!"

The old man seldom refers to him by his first name.

"Yes, sir?"

Sigerson looks stern at first, then smiles.

"Whatever you do, in the end . . . be a good lad."

"I promise I shall, sir."

But his first stop on the way to Belgrave Square is for distinctly evil purposes. His pockets are empty again, and he is planning a robbery. In the late spring, while living on the streets during his pursuit of the Whitechapel murderer, he had successfully stolen from a shopper at busy Smithfield

Market. He'll try it again. If he is caught, he will be instantly arrested, and there are many Bobbies in the markets. His whole future hangs on his light-fingered skills.

The last time, he had a full day to pick his victim and had chosen a female servant who was new to her market job, who set down her baskets while paying for her goods, giving him an opportunity to swoop and then disappear into a thick crowd. He doesn't have the luxury of time now. No easy targets appear. It is very late afternoon and the last day of a bleak November so the market has a sparser look: fewer stalls, limited vegetables. *Should he really try this? It's too risky.* But he must. He walks down a makeshift aisle in the middle of things, with barrows and carts lining it and vendors crying their goods in a crowded din. He sees a fish-monger, a poor old man with sores on his ruddy face, with long hair and a beard, wearing dirty, over-sized clothes . . . who turns his back for an instant. Almost unconsciously, Sherlock snatches two fistfuls of fish, already gutted and wrapped in newspapers, and is lost in the crowd before the man even notices.

He is halfway to Belgravia in minutes, his hands red and freezing as he clutches the ice-cold goods. He doesn't feel proud of what he's done. What had possessed him to steal from that poor old man? He at least could have chosen a different monger, but he had been thinking about no one but himself. *It is done*, he tells himself; *it is useless to worry about it now. This could be the means to help Paul Dimly.* That thought reassures him. *It is time to move on.*

Belgravia nears.

His father's admonishments about observing are deeply ingrained in him and have been re-emphasized by Sigerson Bell. But listening skills are almost of equal importance. Both his mentors agree. "Listen to what everyone in the world tells you," Wilberforce Holmes once said, "whether it is a royal declaration or a shout in the street." He had tuned his ear to the constables when they discussed the Rathbone ball and listened to every syllable as Miss Doyle spoke of the contents of the great house and the servants who worked within.

Footmen are the most costumed of all the domestic help in a nobleman's home. They dress in distinctive uniforms and wigs, with white stockings, and breeches. They are supposed to be tall and are often young. Irene described one who was very young, a sort of apprentice, only used on busy occasions. Thin and with strands of black hair just like Sherlock's evident under his wig, he also had, as Irene recalled, a rather prominent nose. Holmes's own proboscis, he has to admit, is not without prominence.

Sherlock is certain that this boy will be working tonight. He assumes that many on staff hardly know the lad and that the Rathbones, who barely recognize their own daughter, are certainly not apt to be well acquainted with one of their infrequently employed servants.

The little private ball and masquerade will be preceded by a meal. That will be helpful too. He walks quickly into Belgrave Square carrying his fish. The sun has already set. Supper time is fast approaching. He waits in the park and watches the guests arrive – they must all be indoors before he makes his move. When he nears the great house a short while later, he sees a sort of parade through the tall windows at the front: bejeweled ladies with low-cut dresses, and perfectly groomed gentlemen in dark suits and white silk cravats, all carrying masks and paired off with carefully chosen partners, descending the pink marble staircase from the drawing room. In moments they will be in the dining room, ready to eat. Then they will remove to the upstairs again, to the ballroom. He needs to act smartly.

He gets past the liveried coachman standing guard outside by pointing to his newspaper-wrapped fish. He grins at him, holds his nose, and motions to the house with his head.

Wealthy homes have big kitchens in the basement and Irene has told him exactly where to find this one. He shoots down the stone stairs and opens the door without knocking, as if he were meant to. There is a mass of servants scurrying about in a sort of ordered chaos, frantic as the supper hour descends on them. It is very loud. He can disappear in here, whether fish is on the menu or not.

"Confidence is the key to anything you do," Sherlock once heard Malefactor tell his charges. Holmes had been hiding in the bushes at Lincoln's Inn Fields, fascinated, in those days, with the underworld.

The boy knows that his rival was right. He has to be bold now and act as though he is exactly who he pretends to be.

He spots the cook, a big-bosomed, middle-aged woman wearing a white apron and dress, who is sending her assistants and other servants off in all directions. Sherlock holds the fish in full view in front of his chest, but turned away from the cook (since she is in charge of the menu), and heads toward an unattended wooden table that looks to be filled with food for a later course. Just as he hoped, no one questions a delivery boy's presence and he sets his smelly load down and has both hands free.

Then he spies his prey; the young footman who looks a little like him. Dressed in the scarlet Rathbone uniform, he is waiting to take the hors d'oeuvres of imported oysters up to the dining room, and is staring longingly down at them in the manner a groom might regard his bride.

Seventeen years old, missed a small streak of his father's working-class grime on his left cheek. Hungry, as befits his class. First few weeks on the job . . . and shall eat at least one oyster on the way up the stairs.

Sherlock slips over, his hand on the vial in his pocket, and stumbles, falling into the big plate of oysters and deftly knocking one to the floor.

A kitchenmaid turns and glowers at him.

"Many pardons, mum," he says, reaching down to pick up the morsel.

"No one is eatin' that 'un, you savage. Throw it out and be on your way."

"Yes, mum." But his eyes are on the footman, whose eyes are on the oyster.

"I have a rule," whispers Sherlock into the other boy's ear as he rises. "In fact, I am the originator of it, mate. It's this: once a portion of food strikes the floor, it can be eaten within three seconds, no later. That's the 'Three Second Rule.' The time grows longer dependin' on your poverty, as your lodgins is deeper in Whitechapel, Stepney, or the Isle of Dogs."

The young footman grins, takes the dirty oyster from Sherlock's open hand, holds his head back, and quickly tips the contents into his gaping mouth. Sherlock sees the brown, powdered opium enter with it and the footman's Adam's apple bounce in his gullet.

"I shall be off."

He waits outside, around the back, at the rear kitchen door, hidden from the view of the coachman out front. No more than five minutes later, the footman staggers out the door, perspiring heavily and feeling drowsy.

"Anything wrong, mate?" asks Sherlock quietly, offering his shoulder.

"It's you, boy. I am seeing strange things . . . I am feeling . . . feeling . . ."

Sherlock takes his full weight when he collapses and drags him into the nearby stable. Stripping down to his underclothing, shivering as he works, he is in the footman's uniform in minutes. Not a perfect fit, a little large and loose, but it will do. His calves don't show as well as he'd like, and it takes him a while before he has the wig on just the way he wants. He'd like a mirror. Then he chides himself. *Stop fussing. Stop delaying.*

He practices for a minute in the stable, remembering the typically proud bearing of the young footman, his gait, and his haughty expression. He takes a deep breath, opens the stable door, and makes for the kitchen. *Confidence.* Sweeping indoors, he heads directly toward the food.

"Barrymore! Barrymore, where are you?"

That must mean me.

He keeps his eyes averted from the kitchenmaid, who hands him a full plate and directs him toward a doorway that leads to a set of stairs. Sherlock is to take the food up to the dining room. This is what he was hoping for; an acceptable reason to not only move up a floor into the main part of the great house, but a chance to observe all three members of the family, too. From there, he intends to somehow find his way farther up . . . and enter Lady Rathbone's bedroom. But first, to the dinner table, where he can consider the conduct and attitude of the Rathbones and their daughter *and* listen to the conversation, which will surely be about the robbery. *What else would they all speak of?* He may hear details that the papers don't have. But he can't spend long there – his goal is the bedroom.

Then, a daring thought occurs to him. What if he tried to say something to Victoria? Just a few whispered words in her ear as he walked past, mentioning Paul Dimly's name – it might save the little boy's life. If she is as kind as Irene says, she might find a way to respond. But he dismisses this before he reaches the room. It could endanger the whole case.

The impossibly long wooden table gleams beneath massive chandeliers, attended by two elongated rows of diners. There are indeed paintings in every appropriate place on the walls and the silverware is conspicuously shiny.

Everything has been replaced. The guests seem to be almost glittering: ladies in white and men in black. Sherlock realizes his mouth is hanging open, and closes it.

He isn't exactly sure what a footman's job is in a dining room, but quickly spots another man in uniform serving the guests over their right shoulders and then standing with his back against a wall. That servant doesn't look anyone in the eyes and the guests don't acknowledge his presence. Sherlock follows his example. Then, up against the wall at about the midpoint of the table, so he can see both ends, he listens, heart pounding.

At first the talk is merely niceties and little jokes, as the food is consumed, stuffed into big mustache-adorned mouths by the men, daintily set onto darting tongues by women. Distended stomachs bulge inside suits and dresses. Way down at the far end, far from her parents and anyone her age, in the seat of honor, sits Victoria. Sherlock observes her out of the corner of his eye.

It is intriguing to see her at a reasonably close distance and in this setting. She has that distinctive strawberry blonde hair, those fine, high cheekbones that he's seen in the illustrations in the papers. But there are things about her that surprise him. She appears a little older than he'd thought she'd look. She rarely looks anyone in the eye; she seems to be alone, though she's in a crowd. It is almost as if she can hardly wait to leave. There's something about her that disturbs Sherlock. Something isn't right with Victoria Rathbone.

Sherlock also watches her mother, who is almost right in front of him.

She is as beautiful as Irene said and is dressed to the nines today, gems glittering around her neck. Her hair is similar in color to Victoria's and he can see a line of resemblance: from her to her daughter to Andrew Doyle and even Irene. Lady Rathbone's brown eyes are indeed a little cloudy, but the way she focuses them to examine things makes her beauty even more bewitching. The use of a long-stemmed, bejeweled lorgnette that she raises in order to gaze at people or objects farther away adds an upper-crust air that she obviously cultivates. But she rarely speaks to anyone for more than a moment, and Sherlock doesn't hear her mention her daughter or see her as much as turn in the girl's direction.

Holmes peeks the other way, toward the opposite end of the room, to the lord at the head of the table. Rathbone barely looks at anyone either, even when he is holding forth on subjects of impressive importance, which seems to be often – his chin is thrust out and his nose elevated. His red-veined face is only partially evident beneath the mustache, mutton chops, and beard that cover it. He never glances down the table to regard his daughter either, but *his* inattentiveness to her existence is somewhat surprising, given Victoria's avowal that her every wish is his command. They sit so far apart here, their conversation might be best conducted by telegram.

For an instant, Sherlock thinks of his own parents, of his mother hugging him, gazing lovingly into his eyes. But that memory hurts, so he rejects it and returns to the task at hand.

Most upper-class people barely know their children, he reminds himself. They have them reared by nannies, educated by governesses. The way Victoria is being treated may not be so unusual.

Then, a guest actually speaks to her.

"It is a joy to have you back, my dear," intones a white-powdered old woman in a loud voice and with a feigned smile. Her face is like a mask and she isn't turned in the girl's direction.

"Yes, yes," says Lord Rathbone, his big, bullish tone sounding forced, as if he knows he must appear courageous and confident the day after his latest setback. He notices a wayward thread on his sleeve and plucks it off. "She is a good girl, is Victoria, very brave through it all, as I taught her to be, and as I admonish our nation to be. Look at her: she has been matured by all of this. She looks as though she has aged several years."

He doesn't glance her way, nor does anyone else, though Lady Rathbone smiles and acknowledges the expressions of admiration Victoria receives from her female peers.

"Your robbery is an incident of national significance," states a young man clearly.

"Yes, yes, I suppose it is." The lord caresses his big whiskers and smoothes down his hair, combed straight forward to hide his balding scalp.

"We must find these evil perpetrators, and the ones who absconded with your daughter at the end of the season (how barbaric of them to choose such a time), use the maximum power of the Force, spare no expense, and hang them all, as you say, publicly."

"That may not be the way very soon, unfortunately, my good man. Even Newgate Prison has taken to executing indoors, out of sight. One may never see a public hanging in London again."

"Perhaps they can make exceptions on this occasion."

There is a round of laughter. Even Lord Rathbone can't hold back.

Sherlock uses his peripheral vision now. He tries to see as many diners as possible and how they are reacting. This robbery was performed by someone who knew the Rathbones, their habits, their whereabouts, their possessions, their home, and how to get in and out of it. The best suspects may well be . . . seated at this very table.

Who is the bold young man who brought up the subject of the robbery? That gentleman continues to talk, almost dominating the conversation, returning it to the crime when it wanders, and insisting on severe punishment for the criminals.

Either twenty-seven or -eight years of age, and obviously single by the attentions he is paying to that plain, fawning female next to him, who is certainly not his wife. Her accent is American, her glowing, low-cut dress and diamonds expensive. He's of high breeding but there are minute threads frayed on his shirt collar, which looks a little yellowed, as if it has had too many washings. His black hair appears to have been combed a thousand times. Is this a man in search of a rich wife? In search of money? He seems at home in the Rathbone mansion.

But Sherlock wonders. *This sniveling sycophant doesn't seem capable of conceiving such a robbery.* Holmes is wasting his time, getting off on the wrong foot just as he did in St. Neots. He doubts there is anything else to be learned at this table – he must get to the heart of the matter, upstairs. The other footman is removing a few plates.

Lady Rathbone hasn't touched her food for some time. She appears to be finished with this course despite the fact that most of her meal is still sitting there. Sherlock leans over her right shoulder. She smells like lemons. Her skin looks like butter. He lifts the plate and glances toward Victoria. Strangely enough, she is looking back at him. Their eyes meet for an instant. It is a strange thing for an upper-class woman to do. She turns away quickly. Sherlock notices her plate. Every morsel has been consumed, the only serving to be so thoroughly attacked. She must be hungry. He glides over, lifts her plate and observes her, just inches away. She appears to be trembling. That's strange, too. But Sherlock doesn't have much time to think about it.

He is careful to leave the room alone. Out in the hall, he glances around, sees no one, and steals up the stairs, dinner plates still in hand. Once he is on the next floor, he slows down, making sure his footfalls are soundless. The richly colored carpets that cover every inch of the hall help. Lady Rathbone's bedroom is one more storey up.

When he gets there he finds that the door is closed, but not locked. He shuts it behind him and turns to the room. It is like being in an illustration from a society maga-zine. Parts of the upstairs hallways had looked a little empty, stripped in places of valuables: a painting gone here, and a vase there. But this room is different. It smells of lemons just like its inhabitant and is filled with so much furniture, so many plants and flowers, and the walls and floors are so densely decorated that it seems as though it will be difficult to move about. He takes a step . . . *and sees someone!* He almost drops the dinner plates. But it's his image in a mirror. There are mirrors everywhere. He regards himself for a moment, thinking he looks fine in the footman's costume.

Get on with it.

He sets the plates on Lady Rathbone's four-poster bed where they almost disappear into the soft red covers.

Why did the thieves not come here?

He makes for her dressing room.

Downstairs, Lady Rathbone is thinking that it is time to announce that she is feeling a little uncomfortable, that she needs a moment to refresh herself in her boudoir. She excuses herself, leaves the table, and glides through the door to head upstairs.

Sherlock is surprised at the dimensions of the dressing room. It is nearly as large as the bedroom and twice the size of his family's entire flat in Southwark. This is where she would keep her valuables, so he must look for any sign that the thieves came here. Perhaps they only wanted her room to *appear* untouched. But it doesn't look like anything was disturbed in any away; nothing has the look of being fixed up after a robbery. *They didn't come here.* What is it about Lady Rathbone that made her alone exempt from the culprits' thievery? An intriguing thought passes through his mind. *Is she involved? If so, is there something in this room that connects her to them?*

He doubts that Lord Rathbone enters this room. In fact, there is no sign that any male has *ever* been here. It is feminine in the extreme: scented and pink and red. Rows of dresses hang from several wardrobes. He opens a dresser drawer and turns away . . . it is full of underclothing and corsets!

❦

Lady Rathbone tries to climb the great house's stairs as often as possible. A lady should look white and delicate, and she has labored to make her face seem so. Her arms, too, are like porcelain. But she doesn't want to be flabby in her unseen places, like so many of her peers obviously are, so she often climbs and descends these stairs, back and forth. She makes sure no one sees her. Under her flowing dresses and crinoline, the muscles in her smooth white legs are strong and taut. The captain likes her like that.

Everyone is on the lower floors, so she goes up and down this flight twice. But she doesn't like feeling fatigued.

She can hardly wait to be in her dressing room and to loose her stays for a moment. She approaches her bedroom door.

Sherlock has found something. Sticking his head into a wardrobe he notices a little heap on its floor, pushed into a corner. It is two gloves, one obviously a gentleman's, the other a lady's. They are placed so they are clasping each other, all the fingers entwined. The man's is a military glove and the other is Lady Rathbone's – it smells of lemons. The boy's head is so far into the wardrobe that he doesn't hear the bedroom door when it opens.

She may not have the very best vision, but she spots the plates on her bed immediately. Her heart begins to race. *Who is in here?* She whirls around but sees no one. Then . . . she notices that the door to her dressing room is nearly closed. It is never left that way. She rushes over and pushes it open. A footman is leaning into one of her wardrobes! He turns to her with a start. She is about to scream, but sees what he is holding in his hands and almost faints.

Sherlock Holmes cannot believe he has been caught. How could he be such an imbecile, so careless? But he immediately realizes that he is in luck. Lady Rathbone obviously doesn't want to scream, doesn't want to draw attention to this intruder in her dressing room. *Why?* He must figure out *exactly* why immediately: bring his powers of deduction to bear more efficiently than ever before. *Be calm. Be clever.* If he can't outsmart her, he will be tied to the Rathbone robbery and live the rest of his existence in jail or worse. He thinks of the punishment the lord spoke of in his boasting talk at the dinner table. Sherlock's life may depend on what he says in the next minute.

She is staring at the gloves.

13

THE SECRET

"What are you doing, young man?"

"I think you are well aware."

"What do you know? Are you a blackmailer?"

Her voice is curiously different from the one she employed in the dining room. There is no forced accent.

"Perhaps we can make an arrangement. Tell me his name."

"I shan't. Do as you will."

"All right. I will take these items with me. And you will allow me to leave with them because if you try to stop me, I will alert the household. We shall be in contact by post. The cost for the return of the gloves will increase by the day. Or, you can tell me his name – and give me those gems around your neck – and I will return the gloves to you now, *the military man's and yours.*"

"His name is . . . Captain Waller," she finally says, her voice choked with emotion. She reaches up to undo her necklace. It is such a feminine motion, so sweet and vulnerable. Her face colors and a tear plops onto her cheek. Sherlock almost feels sorry for her.

She is so flustered that she is having trouble undoing the clasp and sits down at her dressing table. He approaches to help her. She looks at him in the mirror, up close, and squints. Then she raises her lorgnette by the stem and whirls around in her chair to examine him.

"You aren't a Rathbone footman! You don't *know* me! You are a common burglar! No one will believe you! Give me those!"

She snatches the gloves from his hands . . . and screams. Sherlock can hardly believe how loudly she shrieks. It isn't the sound of an upper-class lady, but the caterwaul of an enraged and aggrieved woman filled with suppressed passions.

He runs into the bedroom with Lady Rathbone in pursuit, well aware that she could knock him to the floor and jump on him without thinking twice. The windows in the room are long and wide, going from knee-high height to within inches of the ten-foot ceiling. One of them is slightly open – ladies like to keep their rooms cool; it is good for the skin. Sherlock rushes to it, grasps the sash in both hands and shoves it up. It barely budges. But his thin frame is his ally again: he can just get through. He struggles out in a flash, forgetting that he is three floors up. Lady Rathbone grabs one of his feet. He can hardly believe it . . . a belle of the London social scene has him by the leg! He can hear servants shouting as they ascend the stairs. He kicks at her, connects with something soft, and feels her release him and fall to the floor. He looks out into the cold, dark night. *Oh-oh*. The ground is far below. The dim lights of all of west London appear to be glowing in the panorama. He can see where the gray flat roof of Buckingham Palace is lit, not far away.

There's a big oak tree about three or four feet from the window. He stands up on the wide sill and leaps. But the branch he aims for is too far away and he misses it and falls through the tree, smacking his arms, his head, and his rear end. *Stay calm.* He looks down, notices a big branch approaching, and seizes it! It makes his hands burn, but he hangs on. Breathing heavily, his heart pounding, he takes a moment to gather himself as he swings from the limb.

"THIEVES! ROBBERY! VILLAINY!" he hears voices shouting. Word has spread through the house and is beginning to spill outside. Sherlock looks to the ground. He's about eight feet from the grass. He lets go. The impact of the landing makes him shudder from his toes to his skull, but everything stays intact. He gets to his feet and runs, aware that several of the house staff are already outside and coming his way.

"Barrymore?" says the cook, who is standing on the lawn with her eyes bulging.

Sherlock knows the area at the front of the house well. He stumbles up the walk, kicks open the black iron gate, and rushes toward the road in the bitter early winter day. The fog hangs in yellow clouds under the tall iron gas lamps on Belgrave Square. The park looks wet and coldly tropical. He heads for it: across the cobblestone street, through the open entrance, onto the criss-crossing paths on the grass under the trees. There is an increasing number of running footsteps behind him, a herd of pursuers.

One of them will catch him, there is no doubt. He cannot get away from that many young men at full gallop. He is done.

Then he trips! But not over any object on the ground or his own feet. It is someone else's foot. Sprawling on the grass, he whips his head around and sees those pretty, patent-leather boots with buttons. He also senses someone rushing out from the bushes nearby. A small boy in a dirty red coat is darting away in the same direction Holmes was going.

"Sherlock!"

Irene Doyle is squatting behind a row of hedges, beckoning him to stay low and come with her.

He doesn't have to think twice.

Rathbone's servants race past in hot pursuit of the smaller boy.

"We shall go this way." Irene nods in the direction Sherlock came from. They wait for all the pursuers to pass. She reaches down and takes his hand. It sends a thrill right up his arm to his shoulders and into his chest.

"Come on, Sherlock! Hurry!"

Finally, he moves, following her onto the street. In minutes they are out of the square and heading away from Belgravia. Irene hands him something – a bundle she had been carrying. Before long, they stop. They are at the high wall that runs along the gardens at the rear of Buckingham Palace. The street is well lit here and they are standing close to each other. Her face and hair glow in the lambent light. She is trying to seem distant and business-like.

"You should put those back on – your coat, at least.

You can't walk around the way you are. We'll throw the footman's coat into a dustbin."

His clothes? But they were in the stable at the rear of the mansion.

"How did you know . . ."

He steps back from her.

"You were watching me?"

"No . . . I wasn't. Believe me. I have no interest in *watching* you. I –"

"Someone was." *Malefactor.*

"No, he wasn't. Not . . . exactly. He was watching the house, not you. Then you came along, pretending to be a fishmonger's boy. He left as soon as you were inside. But I wanted to see how you made out, so he asked the littlest Irregular to keep me company – the wee fellow has a bit of a shine for me. Then I saw you climbing out of the upper-storey window and hightailing it over here. I figured they had you – it is in my interest to keep you in this game. It occurred to me that the little one was wearing a stolen red coat not unlike your footman's uniform. So I asked him to lead the servants on a wild goose chase away from here. He always does what I say. He will stay far in front of them. Believe me, he will never be caught."

She smiles weakly.

"So . . . you've told him."

"Not as much as I told you."

"He has no interest in helping you, Irene. Don't deceive yourself. His interest is in other things: in being near you . . . in my destruction."

"I just want someone to solve this. It just needs to be done."

They had started walking again, but Sherlock stops. "Thank you for coming to my rescue, Miss Doyle. Now, I must be on my way."

He turns to go.

"Sherlock, you know I would rather this was different . . . and I hope it is you who succeeds."

"If you told that snake *anything*, then you told him too much. I kept you at a distance in order to protect you, Irene, but now you . . ."

"I . . . *what*? Say it Sherlock, even if it is an awful thing, say it. Say something with some passion in it to me. You have become so cold."

He had lost his temper and was going to say that she had turned into his enemy. But now he looks into those beautiful brown eyes and can't do it. It isn't true. He turns away so he won't see her when he tells her what he has to say . . . this final time. It isn't a moment for bitterness, just time to be brave, for the bare truth. His life cannot be like anyone else's. He remembers holding his dead mother in his arms.

"There will never be another time when I will need you in any way. I work alone."

A cloud passes over her face. Deep pain and resentment wells up inside her.

"You will regret this, Sherlock Holmes!" she hisses, in a voice unlike her own.

14

Sherlock lies in his wardrobe that night feeling lonely. He still has Sigerson Bell as an ally, but no one else. He wonders if that is really the way it has to be. Will anyone ever understand both him and what he believes in? It would be wonderful to have a companion – a mate his own age he cares about – someone to help him in his lifelong quest.

But he can never have a girl for a close friend . . . or a wife . . . everyone must be kept at arm's length. He wishes it wasn't so complicated. Alone and in the dark, he lets the tears slip down his cheeks. Soon there are many of them. He turns to his rough hempen pillow to muffle his sobs.

The next day is a Sunday, but he is up early with an expression of resolve on his face. He knows he should act slowly and meticulously, but the fact that Malefactor was right outside the Rathbone home makes that a losing proposition. He has some leads and he must follow up on them immediately.

This crime has something to do with Lady Rathbone. What, he doesn't know. But he can't pursue her anymore, at least not directly. *What else? Who else?*

Victoria.

Something isn't right about her, he is sure. What if he watched her . . . or even found a way to engage her in a brief conversation, an exchange of just a few words that he controls? On the surface, that seems impossible. But perhaps there is a way.

He needs to go back to Belgravia and figure it out: stay in the park in the square, well out of sight, watch the house, wait for Victoria to come out, observe her movements, follow her, or discover how he might actually approach her. And if he succeeds, he should mention Paul Dimly. He can use the little boy's name: her heart will melt when she recalls him and then perhaps she'll talk to someone like Sherlock – he can take advantage of her momentary indulgence to ask his questions. They will have to be expertly conceived.

He leaves without breakfast, before the apothecary is awake. When he gets to the park, he doesn't have to wait a minute to get started – there is a surprise as he settles by a tree in the square to watch. Though the big mansion doesn't appear to have roused yet, Victoria Rathbone is stepping out the wide front door . . . alone. And not just for a breath of air – she is wearing a fancy coat and bonnet, as if she dressed in the night and is going somewhere at this early-morning hour. But no carriage awaits her. This is decidedly strange. It is unusual for a respectable lady, especially a young, unmarried one, let alone one recently traumatized, to be by herself outside in London. Irene Doyle has certainly been known to go out alone, but she isn't of the Rathbone's superior class, and was raised by a father who encouraged her to be independent.

Sherlock tucks himself behind the tree and observes, rubbing his hands together to keep warm.

He can see now that Victoria is carrying a big bag, a portmanteau, showing surprising strength in her pale arms. Her breath is evident in quick little cloudbursts in front of her face. She closes the door gently, as if she hopes it won't make a sound, looks carefully around the front lawn, back up at the big, bulging bay windows on the front of the house, and then walks briskly along the front walk toward the gate. *What is going on?*

An idea rushes into Sherlock's mind. He steps out from behind the tree and darts across the road. London's street children often do little favors for the rich for coins.

"Hansom cab, me lady?" he shouts.

Victoria Rathbone stops dead in her tracks. One of her hands moves to her lips, as if to shush him. But she arrests it before it reaches her face, turns sharply toward the house, and begins to scurry back. Sherlock can't believe how quickly she moves. In a flash, she returns up the walkway and into the mansion. There isn't a second to even mention the little boy's name.

Sherlock doesn't have an inkling about what this means, but he knows it isn't advisable to stand there trying to figure it out. He takes to his heels.

Did I frighten her? Was it simply that? Are there servants pursuing me again? He glances back as he flees. No one seems to be coming, but he keeps moving, just in case. *Was she really leaving the house alone? Why did she run back?*

It doesn't make sense.

Holmes maintains a quick pace until he is all the way to Trafalgar Square. There, amidst the beginnings of a crowd of Sunday tourists in the cloudy, early-winter morning, he blends in, becomes anonymous. He huddles against the stone plinth of a statue and thinks. He eats some chunks of bread he has brought from the shop. The crowd grows. Out in the teeming colors of the masses in the square, he hears people arguing, vendors shouting, the pigeons cooing, vehicles rumbling on the streets, church bells tolling nearby. It is so loud that it almost hurts his ears. He thinks he sees an Irregular, that little one, peering at him from among the tourists. But when he looks carefully, he can't be certain. He makes the scene go silent. It all fades, faces blur, and even smells recede. People move, speak, shout . . . without a sound. He concentrates. *What isn't right about Victoria Rathbone? How does it fit into what he knows about the robbery?*

All he really has is her unusual behavior, her mother's secret, and a vague profile of the culprits and how they pulled off their crime. It worries him that Malefactor might be well ahead in this game.

He tells himself that he should do something to clear his mind.

He decides to go to Stepney. He isn't sure why.

Stepney lies east of even Whitechapel. There are many roads that lead to it, and all that come from central London are treacherous for a boy out on his own. The city is filled with pockets of poor, violent neighborhoods, and generally things get worse to the east or south.

Sherlock decides to steer clear of Whitechapel itself. He has had enough of his father's old Jewish territory and those dark alleys where he came face-to-face with his first gruesome murder. Instead, he will walk nearer the Thames. He strolls toward St. Paul's Cathedral and then swings south to the water, amazed, as always, at the number of churches in London. They are mostly dark and medieval, awe-inspiring temples to goodness standing amongst all this evil. He passes London Bridge and the ancient Tower of London, still thinking about Victoria and her mother. He veers slightly north to avoid the docks and the hard-living Londoners who lurk there, but soon is in places where he must be on his guard anyway; where anxious people in search of a living eye their marks, where crowds of children walk about in rags, begging from strangers. He darts through Shadwell, slows past a Friends Meeting House, feeling a little safer, but then moves into Stepney. Here he must be alert again.

Irene had said that the little boy was in the Ratcliff Workhouse, which Sherlock knows is near St. Dunstan's Church. *What sort of parents did the child have? A young girl who couldn't keep him? Paupers who couldn't either?* Sherlock begins to chide himself for being here. This has nothing to do with the robbery, and he's wasting his time. Malefactor is likely hard at work. Did he come here as a way to be close to the one person he dearly wants as a friend, but has pushed away for good? Perhaps he might see her.

He walks up Stepney High Street, feeling more secure where the road is busy, and sees St. Dunstan's up ahead, lording it over both its expansive green grounds and the dirt-poor neighborhood.

It is like a castle from the Middle Ages in a modern, knightless world. Church services have just ended and the property is nearly deserted. He steps gently across the grass and sits on a bench near the grand stone stairs, pausing for a few moments, thinking about the case, his mother, whether or not he really wants to see Paul Dimly, and if he would be allowed into the workhouse anyway. The sun is straight above him in the cold noon hour. He stands and walks up the many steps to St. Dunstan's entrance and tries the big wooden doors. They are locked. Looking north from this elevation, he sees the back of a rundown, two-storey building that looks like a patched-up stable, the words "Ragged School" near the roof. *Didn't Irene say that Thomas Barnardo ran such a school near here?*

When he walks past the school a few moments later, he spies a young man stepping through the doors into the street. He wears a plain but respectable suit, round, wire-rimmed spectacles and the beginnings of a mustache. His appearance sticks out in these surroundings and there is something about him that strikes Sherlock as rather brave. A child nears, dressed in a filthy garment more like a potato sack than a dress and wearing a spit-polished pair of men's black boots. The young man pats the little girl on the head. Her hair hangs in greasy strings and is likely crawling with lice. She clings to him, but he admonishes her, makes her stand up straight. Sherlock hears the word *Jesus*. Ah, this is his man.

Holmes approaches. He wouldn't do this with just any gentleman of Barnardo's middle-class stature. Most citizens of his ilk, encountering a desperate-looking boy in a threadbare suit, would shout at him or strike him or run. But he knows Thomas Barnardo is different.

"Excuse me, sir."

"Yes, my good fellow. Are you in need? The lord . . ."

"I am a friend of Irene Doyle's."

There is a pause.

"You are?"

"And I would like to see Paul Dimly."

"Ah, Dimly. That is not his Christian name, young man. Better to simply call him Paul, like the saint. A friend of Irene Doyle's, you say. Would you like to help the child?"

"Uh . . . yes, yes I would."

"And how will you do that?"

"I . . . uh . . . I don't know, sir. I haven't figured that out yet."

Barnardo smiles.

"Come with me."

The Ratcliff Workhouse isn't a particularly large version of those mostly black, soot-encrusted, granite or wooden monsters that stain London every few dozen streets or so. It is built in a *U*-shape, on three floors, with Spartan accommodations, a large work area outside, and a cavernous dining hall in the basement. Paul Dimly lives alone in a very small room on an upper floor once used as a broom closet. He has no one to live with and would shun company anyway.

When Thomas Barnardo ushers Sherlock into the little room, they are startled to find it empty. After a moment of panic, the kindly man realizes what time it is, and that the little boy must have been taken down to dinner. The dining hall (though it is hardly fitting to call it that) is tall and long and cold and filled with crude, wooden tables set with tin plates and cups. At a thick counter at the front a burly male cook is ladling out a lumpy, dark stew. It seems to have a good deal of cabbage in it, for the stench of that vegetable fills the fetid air. Sherlock spots a small, scraggly Christmas tree, undecorated, on a wooden pedestal, just over the cook's shoulder. He has forgotten that December has just arrived, and a dart of pain pierces his chest – his mother always celebrated Christmas and his father used to join in, too. This will be his first year without her, without his family.

Paul Dimly isn't difficult to find. He is the smallest being in the room. Sherlock is alarmed at his size. He seems no larger than a dog, a living Tiny Tim. And he crouches over his meal, not touching it, pulling himself into a tight ball in the cold, as if he were trying to get back into his mother's womb.

"Paul," says Thomas Barnardo. "I've brought a friend of Miss Doyle's to see you."

Sherlock thinks the boy moves a little at the sound of Irene's name, but he doesn't look up. His dirty, reddish-blond hair is so thin that he seems to be balding. He has no shoes and his torn workhouse uniform is the color of dirt.

"Oi!" shouts a rough from across the table: he's a few years younger than Sherlock. "'ere's a bloke to look at you." Paul doesn't respond. "Look up! Dimly!"

As other nearby boys laugh, Paul stares up.

It nearly makes Sherlock Holmes cry. The little one's enormous eyes are a beautiful deep brown like Irene's and seem to fill up half his face, but they look right through his visitors and can't focus. The lids are swollen and turned inward, the iris and pupil, even the whites, are covered with dirty clouds like those that dominate London's winter skies. The mists that still float across Lady Rathbone's similar brown eyes are nothing compared to this. The child seems as though he is already blind.

"He can barely see your face," whispers Barnardo, "I would guess he has little more than a week . . . then he won't see anything at all."

Sherlock wants to leave the hall. He *must* find a way to talk to Victoria Rathbone. *Now.*

But there is another concern inside him. And it worries him. He is just as excited about gaining Irene's admiration, the adoration of London, and the envy of Inspector Lestrade, as he is about helping this forlorn child.

He feels he should say something to Paul Dimly before he goes. As he regards him again, he notices that more than his eyes are like Irene. He has her high cheekbones, a face that somehow looks fine and well bred. He is remarkably like Lady Rathbone too, now that Sherlock considers it.

"Is that your hat?"

Worried that the bullies would enter his room and steal it, little Paul has brought his precious hat with him again.

"It . . . is his father's," says Mr. Barnardo, smiling at the child.

Dimly's eyes are resisting tears so the young doctor steers Sherlock away, but not before Holmes examines the boy's treasure as best he can, half-hidden as it is in two small hands. *A cocked captain's hat, deep blue with a camel hump in the middle, flattening at either end. Royal Navy. Initials on the brim . . . first one . . . can't see it . . . second . . . W.*

Mr. Barnardo walks down the creaking staircase with Sherlock, his hand on his shoulder.

"There are many children like him in London, you know. We cannot help each and every one. He may be lost. But we can, all of us, attempt to reform the society in which we live. That will change everything in the long run. There are several ways to do that, even the poorest can help. The first and most important is to turn to our Lord Jesus Christ for guidance and admonish all others to do the same. The second is to petition our government to care for our poor, to enact . . ."

"Sir," says Sherlock.

"Yes, young man?" There's an air of expectation on Barnardo's face.

"Who was his father?"

"Paul's? I have no idea. And neither does he, I should think. He was adopted by a man and wife who died of the cholera about a year ago. He was brought here by the parish beadle."

"How old is he?"

"Just five, God bless him."

Sherlock's questions have a purpose. And the answers are putting a shocking possibility into his mind. *The boy looks like Lady Rathbone. He has her eye problem. She disappeared for many months five years ago. She loves a captain whose last initial is* W . . . *the same letter on the little boy's hat.* But it is a laughable notion and he rejects it the instant it enters his mind. This is simply a series of coincidences. *Impossible.*

"There he is now."

Sherlock looks up to see the fat, uniformed beadle on the staircase landing, speaking to one of the workhouse nurses, twirling the mustache on his red, fleshy face, trying to impress her with a long-winded story filled with the biggest words he can muster.

"Beadle?"

The man turns to Mr. Barnardo, annoyed to be interrupted.

"Can you tell us about the little one with the eye infection?"

"Who wants to know?" He glances down his nose at Sherlock Holmes.

"I do," says Barnardo.

"Yes . . . well . . . Paul Dimly . . . I got word of 'im about a year ago, I did. 'is folks passed from the cholera and 'e was left alone in that flat they was living in."

"Where?" asks Sherlock.

"Believe it was on White 'orse Lane," says the beadle reluctantly.

"You have such a sharp memory, you does," says the nurse, smiling up at him. He clears his throat.

"North of 'ere just south of Mile End and the Jews' 'ospital, two buildings up from where White 'orse Lane meets Friendly Place, beside O'Neil's green grocer shop."

"Thank –"

"And they weren't 'is own folks. They was old. Others around said they was distant relations to a captain in the navy who 'ad fathered the lad . . . gave 'im to 'em. 'e was from the 'igh end of the family, such as it was. Doubt the truth of that, though. Poor folks talk."

When Barnardo turns back to the boy, he is gone.

White Horse Lane is a thoroughfare to the north of St. Dunstan's Church. It runs straight up to Mile End, which is the eastern part of Whitechapel Road. It isn't the best neighborhood, but not the most frightening, either. Sherlock even spots an unkempt little park nearby.

It seems impossible that this desperate child in that dark workhouse could have anything to do with Lady Rathbone. He tells himself it is ridiculous one more time.

But the more he thinks of the lad's face . . . and then hers . . . the more the two look alike.

It doesn't take him long to get to the intersection of the streets he seeks. He sees the Jews' hospital up near Mile End and spots the Irishman's green grocery. He counts two buildings to the north. The residence he is looking for is obviously tenanted by more than a single family, one to each of the three floors. It is a non-descript lodging, neither poverty-stricken nor comfortable. There are two boys playing skittles on the street nearby, both about ten years old, dressed in threadbare trousers and shirts, but at least fully clothed and not barefoot. *Perfect. Never ask questions of adults.*

"Do you lot know of the family that used to live here?" asks Sherlock pointing at the house in question. "The old folks who had a boy?"

"The Wallers?" says one lad immediately.

It sends a chill down Sherlock's spine. "The Wallers," he repeats in a monotone.

"That's what I said, you prat. Are you deaf?"

"And he weren't their son."

"No?"

"Me mum says he was a bastard."

"Heard that too. A navy man, his real daddy was. Wallers had no folks left around here when they died. They croaked awful sudden like. The beadle came and took the boy away. It was winter time and he was freezin'."

But Sherlock is barely listening. He is thinking of Lady Rathbone, fear on her face, admitting to the name of her secret lover.

Captain Waller.

Within an hour he is on Montague Street, tingling with excitement, anxious to tell Irene, barely able to wait and see the look on her face. They may never be friends again, but at least he can have her admiration.

He is certain that what he has learned will save little Paul's life. The child was given away at birth so Lady Rathbone likely doesn't know where he is or even that he is alive. But if it is at all possible for her to help him now, she will surely move heaven and earth to do so. What mother wouldn't? And even if she can't, the Doyles can now take little Paul into their home – *the child is their relation.* And there's still another possibility . . . they could all *force* Lady R. to help them. The facts are there for the three of them to blackmail her.

He wants to speak to Irene alone.

It's been another cold, rainy day. There is green Christmas holly on the Doyles' front gate. He squeaks the gate open and walks quietly up to the doorsteps. Looking down, he finds Mr. Doyle's footprints on the muddy surface, heading out. If she's here, she is on her own.

Then he hears something startling.

Singing . . . coming from a second-storey room of the Doyle home. And though it is beautiful, it isn't an opera piece or a hymn. It's the lusty sound of a music hall ditty:

"I love you like
You love me

We're so alike
Don't you see?

But gems and pearls
Would make it better
Gems and pearls
In your next love letter."

Though he is surprised to hear such a song in the Doyle home, that isn't what is startling. It's who is singing it. Irene's voice, a voice Sherlock never dreamed she had, sounds remarkable: strong and clear, filling the risqué song with bold intent. For a moment, he forgets what he has come for. Then he picks up a pebble and tosses it at the window. The singing ceases abruptly, the window opens, and Irene looks down. At first she appears embarrassed, then angry.

"Go away."

"May I come up?"

"Up? . . . Here?"

"Yes. I have something very important to tell you."

She hesitates, but then disappears from the window.

In minutes they are sitting far apart on the settee in the morning room on the ground floor and Sherlock is feeling a sort of homesickness. He glances around at the familiar furniture, the warm, wood walls. This was where he and Irene used to talk. But today she is close-mouthed. And she barely looks at him.

"Was that you singing?"

"No."

"Then who was it?"

"None of your business. Why would you care, anyway?"

"I didn't know you –"

"I have always wanted to sing. I told Malefactor about it and he encouraged me."

"I see."

"Father wouldn't approve, but it appeals to me."

"He is a wise man. That is not the sort of song –"

"What did you have to tell me?"

Sherlock isn't sure how to begin. "I went to the Ratcliff Workhouse."

She steals a glance at him. "You did?"

"Irene . . . I think I have uncovered something about little Paul, something incredible, utterly inconceivable, until I put together some facts."

"Tell me, and then go."

He describes what he found in Lady Rathbone's room, the navy captain's gloves entwined with hers, her admission that her beau's name was Waller, how the boy's birth occurred at the same time as her longest disappearance from home, their similar eye problems, similar appearances, and the house on White Horse Lane belonging to aging caretaker parents with the same last name as the captain, people who adopted their child from a relative in the Royal Navy.

Irene is stunned. She stares into the distance for a long time after he finishes.

"That explains why the boys are like twins," she finally says.

"I beg your pardon?"

She goes upstairs without saying a word. Sherlock follows. They enter the master bedroom. She opens a closet and brings out a framed painting.

"What are you –"

Irene turns the painting around so he can see it. The image floors him.

"Why . . . it's Paul Waller. Why is he dressed like . . . how could you –"

"It's not Paul Waller . . . it's Paul Doyle."

"Who?"

"My brother."

"Your what?"

"When I saw that child in the workhouse I couldn't believe what I was seeing. My brother had come back to life . . . Paul is a favorite family name . . . this explains it all."

Her story is long and filled with emotion. She recounts how her brother's death tore her father apart, how the boy was never spoken of again, especially after she was born and her mother died; how she has striven all these years to be an heir who will make her father proud.

"That's why I couldn't tell you or anyone else why we wanted to save him."

"But you can save him now. Go to Lady Rathbone, Irene. Tell her about her son. She will help cure –"

"Sherlock, you know even less than I imagined about the upper class. She can never acknowledge the existence of a child born out of wedlock, not to anyone, not even in secret. If it ever became public, it would destroy her and be the death of her husband's political career. And my father would never consent to forcing her to do anything with this information; that isn't his way. In fact, I doubt he would be party to even speaking of the child's existence in her presence."

"Then, just tell *him* what I told you. He would adopt Paul now, wouldn't he? His own relation? Even if the child's eyes cannot be healed, he will have the two of you . . . and all of this." He looks around at the beautiful room.

She blanches and doesn't say anything. He had expected her to be overjoyed.

"Irene?"

"Yes . . . yes, I suppose that is what we should do." She gives him a frozen smile, turns her back and stands gazing out the window. The master bedroom looks out over Montague Street. The thought of being replaced in her father's affections stands before her. His son will return.

"Sherlock!" she says suddenly, seeing something through the window. "My father is coming!"

She shoves the painting back into the closet as they rush out of the bedroom and down the stairs.

"I don't understand," she says, "he was supposed to be away all day. He looks like he's in a hurry. I wonder if something is wrong. Maybe it's the robbery. Maybe the thieves have been found!"

By the time they reach the ground floor, they can hear Andrew Doyle opening the front entrance. Irene pulls open a closet door in the hallway, grabs Sherlock by the shoulders and shoves him inside. He listens in the darkness.

"Irene!" Mr. Doyle exclaims, out of breath, barely into the vestibule. "You will never believe it! The news is all over London!"

"Calm yourself, Father. You are too excited."

"It's Victoria Rathbone!"

"What has happened?"

"She has been kidnapped . . . *again*!"

PART THREE

ABDUCTION

herlock Holmes doesn't wait for the Doyles to get to the other end of the hall. He opens the closet, quietly rushes to the entrance, and flies down the front steps into the London day. He hits the streets on the run. At first, he doesn't even know where he is going. He's just moving, and his mind is racing, too.

Kidnapped . . . a second time! What does this mean? What does this MEAN?

He has to get somewhere. He must do something while the criminals' trail is fresh. But where should he go and what should he do? He is betting that he is uniquely positioned to solve these crimes, knows things that the police (and hopefully the Irregulars) don't. It is essential that he act immediately. These villainies may very well be connected. What if he solved the robbery *and* located Victoria? She is out there now . . . to be found.

Little Paul is facing blindness even if the Doyles adopt him, but if Sherlock can throw light on both crimes, *all* will be well: Victoria will get the physician to work his magic and Andrew Doyle will be even more grateful to him than he would have been before . . . the gift of sight will be gained for his adopted son. Sherlock's future will be made. His heart pounds.

Be calm.

He stops running as he turns onto Great Russell Street. Breathing hard, he walks up to the elegant stone steps of the Roman-looking British Museum and sits down. *Think. Quickly, but without error. What must I do?*

What do I know? Two thieves, two carriages, intimate knowledge of the inside and outside of the house, mother with a secret, daughter acting strange, leaving the house on her own. But none of that still seems to go anywhere, so he sets it aside. *What else? Think of both crimes.* He remembers what Lestrade said when he found Victoria the first time. The culprits had held her somewhere on the southern coast. That tells him little as well. But . . . what is his instinct saying? Perhaps he can put that together with the facts. He feels there is some connection between Lady Rathbone and the robbery. It would explain the most singular fact about the crime: why the thieves didn't so much as enter her room. *Lady Rathbone . . . her lover . . . and that crime . . . either crime.* How do they all go together? His mind slips back to the police information again. *A place on the southern coast?* He goes from east to west remembering coastal towns and cities. Folkestone? Eastbourne? Brighton? Portsmouth?

A connection sounds loud and clear.

Portsmouth. . . . It's the home of the Royal Navy.

Captain Waller.

Sherlock gets up and heads home.

Lady Rathbone's secret lover may very well live in the city where Victoria was held! The police may be flying there now: frantic, Lestrade is surely at the end of his rope. The boy smiles. *If the Force indeed found Victoria in Portsmouth, they will hope to pick up the trail there now – but that will be all they have. On the other hand, I may know the identity of the mastermind himself.* Waller won't have left England. He, or anyone else who is holding Victoria, knows she is valuable only if he keeps her in his hands, stays close by. All Sherlock has to do is locate him – a captain, distinguished or not, will be traceable in Portsmouth. *Follow him.* Perhaps Victoria is hidden in a secret navy location.

But first, Holmes has to find a way to get there. He cannot walk all the way to Portsmouth.

He must go back to the shop and tell Sigerson Bell his plans. He wants to get the old man's blessing to be away this time and perhaps even gain his aid. The apothecary helped him with the Brixton gang case and recently allowed him time to investigate the Rathbones. Even so, this might be going too far. Tomorrow is Monday and a school day, the beginning of the week when Sherlock is particularly needed at work. Nevertheless, he is adamant that this time, he will do things right. He must speak to his friend. Whatever happens, it must be decided immediately.

The sun is setting as he reaches Denmark Street. The minute he enters the front door to the tinkle of the bell, he senses that something is different. It is strangely silent throughout the shop, especially in the laboratory, but despite the boy's acute ability to observe, he can't spot anything out of the ordinary. He simply senses it. Bell is sitting at the wooden lab table, mixing some sort of viscous green liquid with brown. *Our Mutual Friend* rests by his side.

Sherlock is ready to explode with his news, lay all his evidence and desires before the old man. But as he opens his mouth, Bell frowns, sets both torts down gently, and puts his finger to his lips, asking for silence. Sherlock looks around again, not understanding what is going on. They both sit quietly for a few minutes, Bell regarding his pocket watch and glancing upwards every now and then, Sherlock standing still, but wanting to pace, to scream out his news. Eventually the boy gets the feeling that there is someone else in the room. He thinks he can even hear a rhythmic breathing. But no one is evident.

He can't hold back any longer. He needs to get to Portsmouth. As his lips begin to form his first word, the old man vigorously throws up a hand and gestures with a single digit, demanding just one more moment of silence. He nods toward the ceiling. Sherlock looks up.

A man is suspended upside down from the part of the lab where its roof peaks to an arch, more than twelve feet high. The boy instantly recognizes him as one of the greatest acrobats in the world. The one and only Thomas Hanlon is hanging from Sigerson Bell's laboratory ceiling like a bat: he of the spectacular Hanlon-Lees troupe.

"Good day," the star says sullenly. He is dressed in a dark suit with a yellow cravat and has black hair, parted in the middle. Though his face is flushed red, he seems perfectly relaxed.

Sherlock's heart sinks. He won't be able to say a word about the case until the acrobat leaves.

"I have been treating Professor Hanlon for feeling low," says Bell in a remarkably calm voice, as if he is trying to soothe all three of them. "He was, as you might know, the victim of a horrific accident in America a few years back, during which a portion of his skull was knocked in. He now suffers from depression of the brain. My solution is an injection of ape adrenaline, followed by a good hanging to let it all shake down into the medulla oblongata. You may extricate yourself, Mr. Hanlon."

The great gymnast pulls his feet out from the rafters without even reaching up. It seems to take almost no effort at all. In an instant, he is falling, but he twists in the air and lands on the soles of his shoes. He walks calmly toward Bell and deposits a coin on the table.

"Feeling better, Mr. Hanlon?"

"A little livelier, yes." His voice is a monotone.

"Thinking too much about oneself is part of the disease, sir. It makes an individual morose."

"But when one is at the top of one's profession, one has little time for others. One must dwell on one's own work, one's destiny," says Hanlon. "You wouldn't understand . . . though I appreciate your help."

The intrepid acrobat leaves the shop.

"I have my doubts about him, Sherlock," says the old man, "He has done some sort of irreparable damage to his brain. I give him less than a year to live."

"I need to ask you something," says the boy impatiently.

"Always ready for interrogation."

"It is about the Rathbones."

"Ah!"

"I must ask you if –"

"I have a question for you first, my boy. Sit down."

Sherlock sits, his heels tapping anxiously on the floor.

"Why do you do these things?"

The boy doesn't like the tone of the inquiry. It seems as though the old man may be about to put a stop to his opportunity at the very moment when he most needs his support. Bell opens a door in his glass cabinets, takes down the jar of opium, and looks meaningfully back at Holmes.

"Uh . . . uh . . ."

"That doesn't sound like a good reason."

"I . . ."

"Is it for the attention it may bring you? Is it to help these superior-class folks? Is it *really* in the cause of justice?" Bell looks over his eyeglasses at Sherlock Holmes, then turns back to the opium jar, seals it up again and returns it to the cabinet.

"I . . ." Sherlock begins, and then thinks. "I would like to help a little boy."

Sigerson Bell turns sharply back to his apprentice with a look of intrigue.

"Go on."

"There's a child in a Stepney workhouse, five years of age, by the name of Paul Waller, who needs medical attention to his eyes. He has a terrible, apparently untreatable infection. His corneas are cloudy and his lids are swollen and turned back. They say he will be blind in a week. Lord Rathbone has the power to help him. He can put the boy into the hands of his personal physician, the only man in London, perhaps in Europe, who can cure him. Victoria Rathbone has promised to make her father do it. But . . . there has been sensational news . . . she has been kidnapped again!"

"I know."

"You do?"

"I have my sources."

Sherlock is a bit taken aback, but he goes on.

"If Miss Rathbone cannot be found, then the little boy will go blind. But . . . I may know the identity of the fiend we all seek. And I think I can locate him."

"And you want to do this for the cause of the little boy?"

"Yes, sir."

"That settles it then."

"It does?"

"Whatever you wanted to ask of me, the answer is yes."

"It is?"

"I am guessing that you want to go to the southern coast . . . Portsmouth?"

As Sherlock looks at him in disbelief, the old man spins like a whirling dervish and advances toward his little strongbox.

"Yes, I too would make a devilishly good detective," he smiles. "The first train available to you is the six o'clock morning express. Fare by the London and South Western

Railway will be one pound return. Take this and be off with you." He hands the boy a couple of coins. "School and this shop shall await anyone with such lofty goals."

An idea occurs to Sherlock.

"Would you come with me, sir?"

The old man is as agile and alert as a rabbit. He wouldn't be a burden, and his quick mind would help the boy at every turn of the Portsmouth investigation. There shouldn't be much danger in this outing, and Sherlock likes the idea of having a companion, especially in the person of his dearest friend.

But Bell's answer surprises him.

"No," he says instantly, "no, I . . . uh . . . I have . . . work I must do." He looks like someone who is hiding something. A guilty expression spreads across his face.

I know he can spare the time. What is he up to? And how did he know about Portsmouth?

"Now, I would suggest to you that you clean up this shop and then take to your bed. You have much to do in the south, a long day ahead of you. You must be up early and on your way. *Shoo!*"

❤

The old man usually rises before the boy in the mornings. Holmes is given to lingering in his wardrobe, pondering his life and then spending a good deal of time at the mirror. Today, Bell is up long before him. Just as Sherlock appears, the apothecary quickly throws a cloth over a vial of liquid ammonia and a shard of yellow sulfur, with which he had obviously been experimenting. He then motions to the table. The boy's breakfast is already waiting: a display of fried liver and buttermilk arrayed in mortars and tubes. The minute the apprentice has swallowed it, Bell begins rushing him.

"Now go. Go, go, go!" He says, almost shoving the boy toward the door. But just as Sherlock walks through it, the old man takes him by the arm.

"Are you sure that you are doing this for the child?"

Sherlock considers his answer for a few seconds. "Uh . . . yes, sir."

When Holmes is almost all the way down Denmark Street in the cold and bustling London dawn, he glances back at the shop. He isn't sure, but he can almost swear that the front door is held open a crack and one lens of a pair of field glasses is eyeing him as he walks away.

Within the hour, Sherlock Holmes is speeding toward the southern coast.

THEIR PORTSMOUTH LAIR

As the first morning train on the London and South Western Railway from Waterloo Station pulls into the Portsmouth terminal, an hour and a half after departure, Sherlock gets up from his seat and walks toward the doors. He is clutching the backs of the wooden third-class benches, staggering about as the locomotive chugs to a halt, warily watching the passengers, anxious to get out.

He wants to be down near the dockyard *now*, the area where the Royal Navy has its barracks, its officers' mess, its magnificent ships in the Portsmouth Harbour. He is telling himself that he has made the right choice coming here. A southern coastal town? A captain in the navy? That *must* go together. But he has begun to have doubts. His faulty reasoning in St. Neots still affects his confidence, and all the time he had to think on the train has made him wonder why he is assuming that Waller must be involved in either of the crimes. There is really no sound evidence, just clever guesswork, and he remembers how his father felt about guessing. But Sigerson Bell thought Portsmouth a good choice, too.

Why, he isn't sure. Because it is a city known for its crime, the best of all the port towns for getting away by sea?

Then he spots something that puts all his doubts on hold.

There's a youth, a little older than he, stepping down from the second-class carriage ahead, glancing around in a suspicious manner. Sherlock smiles. The lad wears a beard and mustache. Definitely wears it. Underneath all that hair, Holmes detects a ferret-like face.

He follows young Lestrade along the platform under the curving glass ceiling, through the beautiful booking office and out of doors. On Station Street, he buys the morning edition of the *Portsmouth News* from a vendor, something to hold in front of his face should his prey suspect a lurker and look back. Lestrade must be on his way to the very spot where Victoria was found the first time she was kidnapped. He will lead Sherlock right to it! Searching for Captain Waller can wait.

Lestrade, heading south and slipping in and out of crowds of pedestrians and often glancing back, is sticking to a main thoroughfare, but when Sherlock looks down side streets he sees the tightly packed neighborhoods for which this gray-and-brown city is known. They house its tough, sea-faring class. This is where Charles Dickens came from and it seems fitting. There appear to be pubs on every corner, drinking holes for sailors, and a sense of danger hangs in the air.

Sherlock expects his guide to take him toward the dockyard or into the heart of the city. Instead, he is heading south in the direction of the green Commons and the suburb of Southsea, a newer, middle-class area much more genteel than the center of Portsmouth. It isn't where one would have expected to find much criminal activity.

Sherlock starts to think, and this time, it's a mistake. Suddenly, the junior Lestrade isn't there. Holmes picks up his pace, anxiously searching the crowds ahead. The streets aren't nearly as busy here: he can see everyone in front of him, respectably dressed folks bundled up in early winter clothes . . . and not one of them is his quarry. He approaches a park. Disgusted with himself, he slouches down on a bench.

"May I be of assistance?"

Young Lestrade is standing right behind him.

Sherlock starts. "How . . . Master Lestrade, nice to see you."

How does he do that!

"On a seaside visit, are you? Perhaps the ferry over to the Isle of Wight?"

"You know why I am here. We might as well continue our walk. I shan't cause any troubles. I simply want to see where she was found."

"I don't have the slightest idea what you are talking about."

"So, you are on holidays, too?"

"Yes."

"A stroll through lovely Southsea?"

"Without question."

"A walk along the boardwalk?"

"Absolutely."

"In the early winter breezes?"

"One can't be choosy."

"In disguise?"

Lestrade doesn't respond at first. They look out across the park.

"You must turn around and go back to London, Master Holmes."

"I will not."

"Oh, but you shall. Or I will call a constable to send you on your way."

Lestrade sits down beside him, smiling.

"What will be the charge? I am causing no harm. But you . . . you are a boy in disguise. *Very* suspicious. Does anyone know you here? Perhaps it is I who should call the police?"

The other boy glowers. "Then I shall notify my father and the detectives who are with him."

"Thank you for informing me of the presence of your father in this city, and should you do as you say and speak to him, I will have reason to doubly appreciate you . . . for you will lead me directly to the scene of the crime. . . . I assume that is where your father is?"

"I will not lead you anywhere!"

"Then . . . we shall wait."

The two boys sit on the park bench for a full half hour without saying a single word. But it is Lestrade who is first to suffer from a case of the twitches, then a distinct coloring in his face. He rises to his feet.

"All right! You have me . . . this time!"

"Master Lestrade, you could simply return home and I would be none the wiser as to the location of the scene."

"You know I don't want to do that! You know I want to be part of this!"

"Yes, I do. Who wouldn't?"

"Here is the deal we shall strike. You may follow me, but only at a distance. You must not enter the building, and you must not speak to my father or let him see that you are in the city. Your presence will be our little secret."

"Agreed."

"This thoroughfare is called King's Road. In about five minutes we will turn off it and go downhill in the direction of the water. Our destination is a small street called Bush Villas, the address is number one. I shan't speak to you or see you again in Portsmouth or anywhere nearby. Good day."

He stalks away at a great pace.

Sherlock keeps him in sight, but slows when they near the crime scene for he sees the lean figure of Inspector Lestrade far ahead, coming out the front door of a three-storey brick home. The detective's son nods to his father and enters the house, glancing furtively back to make sure Holmes is nowhere in sight. He has stopped in the alcove of a church nearby and is considering how to proceed. *All is fair in love and crime.* The English Channel isn't far away and a cool breeze wafts in from the water. Gulls cry above.

This is a strange neighborhood indeed, in which to keep a kidnapped girl. Instead of hiding her where all sorts of skullduggery is a daily occurrence, where one could vanish into the snaking streets and alleys and hole up in a grimy, little flat, where grappling with a struggling victim wouldn't make a scene or cause others to run to her aid, where lips are sealed . . . they chose this middle-class area with it's wide-open vistas. *Why?*

What if she wasn't struggling?

Lestrade is speaking to a man in a suit with a checked waistcoat, who carries a top hat and walking stick. The detective shakes the man's hand and sends him on his way, then reenters the house. Sherlock steps out from the safety of the church and approaches number one Bush Villas. From a first-floor window, the younger Lestrade spots him and frantically motions for him to leave. But Sherlock is watching the well-dressed gentleman briskly pacing away, regarding the other houses as he goes, heading not into Portsmouth central, but toward the wealthier residential areas in Southsea.

About fifty years of age, lives nearby. Self-made: those born to wealth don't walk so industriously. Interested in other houses . . . the landlord!

Sherlock is off, rushing along the footpath after the gentleman. Upstairs in the window, Lestrade Junior is aghast. Holmes follows for a while, until he is sure that he and the landlord are out of sight.

"Sir!" He finally shouts.

The gentleman turns and looks down his nose at the boy.

"Inspector Lestrade . . . he sent me with a message. He has a few more questions for you. I am to bring back the responses."

"You are? I thought this was secret stuff. Why didn't he come himself?"

"Doesn't like to run."

The gentleman laughs. "Yes, I can imagine that, our Lestrade."

"And he prefers unlikely messengers. I am not what I seem, you will understand."

Susceptible to flattery, thinks Sherlock as he watches the man straighten his waistcoat.

"What would he like to know?"

"He wanted me to say, firstly, that he was impressed with your keen memory of the events in question."

The gentleman smiles.

"It is nothing. I make it a habit to train my mind. I am told I have a large bump of mnemonic recall on my cranium. Ask me anything, and I shall see what I can do for the Inspector by way of retrieving files from my brain banks."

"When did you let this house to the people who were holding Victoria Rathbone?"

"He has already asked me this!" snorts the gentleman. He looks suspicious.

"Inspector Lestrade is very thorough. He finds that by asking questions more than once, new things come to light. You might add something? There are several other queries. He just asked me to start with this."

"Yes, yes. I've noticed that about him: a repetitious sort. Well, as I've said, I let the house to two gentlemen for a one-year period some time ago. But they only appeared the very morning she was discovered. Curious that. I saw all three of them when we transacted our business. She was wearing a dark veil over her eyes." The man leans closer to Sherlock. "These are things that were never published in the newspapers, you know, just between me and the good inspector."

"You are sure it was two men?"

"Of course, I am sure, you young fool."

"I am merely a fool's messenger, sir."

The gentleman laughs.

"You are a saucy one, young buck. And well-spoken. You know, I had very little when I was a child, too."

"So, just the two men . . . and the girl?"

"Yes, though I did have a feeling."

"A feeling?"

"Don't like to mention such things. Feelings are rather feminine, don't you think?"

"Then let us call it an instinct in your gut. What was it?"

"Well put, my boy. I didn't say this to Lestrade, of course. But nevertheless . . . I had the feeling . . . tell him it was that instinct in the gut sort of thing . . . that someone else was pulling the strings, just by the way the two men kept consulting each other, weighing things, as if wondering how someone who made the decisions would react."

"Someone else? Perhaps a local man?"

"That would be my guess."

"And the lady, sir, she made no effort to signal to you that she was being held captive?"

"Yes, that is correct."

"That is singular, indeed."

"Lestrade thought so too. And the two gentlemen, they vanished without a trace."

"Almost as if they had intended it all," says Sherlock under his breath.

"I beg your pardon, young man?"

"Nothing, sir, just chatting with myself. Bad habit. Thank you for your cooperation. Inspector Lestrade thanks you as well. I shall be sure to tell him about your 'instinct.' You have remarkable powers of recall indeed!"

The landlord steps away from Sherlock at an even quicker pace, his chest puffed out. But the boy is already rushing back to the house. There is something else he wants to know and he has to get into the house to confirm it. From the street, he had noticed that the shutters were closed on the windows in the top two storeys. The boy has also noticed that the cold Southsea footpaths are muddy.

All the policemen are inside. Sherlock walks up to the entrance, climbs the steps, and stands flat against the wall to the side of the locked front door. When someone comes out, it will open toward him. He will have the element of surprise too, always a powerful weapon. It takes a while, but eventually a figure appears. It is Lestrade Junior, obviously a bit bored and looking for some cool Southsea air.

Holmes darts in.

"Sherlock!"

He knows what he wants to see. Making for the stairs, he rushes up the first set, looking closely at the surface of each step. Then he turns on the landing and glances up the stairs to the upper floor. The detectives are conversing up there. Young Lestrade, who has followed on the double, is instantly on him, seizing him and almost throwing him back down to the entrance, trying to do so noiselessly, and then hustling him out the front door.

"You promised me! You will go too far one day, sir!" He is furious, but trying not to shout.

"My apologies. It is my naturally inquisitive ways. They get the best of me at times."

Young Lestrade almost smiles; almost. He shoves Holmes tight to the building.

"You saw something in there, didn't you?"

"As a matter of fact, I did. It may throw some light on this matter."

"Tell me."

"Only if you give me something in return."

"I have given you enough."

"When the police were informed of the presence of Victoria Rathbone in this house, who told them?"

"I can't say."

"Then neither can I. You might have been able to follow up on what I discovered in there. Without it, you have nothing."

Lestrade hesitates.

"We received an anonymous tip from the public due to my father's brilliant idea of announcing . . ."

"In other words, you have no idea who sent it and neither does your father."

"It was from a member of the great English public, who preferred to remain anonymous."

"Not wanting to get involved in this mess?"

"I should think."

"Did anyone see this anonymous person?"

"No. The message came by telegram."

"So . . . it could have come from anyone . . . even, theoretically, one of the culprits."

"What do you mean? Tell me what you saw in there. You promised."

You shan't make anything of it anyway, you boob.

"The crime scene has been sealed since the day the culprits were here, has it not?"

"Yes."

"Know this: all the footprints on the staircases were made by the police and you and your father. I would recognize your governor's bootprints anywhere, and detectives leave distinct marks too. I must be off."

Ignoring the other boy's puzzled expression, Sherlock turns down the front steps of the house and heads for the street. As he does, he hears an upstairs window snap up and the shutters open. A few strides later, when he glances back, he sees Inspector Lestrade's shocked face looking out. It quickly turns red.

"Bring me that boy!" he shouts, extending a finger at him.

But "that boy" has far too extensive a head start and his long, young legs are too much for the otherwise competent members of the Force. He disappears up across the Southsea line and into the city proper, veering and turning down little streets and alleys. Before long, his pursuers give up.

He immediately ponders his next task. Finding Captain Waller is going to be difficult. There are several options. He can go to the barracks or the officers' mess and simply ask for him, but he wonders what his reception might be. Perhaps he should scout out the pubs in Portsea or across the strait in Gosport, the Royal Navy parts of town. He could make inquiries in the taverns a captain might frequent. That's all to the west, through an undoubtedly dangerous area.

But first, he must eat. The apothecary put some sardines between biscuits for him and he can feel them bulging in his suit-coat pocket. He is tired from running and wants a drink, too. There's a public tap near the railway station. That would be a good place to eat; a busy spot where no one can accuse him of loitering.

A short while later he is leaning against the outside wall of the station, munching on the biscuit sandwiches, savoring the strong taste of the sardines, when he sees something that arrests his meal in mid chew. A middle-class woman, dressed in a plain, dull cotton dress and bonnet, is rushing out of the entrance to the station and something is very wrong about her appearance. Sherlock spots it all immediately. She has the upright, proud bearing of someone distinctly above the class of her clothing; there's a scarf pulled up over her mouth and nose, though this noon hour is not especially cold; and under the bonnet, pulled down as it is to her brow, he spies a pair of stunningly beautiful, yet slightly cloudy, brown eyes.

Lady Rathbone isn't more than ten feet from him. Sherlock turns away quickly. He hears her call for a cab and enter it. When it heads out into the Portsmouth streets, he runs after it.

Thankfully, it is a Monday and midday, so the roads are busy and Sherlock is able to keep up. The cab heads toward the dockyards. Before they reach the water, the two-wheeler stops and she alights and scurries into a little town square. A man is waiting for her at a bench, dressed in a dark suit, not a uniform. They embrace and hold hands as they sit. *Early forties, upright bearing, mustache curled at both ends, tall, dark-haired, handsome, though the redness of his nose betrays his fondness for drink.* There's an elm tree not far from the bench, so Sherlock slips over and slides down to the grass, facing away from them, his back against the trunk and his beak in his newspaper to hide his face.

"This is for you," says the man in a soft voice. Sherlock glances around and sees her take a note from him with a smile. But then her anxious expression returns.

"I came as soon as I could."

"Your message said so little. Who are these fiends who are hounding your home and your child? Can't the police do anything?"

"It's more than you think."

"More? What do you mean? How can there be more?"

"We've had an intruder."

"An intruder?"

She looks guilty. "He confronted me. I gave him your name."

"You *what*?" He almost gets to his feet, but she pulls him down.

"It was just a boy. He broke into my room and found our gloves. I don't think he really knew anything, but he demanded your name and I had to tell him or he wouldn't leave, would have alerted the house. He may be after you for money, so you need to be on your guard."

The man glances around. Sherlock sinks into his paper.

"Do not distress yourself over this. You already have your child to worry about. This blackmailer's timing is bad, anyway. I . . . I'm leaving England soon. I would have sent for you today and told you, had you not sent for me. I . . . I'm going to America. Tomorrow."

"No."

"I must. It won't be for long."

"But . . ." She looks him up and down. "Is that why you are out of uniform? What's happened?"

"I've left the navy . . . the only captain in the ranks who didn't have blue blood and in command of the small-est boat they ever floated . . . a sixth-rate vessel . . . it might as well have been a rowboat. It would have stayed that way forever for me. So I've left my post. I'm not of their kind, those prigs."

"You didn't say that when they were promoting you. You charmed them out of their socks."

"Charmed their wives, Pauline, and toiled many extra hours. Let's be honest."

"One does what one must to get ahead. We both know that."

"I hate the blue bloods, all of them. . . . I hate your husband."

"I do too, sometimes."

"But I will show them."

"Show them? By doing what?"

"It's only an expression, dearest. I must be off."

"But I've just arrived. Why are you rushing away?"

"It's simply some business I've arranged. Then I must prepare for departure. . . . I shall write, Pauline. And I'll be back before long. Read my note."

As he pulls her to her feet and embraces her, Sherlock makes a mistake. He rises slightly to see them. The captain is lifting her in his arms and turns slightly. Over his shoulder, she sees a lad peering at them above a newspaper.

"The boy!" she cries, pointing at him.

Sherlock rises, poised to run, but it's the couple who flees. The captain takes Lady Rathbone by the hand and flies out of the square, then lifts her into the hansom cab that still waits on the street. He pounds the roof and shouts at the driver. The cab darts out into the traffic and is gone in seconds.

Holmes stands there, stunned, the newspaper in his

hand. But then he notices that the lady has dropped something. He walks over and picks it up. *The note!* He opens it with trembling hands. This may be the answer to all his questions, to what he and the police and Malefactor and Irene have been pursuing for months. It was obvious from the couple's conversation that the captain is up to something and that Lady Rathbone knows nothing of it. Is this a confession? Will it say why he is leaving the country?

He opens it.

Dearest Pauline, know that I will always love you.

It's a love note, a stupid, meaningless love note. The disappointment is hard to bear. He jams it into his frock-coat pocket and heads back into the center of the city, not sure what he should do next. Try to follow the hansom cab? But it has long since vanished. Return to Bush Villas? But they will be on the lookout for him. In fact, Lestrade may have half the Portsmouth constabulary searching for him.

Within a street or two Sherlock feels he is being followed. Someone is lurking behind. He slips away from the bigger thoroughfares and darts down a small road, then a smaller one, then through alleys and mews, going faster and faster. His pursuer seems to be getting closer. But after a few minutes, he thinks he has shaken whoever is on his trail.

When he finally stops, he leans against a clammy stone wall on a narrow, cobblestone lane, trying to discern exactly where he is. He has run so frantically and turned so often that he has lost his sense of direction. He looks up to see where the sun is, to get his bearings.

But it isn't wise to look anywhere other than straight ahead or behind on the little streets of Portsmouth. Instantly, someone seizes him, and the steely arms that apply the grip aren't covered with blue-uniformed sleeves.

"Just relax, mate, and we'll get you stripped down and on yer way in a wink."

The arms are bare, even in this cold December morning. They are tattooed, hairy, and as thick as mill posts; the breath coming directly into Sherlock's ear from behind, stinks of beer. The thug grinds his face stubble into the boy's cheek and holds him uncomfortably close in an iron lock.

This rough will rip off his clothing, take everything he owns, and leave him battered or dead on this nearly deserted street. He is in a very bad part of town.

Then a memory makes a sudden appearance in his brain and the art of Bellitsu is at his fingertips.

"When a gentleman seizes you from behind, he is almost always an unthinking rough of some sort, intent upon doing you some evil, my boy, but without a speck of fighting technique," cracked Sigerson Bell one day in the lab, wearing his pugilist's tights. "He shall grip you thusly." Bell demonstrated exactly the hold that the stinking sailor has on the boy at this very instant, with his meaty arms under Sherlock's armpits and his hands clasped tightly behind the boy's neck.

"Throw your arms straight into the air!" the apothecary had shrieked.

Sherlock does so.

"Then drop down to the ground and roll away!"

Sherlock slides out of the grip and rolls when he hits the cobblestones.

"Jump to your feet, take a balanced position, and measure your distance. Then strike your opponent with an oriental martial arts kick to the temple." At the time, Bell had performed the feat as quickly as a cat and smacked another skeleton's skull.

Sherlock pivots, dips his hips, and drives the point of one of his heavy Wellington boots into the thug's temple. The man drops like a stone. But the boy doesn't wait to see if he rises.

"Then . . . RUN!!!" Bell had screamed in his high-pitched voice.

Sherlock is off to the races again. He rips down the little cobblestone street and takes the first turn. As he does, he glances over his shoulder and notices someone peering around the corner near the fallen man, as if motioning for him to get up and pursue. It looks like a tall boy in a black tailcoat, and there seem to be a couple of others near his side, one blond, the other dark.

But Sherlock doesn't allow himself more than a passing glance – he is likely imagining those figures anyway. Within minutes, he somehow finds his way directly to the railway station. Perhaps it is his good sense of direction, now regained, or perhaps fear sends him where he needs to go.

There are many daily trains to London and he is on the next one. He huddles on the wooden bench. As the train pulls out, he thinks about what he's learned.

There were two men and a girl here, and possibly a local man pulling strings. They used a middle-class neighborhood, not suited for hiding a prisoner. They were only in the house for part of a day, just for hours, or perhaps minutes because they didn't even go upstairs to the bedrooms. She didn't try to flee. On that very morning, an anonymous telegram was sent to Scotland Yard. The two men were conveniently gone when the Force arrived, though the police got here on the fly. Did someone intentionally draw Lestrade's men to Portsmouth?

But all this reasoning doesn't reveal anything about *who* they are or *where* they are now. And it doesn't mean Captain Waller was involved. He seems to have a secret and bears a grudge against Rathbone – so he has a motive. But that doesn't mean he had anything to do with the crimes.

Sherlock wishes that love note had actually said something. He pulls it out of his pocket to crumple it up and throw it across the half-empty carriage. As he does, he takes one last disdainful glance at it. At that instant the train bursts out from under the station roof into the sun. Its bright rays shine through his window and he catches a glimpse of something on the paper.

A watermark.

It is the barely detectable outline of two faces.

GRIMWOOD'S SECRETS

Two men and a woman in Portsmouth . . . two men and a woman at Grimwood Hall! They indeed used the port city as a diversion! Sherlock Holmes is wishing that the train went right through London and on to St. Neots. It wasn't so long ago that the speed of these locomotives frightened him, but now, rocking back and forth on his seat in an anxious motion, he is trying to urge the train to move faster. But he is conscious of another problem. It may not matter how fast he gets to London . . . for how will he get from there to St. Neots? He doesn't have enough money left for another fare.

Meanwhile, Sigerson Trismegistus Bell is standing on the platform at Waterloo Station, dressed in his bright green tweed frock coat and red fez, holding a big brown canvas bag. He is tapping his foot, waiting patiently, his question-mark shape and colorful attire evident from everywhere in the station (and likely for several miles in any direction). He is at exactly the spot where the third-class cars on the last morning train from Portsmouth will stop. He was here for the one before as well.

Finally, the right one arrives.

Sherlock spots the old man instantly and descends from his carriage with trepidation written on his face.

What does this mean? Is he going to make me come home? Or is it something worse?

"You know, my boy, I was much taken by that riveting tale you told me some time past about the mill in St. Neots that manufactures the only paper left in England with the mark of the two Fourdrinier brothers upon it . . . and your unlawfully breaking into the manor house nearby and what you saw there. I also recall that you disappeared for twenty-four hours at that time . . . without permission!"

He isn't pleased.

"You were in error then."

"I was?"

"Yes, and I'm sure your trip to the southern coast has confirmed that."

"I have been meaning to ask you, sir, how did you know I wanted to go to Portsmouth?"

"Oh! It was the deepest deduction of the most convoluted kind."

"Could you explain?"

"You have the eccentric habit – indeed you are an eccentric boy, never seen the like of it in another human being – of talking aloud to yourself. Whilst I was cautioning you to be silent to allow for the full effect of the bat adrenaline dripping into Professor Hanlon's medulla oblongata, you were mouthing a single word over and over to yourself."

"A word?"

"*Portsmouth.*"

"Oh."

"You now want to go to St. Neots. And I have made a decision. It was a difficult one."

How does he know where I want to go? It doesn't matter. He has had enough of me and my ways. Just when I most need him. What does he have in the bag? My things? Is he moving me out?

"Oh, the bag? That is your dinner and supper, and perhaps enough to break your fast on the morrow as well. Pickled eggs, home-brewed ale with a very light alcoholic content, an onion, some leeks, a kipper or two, a doorstep of bread, and some thinly sliced rabbit. Step this way."

My dinner and supper?

Waterloo Station is one of the busiest in London and even at this late-morning hour the crowds are thick. Folks of every class, soldiers and sailors and railway employees bustle about. Black top hats and brown caps and colorful bonnets float along the tops of the masses. Locomotives emit shrill, ear-splitting whistles that startle the ladies and bounce off the steel-girder and glass roof. The smell of grease and steam and sulfur hangs in the air.

The old man ushers Sherlock away from the long lines of platforms toward the arched openings in the brick wall, which lead out into the booking offices and the cavernous main hall with its high ceiling.

"This," says Bell, as he presses two gold-colored coins into Sherlock's hand while they almost run toward the doors that lead out to the street, "is for you. Get across Waterloo Bridge and take a hansom cab, or dash on foot, or whatever you choose, and be at King's Cross Station as quickly as you can. The trains leave in St. Neots' direction at thirteen past the hour, every other hour. You have enough for a cab, and a return fare, perhaps a little more. Your accommodations at St. Neots are another matter, up to your own discretion, though one has the sense that you may not spend much time upon a pillow tonight."

"But how . . ." begins Sherlock as the cold air hits his face and the sounds of traffic burst into his ears.

"How did I again know where you were bound? It is the diagnostic doctor in me!" shouts Bell proudly. "In fact, it was my deduction that St. Neots was the scene of the crime from the start. I was rather disappointed in your analysis. You are too emotional! Why would they hold the girl in Portsmouth a second time – the city where the police had found her before! But there are *still* many holes in this St. Neots idea, my boy. It's like Swiss cheese! Can't say that I know what you will find up there. It may not be what you think. Now be off with you!"

"Can you come with me, sir?"

That guilty look passes across the old face again.

"Uh . . . nonsense . . . no, I have things I need to do."

The boy is sure that Bell has no appointments for the rest of today, and none tomorrow. *What is he up to?*

Sherlock wonders if it has been wise to tell the old man all about the case. No one, absolutely no one, can be trusted. Malefactor once said that, and the boy believes it – it is one of the few tenets of the young crime boss's philosophy that he accepts completely. Sigerson Bell is being far too nice, too helpful, and trying to lead him north. What, indeed, will be found at St. Neots?

Up on Waterloo Bridge, known to Londoners as the Bridge of Sighs due to the legions who leap from it to their deaths, he takes a few seconds to find the apothecary in the crowds moving on the footpaths south of the Thames below. The old man is easy to spot, even at a distance: scurrying like a big, bent-over squirrel, rushing home as if he cannot spare a moment.

♥

Because Sherlock was at King's Cross just a few weeks ago, it is easy to find the right platform for the train up to Cambridgeshire and St. Neots. He doesn't have to devise plans to evade the ticket inspector, either. He sits possessively in his seat, watching northern London pass by, thinking about what he will do the minute he hits the ground in the north.

He also thinks about Paul Waller. Mr. Barnardo said the child had perhaps a week before he went blind, but it might be a day too, or he might be lost by now. Sherlock thinks of his own poor childhood . . . and of all that Mr. Doyle can do for him. There isn't a second to waste.

But is St. Neots *really* where he should be going? What does he *really* know? He didn't actually see anything in Grimwood Hall that confirmed a single thing. He saw two men and a woman, dark images, illusions, ghosts. Something, however, wasn't right about what he saw, and he is certain that the girl was *never* held in Portsmouth. Then there's Captain Waller's St. Neots stationery. Yes, everything points northward.

But amidst all these puzzles, one rises above the others. It concerns the conduct of the kidnap victim herself. He keeps thinking about her unusual ways at the family dinner table and of her leaving home alone just past dawn the next morning. *What role is Victoria Rathbone playing in this strange drama?*

This time he takes the train all the way into the little brick station at St. Neots. There are only two tracks and platforms, one going north, the other south. A railway employee is nailing green, sharp-leafed holly on the walls. Up above the entrance, the big, white-faced iron clock says it is just past three o'clock. Sherlock is itching to get going, but he has to be smart. It is December 2nd, three weeks before Christmas, and there are still a few hours before it gets dark. Remembering the beasts or whatever it was that lurked on the manor house's grounds and the vantage point that Grimwood's three residents have on their surroundings through their windows during daylight hours, he decides it is best to approach the mansion under cover of darkness.

But there is something vital he should do in the short time he has left. Within half an hour, he is in the field by the Great Ouse River north of town, the paper mill pushing smoke into the cold air not far away. Penny Hunt will be coming home soon. He crouches down in the tall grass.

The sun is getting low when he sees her.

Shouldn't an employed woman, a mother, be happy, perhaps whistling a merry tune? But it seems she is never that way. She trudges forward, her head down. When she is close, he spots another bruise on her cheekbone. He rises. She almost screams, but then her face relaxes a little, just a little, for she is not pleased to see him again.

"Master Bell . . . or Holmes, isn't it?"

"The same, Mrs. Hunt."

"I am at least glad to see that you are still alive."

"I seem to have eluded the curse of Grimwood Hall."

Penny doesn't smile.

"Why are you back, boy? I shall call the constable."

"Please don't." He motions toward the hill. "I did indeed go up there last time, Penny . . . and I need to go there again."

"No, you do not."

"Those are just stories, legends."

"People who live there and go there . . . die. A woman was murdered and a man was eaten alive. There are beasts loose on the grounds. That is NOT a story."

"I have no choice, Mrs. Hunt. I saw someone up there last time . . . then I believed I was wrong about that person's identity. Now, I'm not so sure."

Her face turns white.

"*Who* did you see? Tell me, boy."

Sherlock is taken aback by her tone.

"I can say this. . . . I believe the answer to a serious crime may be found in that manor house."

"What crime?"

He might as well explain. He needs her help and he can't be betrayed.

"The Rathbone case."

She looks stunned.

"Was it *her*? Their daughter?"

"I don't know."

"What do you mean, you don't know?"

"What I saw was through the crack in a door in a dim light so I –"

"Then it could have been anyone?"

"It was definitely a girl and –"

"Definitely a *girl*?" She looks terrified. "My Polly!" She begins to cry.

"Now Mrs. Hunt, you shouldn't assume –"

"What you have is *just* a theory! I *know* my daughter was up there. She was about the Rathbone girl's age, reddish-blonde hair. The blacksmith was certain he saw her on the hill by Grimwood that last night. I dreamed those beasts killed her!"

"Help me, Mrs. Hunt, and I will go there and bring you back answers."

"W-What do you need to know?"

"Has anything unusual been happening in town since I left?"

"There have been people around."

"Yes?"

"They was asking questions, but doing it on the sly. Many folks didn't even know they was in town until they left."

"What people? Policemen? Inspector Lestrade again?"

"No."

Sherlock sighs.

"There was a boy, a tall one with black hair, and two shorter boys with him: a blond lad, very quiet, and a dark-haired one, nasty looking."

Sherlock's heartbeat picks up.

"Did this boy affect a top hat, carry a walking stick and wear a black tailcoat?"

"How did you know that?" gasps Penny. "Are you mixed up in this more than you say?" She raises her voice. "You are just a boy, Master Holmes! How do you know these things? What is going on up there?"

"I want justice, that's all. And if you want answers, you will keep talking."

She pauses.

"They didn't stay long. They were here the day after you were. But that was the last I heard of them."

"Was there a girl with them?"

"A girl?"

"Yes, a . . . pretty one . . . respectable?"

"No, there was no girl."

Sherlock is relieved.

"I never told you this," continues Penny, "I watch the manor sometimes from my little parlor window, especially since Polly went. It is peaceful in my house when my husband is asleep, when he's finally quiet. That's when I watch. I'm not sure why, because it terrifies me so much to even glance up that way. Human beings is strange folks." She touches the bruise on her face. "There has indeed been some funny goings on up there of late."

"At Grimwood itself? What do you mean?"

"All three of them were gone for about a day once."

"They were? When?"

"It was the very day you left. I remember lying awake, waiting for my husband's snores to get deep and loud, so I would know he was completely asleep. Then I got up and went into the parlor. I have a stool I like to sit on near the window and look out. It must have been not long past midnight, perhaps two in the morning. Their lights usually went off a short time after we turned in, about eleven. But that night, after you were up there . . . their lights went out a little earlier . . . then came back on about two, and then went out again about an hour later. It was very strange. I was sleepless that night, thinking about Polly, and about you a little too, knowing you might be up there. I was imagining those beasts on the grounds. I didn't tell you when I saw you at the station the next morning. I was just glad you were going home."

"But you figured they'd gone out in the night?"

"I knew it for sure the next day – someone saw them returning."

That was the day the culprits went to Portsmouth.

"Did all three return?"

"I don't know. But it all went back to normal after that. I could see the dim light, glowing in the upper storey the next night, just a speck, and the other lights on in that area on the ground floor, shining bright, as usual. The lights have gone off and on at their regular times ever since."

"Everything has been exactly the same?"

"When it comes to the lights, yes, but I'd say there has been more activity there the last forty-eight hours or so, more coming and going than usual, but all during the day."

"Thank you, Mrs. Hunt."

"Why are you doing this? You aren't a policeman. Do you know someone who is involved? I doubt it's your father. It can't be the Rathbones, you are poor."

"It . . . uh . . . there is a little boy's life at stake."

"A little boy? Someone you know?"

"It's too complicated to explain. But if this isn't solved, the child will wither."

She puts her hands on his shoulders and tries to make his eyes meet hers.

"It isn't only about the boy, is it, Master Holmes? You have something to gain here, don't you? Tell me the truth."

"Maybe I do. But that isn't why I'm doing it."

"Truly?"

"You should be getting home."

"Are you going to Grimwood now?"

Sherlock isn't sure he should tell her.

Trust no one. Why does she need to know when I'll be there? First, she doesn't want me to go at all, tells me all sorts of strange stories to keep me away . . . but now she has volunteered information as if she wants me to go up there and risk my life. Is this simply about her daughter? Does she even have a daughter? I don't know that for sure. Why does she keep appearing whenever I need her?

He has to trust someone. So he nods his head.

Who IS that girl in the room up there?

18

Holmes's hands are shaking as he eats by the little river: a pickled egg, a kipper, a few leeks, washed down with some ale. He stuffs the brown bag into a depression in the bank deep in the tall grass and begins to walk slowly back into town. By the time he gets there, darkness has descended and the air has grown much colder. He moves on, out into the countryside, then toward the hill.

The sky is black but lit by a bright, full moon as Sherlock reaches that stone wall with the wrought-iron fence on top that surrounds Grimwood Hall. The same lights are on as when he was last here, the same lights Penny described: several rooms shining downstairs, that dimmer glow from the small window in the turret-like room two floors up. He puts the toes of his boots into indentations in the damp, mossy wall and scales it. At the top, he steps over the little, spear-tipped fence and sits, gazing down onto the grounds, which are more visible tonight than last time, not only lit by the dim lights of the few gas lamps in the granite manor house, but by the marvelous big moon.

It is a quiet, spooky sight. Grimwood Hall looms like a dark monster over a front lawn several hundred feet across. He can make out the unkempt hedges, the bushes, the shaggy willow trees, and copper beeches. He wonders how he made it last time: across this ominous wilderness in a much darker night. The hedges appear to be arranged in a maze, designed to be a green-walled puzzle, a game for anyone trying to navigate from here to the house or back. It looks like one could start out to the right, then turn left, then right for a long while, then . . . there's a dead end. How, indeed, did he do it last time?

Then he hears a roar. It vibrates in his chest, turns his flesh to goose bumps and sets off a series of barks and growls.

He had forgotten about that sound.

What, in the name of the God, creates it?

Sherlock shivers. He has to enter the labyrinth, and he has to do it now. Where does he start? If he comes to that dead end, if whatever is making that roar tracks him there, he is finished. He must have simply been fortunate on his first trip. It must have been his natural sense of direction that got him through. It cannot fail him now.

He looks up to the moon in the cold December sky. He will watch it to keep his bearings. His hands, held tighter than he is aware of on the iron fence, are almost frozen to it. He releases them and rubs them together, then pulls the collar of his frock coat up around his neck. Something hisses on the grounds not far away.

But he jumps down.

He doesn't move for a moment after he lands. He squats, very still. He can hear the wind blowing through the trees, but nothing else. A wall of hedges is directly in front of him. He spots an opening to his left. That's where he will enter the maze, then turn right, then left, then keep right for a long while. After that, he isn't sure. He will have to use his instincts when he gets that far and move as directly as he can toward the manor house.

Sherlock looks up at the sky one last time. It is nearly as black as his coat, but filled with glittering stars. They seem to wink at him. Somehow, despite the absence of clouds, it begins to snow. It is like a miracle: a light, gentle fall of flakes that are so sharp against the night that he seems to be able to see the complex design of each and every one.

He gets up and moves quietly to the entrance to the maze.

Instantly, there is another roar followed by a cacophony of sounds, more hissing near his feet . . . and the rustling of something pursuing him! He bends over and runs into the maze: right, then left, then right. The sounds of violins play frantically in his head. In seconds, he is at a dead end. Whatever is after him seems to be gaining! He doesn't care about the Rathbone case anymore or Paul Dimly or anything other than getting out of here alive. But he can't find any openings in the hedge. Beastly sounds are all around him: a gorilla's growl, a lion's roar, and other shrieks he doesn't recognize.

Keep running! Where? Where!

The creature is almost upon him. He imagines it pouncing, landing on his back, ripping his skin, its sharp teeth sinking into his flesh, blood surfacing in great oozing lines: it seizing his neck, twisting him around, tearing open his throat; a gurgling sound, gasping for breath . . . dying . . . eaten.

He cannot find an opening in the hedge!

He tears into it, right into it: its hard little branches ripping his coat and cutting him. He stays on a beeline as he slashes through, and then goes through the next one, straight at the manor house, like an animal frantic to live.

When more openings in the hedge walls appear, he enters them, when they don't, he goes right through again. Finally, he comes out of the maze and sees the alcove at the house with the iron fence around it. He runs toward it through the long grass, leaps, and catches the fence up high. He pulls himself on top . . . and feels something tug – *fangs* – at his boots. But he gets over and when he lands on the other side, looks back. He sees nothing at first, then a pair of glowing eyes, sinister lights, flashing for an instant and vanishing back into the darkness.

He sits on the cobblestones with his chest heaving, sweating in the cold, steam rising from his clothing.

Make yourself calm.

He takes a deep breath before he stands and turns to the arched door in the house. The sound of people talking can be heard inside in the distance. They seem happy.

It's two male voices . . . and a woman's.

When he lifts the latch and pushes, the thick door opens. He steps inside and closes it gently. He's in the vestibule. He knows where to go this time: he must make his way through the grand hall, way down to the end where the smaller room with the bright light is . . . where those three people are moving back and forth, laughing and conversing. Sherlock must get as close as he can. He needs evidence: real evidence.

He approaches the armor that stands against the wall, complete with helmet, sword, spiked ball and chain, but this time avoids it, swinging wide, feeling his way in the semi-darkness, making for that lighted room.

Keeping his back against the wall, moving without a sound, he can soon hear exactly what they are saying.

"Hurry!" exclaims a male voice.

"Pack up!" says another.

"Gone by morning, America for Christmas!" giggles the young woman, rolling her *R*s.

"You will travel lightly, my dear?"

"Oh, heavens no, sir," she sighs, "I shall have the Rathbone fortune with me!"

It's them. There is no doubt.

But Sherlock wants to see them clearly. All he can make out from where he stands shaking in the hall are figures moving back and forth, apparently filling suitcases and boxes.

They are getting ready to leave. Tomorrow morning!

"The captain will be pleased. Everything is on schedule."

Sherlock almost cries out, but puts his hand to his mouth.

"If we were to cut the hands off of England's thieves, there would be no thieves in London!" barks one of the two men in a pompous, upper-class voice.

They all laugh.

"One must be brutal with brutal people."

"Never give them an inch!"

They give a whoop of delight.

Amidst the cover of laughter, Sherlock thinks he can step closer. He inches along the wall, getting almost to the doorway . . . and knocks something over. It's a vase. It whacks against the floor, a single, loud bang, but it is brass and doesn't smash or roll.

"Listen!" says one of the men.

Silence.

Sherlock holds his breath.

"Must be one of those beasts!" cries the young woman, and they all laugh again.

Sherlock picks up the vase and gingerly sets it back on its stand. He should tiptoe out of here, try to get off the grounds, and send word to Lestrade in London. But he can't resist seeing the thieves, confirming who they are: he especially wants to look at the woman. He is right at the door now. Summoning his courage, he peeks his head slightly out to see around the frame, exposing the side of his face.

It is a sitting room of sorts, though it has no chairs. He sees a man . . . wrapping a cloth around a painting.

Young. Perhaps mid twenties. Dark hair and eyes. Slender but muscular. A scar across his left cheek.

He sees the other man, putting handfuls of silver cutlery into a big black bag.

About the same age. Red hair, light eyes. Approximately ten stone, slightly under average height, walks with a limp, left leg.

He can't see the woman. But then she walks across his sightline, coming directly toward him. Sherlock sees her face. He gasps. Then he turns and creeps away, tight to the wall, back down the hallway toward the vestibule. When he gets halfway, he flattens himself against the paneling, twenty feet from the thieves, trying not to make any noise as his chest heaves as though it will burst.

It was Victoria Rathbone!

19

TEMPTATION

She has the same strawberry blonde hair kept the identical way, the same pretty face. She looks the right age. She is even wearing the dress she had on yesterday when Sherlock saw her cautiously leaving her father's Belgravia mansion. *There is no doubt: Victoria Rathbone is working with the thieves! She helped them rob her father! She was in on it all along. She allowed herself to be abducted . . . twice.*

Then another thought comes into his mind and he whispers it out loud.

"If Victoria is down here . . . *who* is in that room two floors up?"

The light was still on.

He moves farther along the wall, tight against it, heading for the entrance of the corridor that leads to the staircase. He shouldn't go up there. *Don't be rash.* He has what he needs. *Leave this instant. Return to town and send for the police and the Times reporter.* Sherlock has the criminals, evidence that Captain Waller is involved, his whereabouts known . . . he has even found the wayward Victoria. It will be a sensation. He will gain Irene's admiration, secure his future, and shame that pig, Lestrade, all in one swoop.

But there is unfinished business. *Who* is upstairs?

When he comes to the corridor opening, he stops. He imagines himself turning here, slipping down the passageway, then into the big room with the beautiful carved staircase with the images of Narcissus on the railings, gliding up the steps, reaching the first landing, and ascending to the next floor. He could head through that maze, find the lighted room, enter it, and discover . . .

It is so tempting.

Don't be greedy. Do this right.

"It was a stroke of luck, you know, *Victoria*, our finding you," he hears one of the men say in the other room.

"For all of us, it was."

"Can you get us that carton in the hall?"

One of the men advances toward the grand hall. The boy retreats silently and in seconds is in the vestibule and then outside, into the bracing air under the gentle snowfall, looking through the vertical iron spikes of the fence, trying not to rush, remembering how the maze twists and turns. Even though he went right through the tall hedges on his way in, he feels as though he knows the maze well enough now to move along its pathways. He can get off the grounds in a flash – he just has to think about the puzzle for a moment.

But something makes him glance back. The big, arched door: *he has left it open just a crack*. The cold air must be rushing in, air that anyone in the hall would feel – he hears footsteps advancing toward it from the inside. He has no choice – he can't stand here remembering how to negotiate the maze.

He scrambles over the fence, lands with a thump on the other side, and races onto the grounds. In a few seconds, he is across the tall grass and into the maze. But the loud smack of his landing must have alerted the animals because almost instantly they are at his heels. He puts his head back and runs. Violins play in his head again. He turns left, right, left, through a hedge, down a passageway, down another, and finally, sees the dim glow of the lights of St. Neots in the sky in the distance above the wall. He makes for it with everything he has, his lungs burning. He executes a leap and reaches for the fence and its spears on top. He misses . . . and falls to the ground.

Sherlock Holmes twists around to face his fate. This thing, this beast – as black as the night it seems, invisible except for its glowing yellow eyes, will maul him and eat him as surely as one of its ancestors consumed that terrible Grimwood lord who murdered his wife.

But the night is silent and no beast haunts it.

Sherlock gets up and rushes for the wall, climbs it in an instant, and gets over the fence. When he is safe, he looks back up at the house to see that dim light upstairs. *There it is.* A shadow moves in the room. He turns and scurries back down the hill toward the town in the darkness, stumbling and falling, his heart pumping, terror and excitement filling his every pore.

He intends to avoid the town and head for his spot by the riverbanks near the paper mill. He can't let the locals or authorities see him sneaking around in the night. Sherlock must hide until the sun rises.

But when he is far out on the marshy fields that separate the town from Grimwood's hill, he hears voices coming across the open space. He stops and listens for a moment, but can't make anything out, just people conversing in low tones, moving, it seems, directly toward the mansion. Either they are poor, or are trying to be secretive because they aren't carrying lanterns.

Sherlock steps quietly out of their path and lies down on the cold, snowy ground, curling up to be both undetectable and warm. The black sky has grown cloudier and he lies very still. Snowflakes land on his face, tickling his nose.

"Shall we take paintings or jewelry, boss?"

Sherlock freezes.

It's Grimsby.

Holmes lifts his head slightly and looks up. He sees three silhouettes: Grimsby's short figure in the middle between a slightly taller and thicker boy behind and a very tall, thin shadow wearing a top hat in front. Sherlock can see the outline of the tails of his coat hanging from his back. He has a thick walking stick in his hand. Malefactor.

There is no sign of Irene.

"What we take is not your concern, Grimsby. I know the value of everything they stole, believe me. We shall have our cut."

"Will she follow us?"

"Shut your gob! You are not fit to speak of her."

"Yes, boss."

"I hate to admit it, but that Jew-boy will solve this. He came here from Portsmouth far too quickly not to know something. He may have the police here by tomorrow. We must get our goods now. And then make ourselves scarce! Pick up your pace, gentlemen."

Sherlock Holmes has always been suspicious that Malefactor's connections in the London underworld run deep. He came to believe, for example, that the young crime lord had some association with the Brixton gang. But is his power, his influence, even greater than he suspected? Is this brilliant boy one of the larger spiders in the web of villainy that pollutes London? Has he made himself invaluable to growing numbers who do dirty business in its alleys and inside its homes? Is his knowledge of the streets, his command of quick, little fiends who can go anywhere and do anything something that even the most ambitious criminals employ?

"You knew exactly when Miss Rathbone would be in that carriage in Rotten Row, didn't you, boss? You knew where they would have to stand to snatch her, didn't you, boss? You knew how Lord Rathbone would respond. That was brilliant, boss. You knew that they hadn't seen their daughter for years, didn't you? You even told that captain that he should get a girl who . . ."

"Close your hole, Grimsby. The captain came to me because I can get things done. If you don't believe in your own brilliance, then it is useless. Pride doesn't go before a fall; it keeps you *from* falling. And word will spread if you have confidence. That's why he was put in touch with me.

But it is not for *you* to dwell on the details of any job. Do what you are told and do it well, and some day you may find yourself in my shoes . . . when I have moved on."

"What if that half-breed gets in our way?"

"Then I shall deal with him."

"Yes, boss," says Grimsby.

They move away and their voices begin to fade into the night, going in the direction of the mansion. Sherlock staggers to his feet, his thoughts reeling. There are so many culprits, so many possibilities still attached to this crime.

He finds his spot by the river and tries to sleep, but tosses and turns all night. Snow falls on him in a cold blanket, and he is freezing. He wants to summon the local authorities up to the manor house *right now* and arrest not only the three thieves, including Lord Rathbone's daughter, but Malefactor and his henchman, too. What an addition that would be to everything he has already discovered! He could wipe a young criminal mastermind from the face of London's underworld. It would free Irene from that rat's clutches, too.

But he knows that the local authorities wouldn't listen to a word of his story – they would arrest him as a vagrant on the spot.

He has to contact the London police and he can't do that until morning. Even if there was a night train that he could take to the city this instant, Malefactor would have made himself scarce by the time they returned.

Keep your mind on what is possible. It is enormous. Get word to both Lestrade and Hobbs of The Times the minute the telegram office opens, have all the culprits in the house arrested – Miss Rathbone has to be caught red-handed – the family's treasures recovered, the captain intercepted. Make sure you are on the scene at Grimwood Hall when it happens. Get the credit you deserve. Secure your future.

But his mind keeps wandering back to the light in that upstairs room and the shadow moving across it. *Is* Polly Hunt up there? And if it isn't her, who in the world are they imprisoning? And what are they doing to her? The thought terrifies him. Is it a kidnapping ring? Or is this person not being held at all: is it a fourth member of their gang? What complex game are these criminals playing? Perhaps they knew he was in the house . . . and the whole manor will be abandoned when he returns.

Whatever the answers, they will come in the morning. But his first job, his duty, will be to speak to Penny Hunt. He dreads what he must tell her and how she will respond.

♥

When the sky becomes lighter, he rises and makes his way into St. Neots. He had watched Penny walk away from the river toward her home several times, so he knows the area where she lives in the north end of town. Cocks crow in the distant fields, his feet crunch on the inch of freshly fallen snow, and he shivers as he walks, his collar up, his shoulders hunched. He enters the town and sees a milkmaid carrying heavy cans on poles over her shoulders, a blacksmith bearing a big sledgehammer opening his shop, and a few other tradesmen moving sullenly along, ready to start their day. He doesn't look them in the eye and tries to act as if he has somewhere to go. Then he spots what he is looking for: a child. In fact, it is one of the boys he met the first day he came here.

"Might I have a word?" he asks softly as the boy approaches.

The lad looks up and gasps. He starts to back away.

"It's you, the London man with the made-up name."

"Sherlock Holmes. It's my real name."

"No, it ain't . . . but that's all right, sir . . . it weren't me that throwed that apple . . . if that's what you're inquirin' about . . . it . . . it were Jack . . . that's right . . . Jack McMurdo . . . 'e lives over at –"

"Do you know a woman named Penny Hunt who works at the paper mill?"

"Mrs. Hunt? I do, sir. Lives down that road right there." He points to a narrow street nearby. "About four homes in, thatched roof with a blue door."

"Thank you, my boy. Breathe a word of my presence, and you will have trouble."

"Yes sir. Is that all you wants? Can I go? I didn't throw that apple . . . I swear it was Jack McMurdo. I can take you right to 'is door!"

"Be off with you," says Sherlock, "and don't throw anything at anyone anymore."

The boy flies away.

Holmes doesn't think he should knock on Penny's door. He doubts he'll need to, anyway: the town is rousing and he knows she will be, too. He isn't standing on the road near her home for more than a few minutes before she appears, holding a dusty rug she is about to shake in the cold air. But it barely seems like her: she is whistling a merry tune and smiling. It puzzles Sherlock.

When she sees him, a look of fear crosses her face for a moment, but then vanishes. She looks up and down the street, back toward the house, and then crosses to him.

"What do you want, Master Holmes?" she asks quietly, still glancing back toward the house. "You shouldn't be here. My husband has a temper."

"Your husband should be trounced by a good man. I am skilled in the ways of self-defense and can do it for you."

"No, you shan't, you silly boy. Life is more complicated than someone your age knows, even one with your wits. But I swear I won't be down in the dumps about anything today. I'm as happy as a clam."

"Well, I am much grieved to change your mood. I have been to Grimwood Hall."

"There is nothing you can say that can upset me, Master Holmes."

"I am afraid there is."

Someone comes out of the Hunts' little home across the street. It is a girl about thirteen or fourteen years of age with reddish-blonde hair.

"Mother?"

Penny smiles. "I will be there shortly, Polly."

Holmes almost falls over.

"She returned last night, and I am over the moon."

Who is in that room on the upper storey of Grimwood Hall?

"I thinks I spent all night just looking at her face. You know, I found that I hardly knew her. Have you ever looked right into the face of someone you love and barely recognized them?"

"I know a family that has that problem."

"I am going to spend every day getting to know her."

"I am in a hurry, Mrs. Hunt. I have two questions I need answered."

She looks back toward the house.

"Ask me anything, Master Holmes. Just ask quickly."

A shout comes from inside the Hunt home, almost a growl.

"Penny! Wench, where is you!"

Polly looks at her mother and reenters the house.

"I must go."

"I will follow you into your home if you don't give me my answers. The fate of a child lies in this."

"And your gain, I'm guessing. Ask me and then let me be."

"I need to wire to the city."

"There's a little post office on the main street, about three doors down after you turn toward London, attached to a baker's. The postman lives above. He has a telegraph machine. He may help you . . . or send you out on your ear."

"And one more thing."

"Quickly."

"The beast that killed the lord of Grimwood Hall . . . what was it?"

"No one knows. But there are stories."

"Of what?"

"A large black cat . . . a panther or a tiger."

Sherlock gulps.

"There is no such thing as a black tiger," he says.

"They say Lord Grimwood went places in India no other European ever traveled. Let me go."

"Good day, Mrs. Hunt."

Before she reaches her gate, she turns.

"Just wire for help, Master Holmes. As a mother, I'm telling you to leave it at that. Don't go back there."

Sherlock finds the post office quickly and bangs on the door. Moments later, a very thin man wearing nothing but yellowing undergarments and a pair of spectacles appears and is, at first, reluctant to be of any aid. But when Sherlock produces three shillings he changes his tune.

"Two shillings for two messages," says the boy. "Another for your silence."

The man nods and goes upstairs to put on a pair of trousers.

Inside the cold little office a few minutes later, the smell of kneaded dough in the air from next door, Sherlock hands the man one shilling, ponders what he should say, and then dictates.

"CONFIDENTIAL. Inspector Lestrade. Come at once. St. Neots. The manor house on the hill. They are here. So is SHE. Will escape before noon. All shall be explained."

The skeletal man stares at Sherlock Holmes, who puts a finger to his lips. The man nods again and receives another shilling.

Sherlock dictates one more telegram, to Hobbs at *The Times of London*. He signs it *Scotland Yard*.

20

GHOSTS

Shortly afterward, the boy is on the marshy field under the rising sun, on his way to Grimwood Hall. He is watching the breaths he takes, as they form clouds in front of his face. He hopes they won't be his last. After he scales the wall again and looks down upon the grounds, he realizes how different it looks in the morning light. For one thing, nothing moves. And everything is silent. *Perhaps all the beasts are asleep. Are jungle cats nocturnal?*

He thinks of what he's read about large exotic felines. There is a book by C.T. Buckland he particularly enjoys. It says that black tigers are myths and that there aren't really such creatures as black panthers; they are simply unusual leopards and jaguars with black pigmentation: if you look closely you can see a black leopard's spots. Though he can't remember everything Buckland had to say, he does recall one thing for sure: big black cats are (and the book had an illustration of one that was twelve feet long), in legend and reality, among the most vicious of all the animals, capable of killing beasts twice their size, and brilliantly camouflaged in the night. He also remembers what Penny said: *Lord Grimwood traveled in unknown lands.*

Sherlock swallows. Perhaps he should just wait for the police outside the lawns. It seems like a smart idea. He gets off the wall and slides to the ground, facing down the hill toward St. Neots, pressing his back against the granite. *Stay here. Wait for the police.*

Before long, he realizes he can't stay put. What if the criminals have abandoned the manor? What if he brings the authorities to an empty house? It would be more than he could bear. And if he stays here, he may never know who is in that upstairs room. He stops himself when he thinks that. *Stay downstairs. Just go into the house, confirm that the culprits are still there. That's all. Hide somewhere safe.*

He climbs the wall and looks onto the grounds again. They remain eerily quiet. He takes a deep breath. *Black tigers and panthers are figments of the imagination*, he reminds himself. He keeps repeating it as he drops inside the wall with a thump.

The cold December wind blows lightly through the copper beeches and weeping willows. He moves into the maze, but not at a run: left, then right . . . he has the passage memorized now. No beasts seem to follow – they must, indeed, be nocturnal. He climbs the fence next to the house and enters through the big, arched door. Nothing is stirring inside. Every one of his lightly placed steps seems to echo.

Father Christmas himself wouldn't be welcome here. There are no signs of holly or mistletoe, no tree laden with candles, no popcorn or cranberry chains on the walls, and Sherlock can't imagine a carol echoing happily along the corridors.

The silence frightens him. *Are they gone? Or are they just asleep?* He needs to know.

Sherlock treads as quietly as he can through the hall and approaches the room where the three thieves were talking last night. He peeks around the doorframe and peers in. It is silent in there, too. He can see the room much better now. It appears to be empty and is, indeed, a sort of sitting room, though all the chairs and settees are gone. All that is evident are large wooden crates, big canvas bags, and suitcases, stuffed full and haphazardly set on the floor.

He creeps through the room, all his senses alert, sees an open doorway to his left and tiptoes through it. It brings him into an area nearly as large as the grand hall, and there – on mattresses stretched out on the floor – are two men, one red-haired and the other dark. Both are fast asleep. The sun has risen and the boy is in clear view. These two are sure to awaken at any moment.

But Sherlock is getting greedy. Now that he is here, he wants to see more. He spots a closed door straight in front of him and makes for it with ghostly quiet. It creaks when he opens it and he freezes, not even daring to look back at the men on the mattresses. But no sounds come from them, so he proceeds into the room. There, on a rudimentary bed under thick blankets, lies Victoria Rathbone.

Leave, says a voice in his head. *Look around*, says another.

Sherlock pushes the door back and keeps it slightly ajar to be sure that it won't creak again. He is now alone with her inside her bedroom, her accomplices just a few strides away. There isn't much in the room besides the bed: just a dressing table with a mirror, a crude, open wardrobe bulging with garments, and a writing desk. A scarlet dress, like the one she was wearing on the first day she was kidnapped, hangs over one of the wardrobe doors. Sherlock steps toward it. Victoria stirs in the bed. He stops.

"Rotting royals from Rotten Row . . . rule . . ." she mutters, rolling her *R*s carefully.

Sherlock stares at her, breathless. Her eyes are closed. She smiles, turns onto her side, and drifts off again. It strikes him that she looks older than fourteen.

He peers into the wardrobe and a curious sight greets him. Beautiful, silk dresses hang on one half of the rack, humble cotton and linen ones on the other. *What is this about?* He moves to the writing desk and sees two stacks of papers piled beside an inkwell and pen.

"Enter by back door," reads a sentence across the top of the first page in the first stack, in what Sherlock is certain is a woman's flowery handwriting. "Kitchen to left downstairs (maids there or on upper floor), dining room to right upstairs on ground floor." He turns to the next page. "Constable painting, third on dining-room wall on right, is most valuable; Turner behind Lord's chair is next, the safe is in the lord's den, first floor behind the watercolor, key in his desk. Lady's bedroom is on second storey, first door on left. Leave it alone. Captain's orders."

Holding the papers up to the light, he can see the mark of the Fourdrinier Brothers.

She was giving the thieves instructions for the robbing of her own home. She must truly despise her father . . . he has nothing to do with her, rarely speaks to her. The ingenious captain recruited her to commit the crime.

Victoria stirs again.

"Blimey," she says in a completely different voice, "the 'ouse is loaded, mates."

Why is she talking like that? At first he wonders if she may sometimes play at being an amateur actress, that accents might be a hobby of hers. But then something dawns on him. *She will need to take on a new name and personality when she gets to America.* It makes perfect sense; she will have to become someone else.

He turns to the other stack of papers. He can tell, by the fact that they have been handled more, that these notes were written earlier.

"Pronounce the *R*s with a roll of the tongue," reads the first line. "Remember, the pitch of her voice is higher than mine," states another. He scans down the page and flips to the next. "Upper class ladies are never alone," says a line written atop that sheet. "Her father will seldom look at me," reads the next line. "I will be expected to hold my teacup with the small finger extended . . . practice French . . . keep walking with a book balanced on my head."

What does this mean? Sherlock turns to the woman in the bed. He quickly casts his mind back over everything he has learned: in St. Neots when he first came here, outside the Rathbone mansion, in the dining room and Lady Rathbone's bedroom, in Portsmouth, and now back here again, especially in this room.

What does this –?

"Eliza!"

The man's shout startles Sherlock and nearly makes him faint.

They are awake and calling her!

The woman stirs, moans, and then sits up in bed, looking toward the door.

Sherlock drops like a swatted fly and lands as gently as he can on the floor. In an instant, he has silently shuffled under the bed.

"Eliza Shaw! Rise and shine! America awaits!"

Is that her new name for her new life?

The door swings open.

"Robert Self!" Sherlock hears her shriek. "Clear out of me room, you cad!" Then she giggles.

"Of course, Miss Rathbone. Now get thee into thy frock, wench, and let us fly to the land of opportunity and wanton behavior."

"Then leave my boudoir, Sir Robert . . . and I shall," she coos.

He hears her rise, sees her bare feet pad across the floor to the wardrobe.

Sherlock is trapped in the bedroom. She will surely see him. *Have I come this far to lose everything? With the police on their way. I should have stayed outside.*

Victoria hums happily as she slides the dresses along the rack. She finds one and begins to disrobe. Sherlock has to escape. *Now.* He glances frantically around the room.

"Eliza?"

It's the dark-haired man with the scar again and this time his voice is serious. It has a suspicious tone.

"I am half-clothed, Robert . . . come in."

She goes to the door with a little laugh.

"Did you leave this open a crack?"

"What do you mean?"

"I thought you always closed the door tightly."

"I do . . . to keep you animals at bay. You might turn into black tigers in the night."

"I am not joking, Eliza, your entrance was ajar."

Sherlock spots a little door of some sort, about two feet high, all the way across the room near the wardrobe. He slides out from under the bed, slithers on his stomach and reaches it. There's a small handle. He opens it quietly and slips inside. He can still hear them talking.

"Are you sure?"

Sherlock is coiled up into a ball in the tight confines holding his breath, but when he glances around, he observes that within six feet this narrow area opens up into a wider tunnel. There is a little hole in the wall near him and he notices that he can see through it back into the bedroom. He is in a secret passageway.

"Look under the bed!" he hears the woman exclaim.

Sherlock starts to wriggle, moves along the six feet of narrow space and sees that he will be able to stand in the wider part. In an instant he is walking along it. He is between the walls.

"No one there," says the man in the distance. "What about in here?"

Sherlock hears him fumbling at the door to the passageway. The boy is near a corner. He turns around it and stops, holding his breath.

"Nothin'."

"You are imagining things, Robert."

"But I –"

"An hour or two and we're gone. You two are the professionals. Stay calm, remember?"

"I suppose I could be wrong. I must be getting itchy to go. It's time to do what I have to do upstairs."

The passageway door closes and Sherlock lets out his breath. The man's last words are ominous. They were spoken in deadly earnest. *It is time to do what I have to do upstairs. What does he HAVE to do?* Eliminate a problem before they flee? One they can't leave behind? Sherlock has to get out of this tunnel without going back the way he came . . . and then get to that upper room. *Foul play of the worst kind may be at hand. Who* indeed, is up there? Sherlock's mind is racing over everything he has seen and heard in the last few minutes.

For a while, it seems as though he may be trapped. He scurries along the passageway and it goes on forever, twisting and turning through the strange house. Every so often he notices holes in the walls and when he glances through them, sees into other rooms. He also finds a tight little staircase going straight up. *Does the young woman downstairs go upstairs this way? And if so, for what purpose?* He is tempted to ascend. If his sense of direction isn't betraying him, he is directly beneath the room two floors up. But he can't go up these stairs and take the chance of getting lost. He keeps moving through the tunnel. He seems to be going in circles in a maze as complex as the one on the grounds. But it finally comes to an end and narrows and shortens again. He gets down on his hands and knees, struggles through another six-foot stretch and slowly opens the short door he finds at the end. He emerges into a den.

There are many dusty, cobwebbed bookshelves in the wood-paneled room. There seems to be no one about. Sherlock scoots across to the outer door and opens it just a crack. He sees the grand staircase rising about fifty feet away and the dark-haired man with the scar rushing to its foot, about to ascend. He carries a scarf in his hand. *What is that for? To bind or suffocate his victim?* The thief stops. He seems to think of something, smiles, and then walks across the empty room to a palatial fireplace. Sherlock is amazed at its size. It looks like it should belong to the queen, like it could heat the entire mansion. The man steps over the old fire screen and stands in the fireplace. Then he sticks his head up the flue: half his body vanishes into it. Sherlock can't see him anymore, or be sure of what he is doing. The man appears to be making a loud noise up the chimney – it is like a roar. When he steps out, he seems to sense something and turns, facing the den. The boy closes the door as fast as he can.

Did he see me?

When the boy opens the door a crack again a minute later, the staircase looks deserted.

Follow him. See what he does. Stop any villainy. Cry out if you must. The police should be nearing.

He wishes he had his horsewhip.

Sherlock sweeps across the room and ascends the staircase, then goes up the next one, and down the hallways, toward the upper room. He knows the way now. When he draws near, he waits at the *T*, peeks around the corner, and sees the man opening the door and going in. Then he hears voices. His plan is to intercede only if the woman cries out. He'd like to keep a good distance away, far enough so that he can stay hidden if everything remains calm. But he can't hear anything from where he is. He moves closer and still can't hear, so he edges right up to the door. He is so cautious, so alert to flee, that it takes him a while to get there and he doesn't think about the fact that silence has reigned in the room for several seconds before he arrives. As he looks through the crack in the doorframe, he sees with a start that the man is coming toward him. In fact, he is just a few steps from the door.

Run!

The boy pivots and flies. He rushes past the adjoining hallway he came from and heads for the next one straight ahead. He'll never make it. He's still ten feet away as the thief opens the door. But suddenly, Sherlock feels as though someone picks him up and carries him . . . it's as if he is weightless . . . he reaches the next hallway and gets around the corner. He has the sensation of being set down and thinks he sees someone vanishing away in front of him; a woman in an old-fashioned dress – no head upon her shoulders.

Holding his breath, he hears the villain stride along the hallway from the door, turn, and walk away down the other corridor. His footsteps grow quieter.

Sherlock lets out a huge sigh. Then he chides himself. *I didn't see a ghost. Nothing picked me up and carried me.*

It is time to stop living in fantasies – he is a detective of facts and data. *There is nothing wrong with my mind. The thief must simply have taken a while to bolt the door – that's what gave me time. It surely must be locked from the outside.*

Sherlock Holmes gathers himself and turns to his task. It is time to find out who is in that room.

He walks briskly down the hallway. He examines the entrance closely. No bolt. Then he looks down. Ah. There it is: on the outside of the door after all, in an unusual place near the floor. *Someone is indeed being held here against her will.*

He unbolts the door . . . and enters.

21

ANSWERS

Everything in the room is clearly visible this time. And so is its only occupant. She is sitting on a settee next to the window, her head down, the same woman he just saw downstairs in bed and whom he glimpsed before in this very room.

It's Victoria Rathbone.

There is a steely determination evident behind her frightened expression. He notices that her necklace is a thick chain with a small bell attached.

"Who are you?" he asks.

"Who are *you*?" she responds.

"I asked first."

"You know very well . . . you rogue!" The *R* is perfectly rolled.

"How can I be certain that you are her?"

"What nonsense is this? Because it is evident, you fool!" Her snotty tone is not without a quaver, but her words are immaculately pronounced. "Are you in concert with those hooligans, or are you a friend?"

"The latter . . . I believe."

"Then, whoever you are, remove me from this room. And send for my father. I shall wait in the dining hall until his arrival."

It's her, thinks Sherlock, *she wants to go home*. Had he observed a brat like this in the Rathbone dining room he would not have thought that anything was amiss.

He casts his mind back again to what he saw in the downstairs bedroom and it all begins to make sense. He decides to try one more question to be certain.

"But perhaps you are just pretending to be her?"

"*No one* can pretend to be me, you idiot!" She stamps her foot and her face goes red.

Ah, yes. We have our girl.

"My name is Sherlock Holmes and I have come to rescue you." He smiles at his turn of phrase. "It is a pleasure to meet you."

"Well, it is *not* likewise. Take me away from here." Her pout has grown across her lips, which are beginning to tremble. "This has been *so* horrible. You can't imagine. I am allowed just four baths a week, I must wear this dress every six or seven days, peasant clothing at other times, and they feed me food barely fit for dogs."

"You look rather healthy to me."

"Do you call no Yorkshire pudding for three months, no oranges, no sweets, healthy? I have been forced to eat mutton and bread and milk and cheese and corn and peas and porridge for as long as I can remember. I have changed my mind. I demand that you take me to Belgravia this instant and let the cooks know I am home!" She sobs.

"No."

Miss Rathbone looks shocked.

"No?"

"You were home just a few days ago, anyway," he smiles.

"I was?"

"And secondly, we must await the police. They shall be along within an hour or two. Let us hope your captors don't flee before the Force arrives . . . or that they don't discover us . . . and murder us on the spot."

Victoria Rathbone gives a little shriek.

Sherlock has put them in a dangerous situation. He can't risk an escape attempt with her. It is broad daylight. And the fiends have placed that little cast-iron bell around her neck and secured it with a chain so that they will hear her if she tries to get away. It is sealed at the bottom and cannot be silenced.

"If they discover us, they can't release us, Miss Rathbone. We would be able to identify them. Your father would pursue them to the ends of the earth . . . and hang them in the London streets."

He walks to the window and peers out. "So, we must wait quietly and hope." He can see St. Neots and the railway tracks running southward through a beautiful rolling countryside. He images the telegraph message shooting along the poles to London.

At that very moment, an hour to the south, Inspector Lestrade is sitting on a special train from King's Cross Station, his son by his side. But he can't just sit there. He rises, shoves down a window, jams his head out, and screams up the tracks toward the conductor.

"Get this iron horse moving, you imbecile!" he shouts.

He has been in an ugly mood all morning, right from the moment the telegram was delivered by an out-of-breath messenger boy. It arrived almost the instant the senior detective entered his office. He is always there early. And lately, he's been in harness even earlier. These last few days have been terribly trying. When the Rathbone home was robbed, the Metropolitan London Police and especially his detective division had been made to look like fools. Now, the girl has been taken again, and he and his men look even worse. There was no sign of her in Portsmouth and he has been completely perplexed. Then came this telegram from that half-breed boy, Sherlock Holmes, he who somehow solved the mysterious Whitechapel murder and, incredibly, handed over the Brixton Gang. Inspector Lestrade cannot, simply *cannot*, allow this child to outdo Scotland Yard again. But that is what the lad is doing. The senior detective knows for certain that the ransom-note stationery came from St. Neots. If Sherlock Holmes is there and says that the kidnappers are in a manor house nearby . . . he may very well be absolutely correct. The boy has been almost flawless in his investigations so far.

"Get this piece of junk moving!" Lestrade screams again.

Then he sees something that makes his day even worse. Hobbs, the bespectacled reporter from *The Times*, is rushing along the platform toward the train.

"Do you know anything about what has transpired here?" Sherlock Holmes asks Victoria Rathbone quietly as he paces in the room, glances out the window, anxiously awaits any sign of the Force coming over the marsh.

"I was kidnapped about four months ago, at the end of the season – such a horrible time to be inconvenienced – and I have been held here ever since."

"You have never left this room?"

"They let me out for exercise and I go downstairs to a bedroom once a day where I am allowed to choose dresses to wear. They are such horrible rags!"

"Are they are kept in a wardrobe – half silk dresses, half what you'd call peasant?"

"How did you know –"

"Why didn't you escape through this window at night?"

"You are a greater fool than I thought."

"Why do you say that?"

"Do you not know about the black tiger?"

"There is no such –"

"Were I to somehow get out this window three floors above ground and climb down the ivy, the beast would hear me even if my bell didn't make a sound. It would track me and kill me within seconds."

"Have you seen it?"

"No."

"Have you heard it?"

"Yes."

Sherlock looks out over the grounds again. Then he remembers something he should have been concerned about long before. To his shame, it has slipped his mind during all the excitement.

Little Paul.

In the Ratcliff Workhouse in Stepney it is breakfast time. Only one small woodstove heats the crude dining hall, and the children, who only eat after the adults are done, can see their breaths as they arrive. The gruel is cold within moments of being ladled into the wooden bowls. Little Paul isn't there. They call out his name but he doesn't appear. A man is dispatched to find him. The child is discovered sitting in a hallway. He couldn't find his way downstairs because everything was a blur.

"I cannot see, sir," he tells the man.

"Do you recall someone named Irene Doyle?" asks Sherlock, turning from the window to Victoria Rathbone.

"I don't speak to any family with that name. It sounds foreign to me."

"She is your relative. Do you not remember speaking to a young lady in your house the day before you were kidnapped, who asked you about helping a little boy in a workhouse in the East End? He is going blind. You said you would make your father help him and have the child taken into the care of his physician, the only man in London who might cure him."

Miss Rathbone lets out a little laugh, which she then stifles.

"My father never listens to me!" she exclaims, trying to keep her voice down. "He has spoken to me no more than three or four times since I turned ten. I was away in India at school for three years. I don't think he laid his eyes upon me from the moment I returned until the day I was kidnapped. Yes, he gives me things to keep me happy, but I would never ask for something like *that!*" She snickers.

"But you told Miss Doyle that —"

"I don't recall anyone named Doyle."

"But you —"

"There are times when you must say certain things to keep up appearances. Perhaps I had some friends visiting?"

Sherlock is stunned and angry. Maybe he should just leave this useless girl here, leave her to her fate, whatever it is. Or perhaps he should go downstairs and make a deal with the criminals, take a cut, and let them get away: Eliza Shaw, the two men *and* the captain.

But then, he wouldn't get the credit he deserves.

"Maybe I should just lock the door and leave you here," he says out loud.

"I don't care."

"You don't care? You might rot up here. Maybe that would be a good thing."

"No I won't, you impertinent boy. That villain, I'm not even sure which one he was – they put scarves over their faces when they speak to me – told me that I will be rescued."

"What do you mean?"

"When he was here, just now, he told me that they will leave food for me for a week. After that, the authorities will be notified and someone will come and get me."

"Do you honestly believe that?"

"Why would he bother to tell me and why would he explain it all in such detail if it weren't true?"

"In detail?"

"Yes, he seemed rather proud of himself. He said that they and a man who shall remain nameless have performed the perfect crime. They would prefer that I live. Within a week, they will be far away, unidentified, and set for life. Did my father *actually* pay a ransom?"

Sherlock doesn't answer, so she goes on.

"They have engaged a London man, a boy really (in his words), who is well connected in the crime world and knows I am here. This boy has been helping them all along and is acquainted with a respectable young lady who is the key to my rescue. It is she who will carry a note to Scotland Yard . . . and because of who she is: they will believe her. I am to be saved on condition that the identity of the London boy remains unknown."

Sherlock reaches out for a chair.

Irene and Malefactor.

"Does this respectable young lady . . . do you think . . . she will know what is in the note?"

"That appears to be the case."

Why would Irene do this? But he recalls what she said to him after she saved him as he fled the Belgravia mansion, when he refused, once again, to be her friend. "*You will regret this, Sherlock Holmes!*" He remembers the expression on her face. She wants to save little Paul. And that's *all* she cares about. But does she want the child in her life? He thinks of how she responded when he suggested that the Doyles adopt the little boy. Sherlock had expected her to be happy; she seemed the opposite. He wonders now if she ever told her father who Paul "Dimly" really is. Does she simply want to save the boy . . . and leave it at that?

Even the kindest heart in the world needs the undivided love of a parent. Moreover, Irene is not immune to the thrills that life offers. Malefactor has certainly been working on her, showing her his high-stakes world. Has he convinced her there is nothing they can do to catch the criminals and that Lord Rathbone deserves his fate? And that he can find Victoria *and* save Paul in the bargain? That might be enough for her. It would satisfy her father, too.

But she is being played for a fool.

Sherlock turns back to the rich girl. He is boiling. She will never help the workhouse boy. Paul will go blind and die. He thinks of the child's enormous, cloudy eyes. He thinks of these criminals getting away with all the loot; he thinks of Lord Rathbone, hard and unforgiving, caring so little about his daughter that he doesn't know her . . . a daughter barely worth knowing anyway; he thinks of Malefactor, gaining in strength; and finally, of Irene . . . lost.

When Sherlock Holmes feels bitter about life, he not only grows furious, but starts to show off. His ego expands with his temper. He decides to exhibit his brilliance to this snobby, hard-hearted girl . . . and say things that hurt her. The entire story of the case of the vanishing girl is in his head now. And no one else's.

"Would you like to know exactly how all of this happened, Miss Rathbone? I doubt your brain capacity is such that you even have a clue."

Victoria looks at him as if she would like to have him sent to the Tower of London.

"First, tell me your mother's maiden name. I believe a former friend of mine once mentioned it to me in passing."

"It is Shaw, if you must know."

"Precisely. There is a relative of yours in this house."

"What?"

"This was never a real kidnapping. These fiends could care less about you or extorting money from your father in that way. They wanted to rob him in a very particular manner. This was, from the beginning, a majestically conceived robbery. A man named Captain Waller, a Royal Navy officer, an old 'friend' of your greedy, ill-deserving mother, who advanced due to his charms and little else, was behind it all. He and two men he employed have been planning it for a long time, perhaps for more than a year. Your father was the perfect target and not just because Waller hated him.

Why? Well, it is simplicity itself, isn't it? Lord Rathbone has a ridiculous view of justice and how to deal with criminals, and just like many of his class, he doesn't really love his children or spend any time with them. He simply loves himself, his position, and his money. Such were the perfect qualities in a victim."

Victoria gives a snort and turns her back on him. But she listens.

"Waller made enquiries in the London underworld and was given the name of the boy you previously mentioned, a rogue with his finger on the pulse of things in the city, one who does thorough research about the rich. The lad found out all there was to know about Rathbone and how to deal with him. Waller was reminded that the lord had just one daughter, not particularly attractive, who was away in India, had been gone for some time. She was almost a stranger to the lord and lady. They concocted a way to snatch her soon after her return to England. But that was still months away.

They developed the key to their plan well ahead of time: they found another *you*. The larcenous boy must have searched out girls in your mother's family; distant relations, near you in age. Or perhaps it was the captain who recalled once meeting a particular girl relative who resembled you. However they did it, they located a third cousin named Eliza Shaw from Manchester way – her accent betrays as much. She was about your size, had similar bone structure, was nearly twenty but adolescent in appearance and able to pass for fourteen. She was a spitting image of you once they clothed her, adjusted the color of her hair, and trained her. They told her their scheme: they offered her the world. And she, of course, surrendered.

Then they searched for, and found, the perfect hideaway: a dark manor house in St. Neots, a nice distance from London, but not too far. The house was said to be haunted . . . no one ever came near it. Man-eating beasts lived on its grounds, headless ghosts inhabited the hallways. They brought Miss Shaw here and continued her early training in how to talk like a spoiled, snobbish, upper-class girl. They copied your dresses, your walk, and your accent.

Then their plan entered the truly clever part. They kidnapped you and brought you here and put you in this room. Every day, Eliza Shaw came up through a secret passageway from her bedroom downstairs and watched you through a hole in the wall."

He spins around theatrically. "Right here!" Victoria's mouth hangs open as he points to a hole, about eyeball-size down near the floor on an inside wall.

"She examined your face, your hair style, the way you walked, and the way you talked when you conversed with the other two men. They always wore scarves in your presence. She even smelled your clothes and copied your scent. When you were allowed outside, she came up to this room and observed you from here as you took your daytime exercise . . . while those nocturnal beasts slept.

Meanwhile, they didn't say a word to the world or the police. They sent no ransom note, nothing. *That* was by design. It seemed like a most curious crime. But they knew your father would not respond. He would give them all the time they needed, play into their hands. And then, when Miss Shaw was ready to become you for a week or two, they sent their ransom note. They gave him three days. Concern about you grew to fever pitch in London and among the police, and especially in the confused mind of one Inspector Lestrade. On the third day, your captors took Eliza to Portsmouth, where the captain lived and had arranged some time earlier to have a home rented in a respectable part of the town, far from any dangers that might interfere with their plans. Portsmouth, of course, lies to the south of London (in the opposite direction from where you really were) and is near the English Channel, so as to appear to be a place for a quick getaway by water. They deposited her there and immediately sent the police an anonymous telegram, a 'public tip.' Inspector Lestrade had asked for one, as they expected, so anxious had he become to solve this crime. The Force came like an army to Portsmouth and found you . . . a glorious day for them and their senior detective."

Victoria is trying not to turn around and gape at him.

"But the entire crime was really about getting inside your father's house, identifying every last one of his valuables, opening doors from the inside, and stealing him blind while he was away. Your mother's room and its contents, dear to Captain Waller, were not to be touched. She was most certainly not the target.

"From the moment '*you*' were conveniently recovered in Portsmouth by the police, the main part of the crime was in motion. Eliza Shaw, thought to be you, and confirmed as such by your mother and father, was inside the Rathbone mansion, free to roam about and make notes, hear conversations about money matters, and discover the location of the safe. I know because I have seen the notes she made."

Victoria can no longer resist turning and staring at him. Who is this boy, this Sherlock Holmes? But he disregards her, lifts his hawk nose slightly and goes on.

"The moment your parents notified Eliza Shaw that they were adjourning to their country home with her, she sent word to St. Neots via the aid of one of those boys in that London gang. She told her accomplices that only two aging housemaids would be in the house that day. She left one rear door unlocked. The fiends pounced within a few hours. They entered the home, immobilized the maids, and found Eliza's notes hidden in a pre-appointed place in the house. They then proceeded to crack the lord's safe and remove all his money, pick out every painting of great value, every bit of his jewelry, his silver, every precious thing . . . to which they were so perfectly directed. They came and went in an hour, and the house was plucked nearly clean!"

Sherlock smiles as he sees the anger in Victoria's face.

"Shocked at the news of the robbery, the Rathbones immediately returned to the city. Eliza Shaw, with her job done, tried to slip away to St. Neots . . . but I intercepted her."

"You what?"

"She is an industrious sort though, so she tried again, not long after I left, and was successful. Thus . . . you were kidnapped a second time!"

Sherlock pauses and regards her intently.

"They are downstairs, the three of them, their cartons and bags filled with extraordinary wealth, the wealth to which you should be heiress – they will sell it all when they get to America and live happily ever after. The captain, of course, will be joining them."

"But they shan't get away! You have notified the police!" She is trying not to shout.

"I have, and a distinguished scribe from *The Times of London*. But they aren't here . . . yet."

The boy looks out the window. In the distance, he can see the steam from a train lifting into the sky as a locomotive whistles across the white-blanketed countryside toward St. Neots.

They are coming.

"You are just a boy. How . . . how do you know all this?" asks Victoria. There is both suspicion and admiration in her voice.

Sherlock puffs out his chest. "I noticed a watermark on a sheet of paper. Then I gathered data and made some simple deductions."

Holmes smiles at her puzzlement, but then his face turns darker.

"What if I were to stroll downstairs and alert them? Cut a deal?" he says. He has had enough of this girl, of Irene Doyle, Inspector Lestrade, Malefactor, and the Rathbones. Every last one of them is an utter disappointment.

"You wouldn't!"

"After all, what have those three really done? They have hurt no one. Even you have not been physically injured, other than being deprived of Yorkshire pudding. They have simply relieved a man, who doesn't deserve to own a farthing, of his ridiculously lavish, unshared fortune. He, who lives in style while nearby children die . . . and go blind."

Victoria says nothing. She actually looks guilty.

"But Master Holmes, you cannot –"

"Be quiet!" orders Sherlock. "I have to think this over." He leans against the sill, staring off into the distance toward St. Neots. He notices that the train has arrived at the station.

Sherlock Holmes, of course, has no intention of notifying the villains. In fact, he is desperate for the police to arrive and is worried that they will be too late. He is staring out the window, trying to will them across that marshy field to Grimwood Hall. He will stay in this room until they get here. All shall be revealed and *he* will be the one to reveal it, with *The Times* reporter looking on. *Credit where credit is due!*

He keeps searching for them. Minutes pass. *Where are they?* Then his heart leaps.

In the distance, they emerge out of the town and onto the frozen field like a small army, all of them on the run. Sherlock isn't sure, but it seems to him that Lestrade is in the lead, a slightly smaller figure by his side. The Force is equipped with dogs: hounds or bull terriers, likely muzzled to keep them quiet, pulling their masters at double speed.

Sherlock has kept back from the window, but now he puts his face right up to it and searches the grounds and surrounding area outside. There are the many trees and the ragged hedge maze and the black granite wall with the fence on top. There is no sign of the sleeping beasts.

The Force keeps coming.

Sherlock notices some movement to his extreme left outside the window. He presses his head against the cold pane and sees two Demi-Mail phaeton carriages in the driveway and a man carrying boxes out to them. Then another man limps forward with a big bag over his shoulder.

What if the fiends spot the police? Will they get away down a back road?

The boy glances at the marshy field again, and as he does, he notices something in the foreground: a top hat peeking up over the mossy wall. It vanishes. But then it appears again. Two other heads poke up this time, too. The first looks up at the window and levels his walking stick at Sherlock.

"Master Holmes, have you decided?" asks Victoria anxiously. She is imagining her fortune vanishing.

As he turns to her, there is a loud BANG! The window shatters and something rockets through the room and is embedded in a wall.

Victoria screams; cold air rushes into the room. In the confusion, Sherlock remembers Malefactor using a thick walking stick last night and it strikes him now that it looked different from the one he usually employs. Holmes has seen thick steel canes just like it in London . . . they sometimes contain concealed weapons . . . *gentlemen carry air guns inside them.*

Malefactor has laid his cards on the table. There is no doubt; he is trying to kill Sherlock Holmes.

On the surface, the boy in the upper room appears

calm, but he is shaking. "Lie down on the floor," he says to
Victoria in an even voice. She doesn't have to be told twice
– in an instant she is just a head and upper body on the pine
boards with a circle of scarlet crinoline dress spread out
around her.

Outside, everything has sped up. The top-hatted head
and its accomplices have fled. The two male thieves in the
driveway are frantic. Through the shattered window Sherlock
hears them shouting.

"That sounded like a gun – close by!"

"Fetch Eliza!"

"ELIZA!! We have to go! Now!"

Sherlock looks to the driveway again. He sees one thief
rushing into the manor, the other mounting a phaeton,
whip in hand. A question enters the boy's mind.

*Was Malefactor shooting at me . . . or was he warning
them?*

Sherlock looks for the young crime boss again. Three
figures are heading for the forest on the other side of the
grounds. No one awaits them at the edge of the trees.
Malefactor must have kept Irene away. He made sure she
didn't see him in action on Grimwood Hill.

The police are nearing and Lestrade is running like a
racehorse, way out in front of his charges, pulling a revolver
from his rumpled brown coat.

At that very moment, a knock sounds on the big front doors of the locked entrance to the Ratcliff Workhouse. An old man with stringy white hair, a goatee and spectacles, wearing a green tweed coat and a red fez is pounding on the doors. He is carrying something in a sack. A grimy concierge is eating thin turnip soup in his tiny office inside. The smelly mixture has been spilling on his yellowed beard and bits of it are hanging there as gets up. "I'm comin'! 'old on to yer knickers!" He staggers out, turns to the entrance, and opens the door.

Sherlock sees Lestrade do something he never dreamed the ferret-faced man had in him: he leaps onto the granite wall in one jump, grips two bars of the iron fence on top, and swings himself up. Off to the side of the house, Eliza Shaw is hustling out the door, wearing "Victoria Rathbone" traveling clothes. The scar-faced villain motions for her to climb into the carriage. The other phaeton, manned by the game-legged thief, is about to pull out.

Lestrade sees them.

"Halt!" he cries, "Or I shall fire!"

The phaetons begin to move.

The Inspector fires his gun and surprises himself: the bullet goes exactly where he intends it to go, right between the first team of horses and their buggy. The phaeton draws to an immediate halt, and the second crashes into it from behind.

"This way!" shouts Lestrade, motioning for his wheezing men to run to the side of the house and intercept the villains. The dogs are un-muzzled and begin to bark and snarl. "Toby!" a constable cries. "Seize them!" Sherlock sees the younger Lestrade arrive, and look up proudly at his father. In the distance, the heaving figure of Hobbs from *The Times* is struggling toward them.

In Stepney, the workhouse door has been opened.

"I am here to see a child named Paul Waller," says the bent-over old man to the foul-smelling concierge.

"Paul Dimly, you means."

"No, Paul Waller. Now, take me to him."

"And who might you be?"

"I am Sigerson Trismegistus Bell, here on an errand from God."

Sherlock crouches by the window and motions for Victoria to remain silent. He doesn't want Lestrade to know he is here, not yet. The plan he has been concocting has a much more dramatic climax.

Outside, the police have taken only a few minutes to bring the villains around to the front door. Sherlock can hear every word.

"An interesting bit of merchandise you lot are carrying," says Lestrade. "Take these two away."

Sherlock peeks up over the sill. He notices Hobbs, far behind, just reaching the grounds and struggling over the wall. Right below the window, Lestrade has turned to Eliza Shaw with a buttery smile.

"And you, Miss Rathbone," he coos, "it is a pleasure to be in your presence again. You shall be returned to your father forthwith."

Neither of the two male villains utters a word as they are pulled away. *Perhaps there is honor among thieves after all,* thinks Sherlock.

"They were making off with me," says Eliza in a shaky voice. "Right off with me!" The *R* rolls perfectly. "I feel I can find my own way home now."

"Nonsense," insists Lestrade, "I shall personally escort you."

"Perhaps just to London, then. I would like to surprise my parents alone."

Sherlock can see that she has a big purse over her shoulder, likely filled with all her incriminating notes.

"That can be arranged," intones Lestrade, doffing his bowler hat at her. As he does, he hears a thump upstairs, coming from an upper window.

"What was that? Are there others upstairs?" asks Lestrade.

"Oh, that is the ghost," laughs Eliza nervously. "The headless lady of Grimwood Hall. Quite famous. Shall we be off?"

"Did someone mention a ghost?" asks little Hobbs as he finally arrives, huffing and puffing. He wrestles a pen and pad from his coat pocket.

"If I might say so, you seem much older in person, Miss Rathbone," interjects the younger Lestrade, "more grown up, that is."

The Inspector rolls his eyes and then frowns at his son. There's another thump from the upper storey.

"There is someone up there, Father."

"Nonsense," says Eliza. "Might you take me to St. Neots station now, Inspector? I am flushed with excitement . . . and *so* impressed with your actions. I may faint if I don't get away. I cannot wait to tell my father."

There's another thump, this time very loud.

"I must conduct this investigation personally, Miss Rathbone. And you cannot leave the grounds without me."

"Yes I can!"

"Excuse me?"

"I demand that you accompany me this instant to the St. Neots train station!" She shouts, stamping her foot.

"Ah," says Lestrade Junior under his breath, "fourteen after all."

"The constables will stay with you. No need to fear. My son and I are going upstairs."

"No!"

He turns to two of his men and speaks softly.

"She is hysterical, gentlemen. Comes under the heading of 'woman.' Restrain her if you must. I shall be back down shortly. This is likely nothing. The window up there looks shattered, so it is probably the wind . . . or that ghost."

The constables guffaw as Lestrade winks at them and he and his son make for the front door. Though very pleased about things, he is also a little concerned. He keeps glancing around the grounds. Where is that boy, Sherlock Holmes? Hobbs is immediately beside them.

Upstairs, Holmes is readying himself for his greatest moment. Fame is about to be attached to his name. All of London will not only know he solved this sensational, mystifying case, but that he, too, was behind the Whitechapel and Brixton solutions. He will reveal everything. His future rises in front of him like a dream.

He hears the front door close and footsteps advancing through the vestibule, down the corridor, and up to the first staircase.

THE VANISHING BOY

The excitement is building inside Sherlock Holmes. His heart pounds harder than it has ever thumped during any moment of danger he has experienced since he first fancied himself a detective. This is not only what he has been working for since the moment his mother died, but really, in a sense, from the day he was born. He is about to get his due.

He strides across the room and opens the door. It has all worked out in the end. He has Lestrade exactly where he wants him. The senior detective will not be able to wriggle out of this one.

Sherlock steps out into the hallway. He can hear the distant voices of the two Lestrades and *The Times* reporter at the top of the second staircase several corridors away. They are trying to figure out which passageway to take.

Sherlock whacks his foot on the floor and then hears Lestrade commanding his companions in the right direction.

The boy can hardly contain himself. How will he put this? He should have something very clever, very dramatic, to say.

"Inspector Lestrade, how nice to see you," he intones quietly, so Victoria won't hear him. His chest, however, is swelling, his eyebrows raised. "Good of you to come. If you step right this way, I shall introduce you to . . . Victoria Rathbone. You say that is impossible, that she is in your custody already? I think not. You see, you have been duped, sir, taken for a fool, a boob, an imbecile. Let me explain."

But as he gloats in the hallway, Sherlock experiences a great surprise. He doesn't like the sound of this pride-filled speech at all. There is something hollow in it, something juvenile.

"*One must pursue things for the right reasons*," he hears Sigerson Bell say.

Back in Stepney, the concierge, who has foolishly revealed to the strange visitor exactly where little Paul Waller is in the workhouse, is in trouble. The ancient, bent-over apothecary will not wait while officials are notified and asked if a visit will be permitted. In fact, he is getting hard to contain.

"You must 'alt 'ere, old fellow," the man insists, placing his hand on Bell's scrawny chest. The intruder begins to push past him.

"I shall do no such thing." Bell looks up the stairs that lead to the first floor. They are filthy. As he glances down, a rat scurries between their feet. "You ought to be ashamed of yourself, sir, and so ought this entire enterprise, so ought England itself. I shall see the boy!"

"I'm afraid —"

But the concierge doesn't finish the sentence. A masterful Bellitsu move results in his chubby hand being removed from the old man's chest and in his falling, face forward, onto the floor, where he remains for more than a few minutes.

Sigerson Bell goes up the steps four at a time, heading for Paul Waller on the double.

Sherlock figures that Lestrade and company are less than thirty seconds from his door. He looks back through the entrance at haughty Victoria Rathbone and then toward the *T* in the hallway just up ahead. That's where they will appear.

Then he hears another voice, a woman's, coming up behind the men.

"Inspector Lestrade!" she shouts. "Don't —"

"Miss Rathbone, you were told to stay with the constables."

Sherlock can tell that Lestrade is undeterred, still walking, coming this way.

"Sir!" he hears two policemen shout almost together. "She eluded us like a cat, and . . ."

"Never mind, we shall all visit this room together."

"I implore you, Inspector Lestrade, don't go —"

Sherlock stops listening. He turns to Victoria again.

"When Inspector Lestrade of the London Metropolitan Police gets here," he says, "tell him everything I told you . . . and leave me out of it."

And with that, he rushes down the hallway, past the *T* and into the next corridor, where he hides around the corner and peers out.

Inspector Lestrade, his son, *The Times* reporter, the two constables, and a protesting Eliza Shaw, emerge into the hallway and turn toward the door. As they approach, Eliza stops in her tracks.

Lestrade notices that the entrance to the room is open. He steps forward. He looks inside. His mouth opens in a gape as wide as the dome on St. Paul's Cathedral.

Though Victoria Rathbone stands behind him . . . before him stands Victoria Rathbone.

Several hours later, long after Eliza Shaw has been removed from the premises in the grasp of five strong-armed Bobbies, after Miss Rathbone stamps her foot and calls Inspector Lestrade every synonym for idiot her little brain can summon, Sherlock enters the grounds. Though the sun is setting, it has turned mild. The snow is beginning to melt.

He looks out over the lawn from the far side of the fence near the arched doorway. It is becoming difficult to see in the growing darkness. The maze is full of shadows. It is time for the night creatures to awake. Fear pulses through every inch of Sherlock's body.

At that very moment, Sigerson Bell is crouching beside Paul Waller. The little boy hasn't been able to cry since he was a baby, but now he is weeping so hard that the tears coming out of his enormous blind, brown eyes seem capable of forming a pool on the floor beneath him. The workhouse employee who had found him just outside his room at breakfast time had been unable to get him to return, so he had left the child in the hallway. The little boy had struggled forward, feeling his way along the wall, seeing only darkness, not knowing where he wanted to go, but going nevertheless. Finally, he had collapsed, his little shoulders heaving.

"Paul?" asks the kind old apothecary.

The boy turns his face up toward him.

"I have here in my bag a solution of carrots and a secret chemical mixture involving liquid ammonia and sulfur, which I once perfected and then forgot, but which I have been working upon assiduously – we will teach you the meaning of that word – for the last few days. . . . Ever since a dear friend of mine told me of your predicament."

"I cannot see, sir."

"Precisely why I am in your presence, my young knight. You see, this mixture . . . it shall cure you."

Sherlock Holmes climbs the first fence just outside the manor house, shaking in his Wellington shoes, looking for black shapes hidden in the night. Christmas is just weeks away – he wants to live. He drops down onto the grounds and heads quickly into the maze. But within just a few steps, right in front of his path, he sees something that makes his blood run cold. It is the head of a massive beast, a face unlike any he has ever seen or imagined! And this time, he cannot escape. Thinking of little Paul and what the child has to endure, he decides that he, too, can look danger in the eye. Quivering, he walks directly toward the creature. Somehow, he must fight it. But as he nears . . . he sees that the horrific face is made by a few branches sticking out at unusual angles in the unkempt hedge. A deep sense of shame consumes him.

He moves again, more slowly. But he isn't much farther through the grounds when he sees another ferocious face. He approaches again . . . but it's just more twisted branches in a hedge. He stands still and thinks back to the thief's strange conduct in the grand staircase room, roaring up the chimney of the massive fireplace. *Roaring!* Sherlock imagines what that must have sounded like outside, blowing in the wind and over the grounds . . . the resounding and echoing roar of some mythical beast.

The criminals had played on others' fears. They had toyed with the likes of Sherlock Holmes, toyed with his deep concerns about himself, his constantly inner-directed worries. There are indeed no such things as black tigers or headless ghosts . . . unless they loom in the fears of a self-centered boy. That poor child in the workhouse was what should have mattered in all of this – and catching those fiends.

Sherlock turns back to the mansion . . . it is really just an ordinary manor house.

He is glad that he won't receive the credit for solving this case. Things must be done for the right reasons. He doesn't need Andrew Doyle's help or anyone else's. He must rely on himself to become what he needs to be.

And so, he makes a vow. He will *stop* seeking more criminal cases or the fame that goes with them. He will leave that for when he becomes a man.

He climbs the granite wall and heads down the hill toward St. Neots: to London and all its evils. But a question keeps repeating itself in his head.

"What if a crime . . . an enormous and irresistible crime . . . seeks out *me*?"

A smile spreads across his face. He picks up his pace.

Praise for DEATH IN THE AIR

Chosen as a 2008 Best Bets by the Ontario Library Association
IODE (National Chapter) Violet Downey Book Award
– short list
2009 Canadian Library Association's Young Adult Book Award
– finalist

"In the first novel, we see many of the characteristics of the adult
detective being formed through his first exciting adventure. In
Death in the Air, this development continues and we get to know
young Sherlock even better . . . This novel is written for the
young adult, but adult readers will also find it satisfying. Peacock
places demand on the reader, expecting intelligence and curiosity.
The fast-paced adventure is a treat."

– *The Globe and Mail*

"Shane Peacock's second novel of the young Sherlock is no less
exciting or authentic than the first, *Eye of the Crow.* . . . Again,
Peacock has remained true to the original spirit of the Holmes
series. Sherlock's pervasive melancholy and his flirtatious rela-
tionship with the underworld of London create yet another
authentic mystery. Peacock has honored the essence of the original Holmes stories while contributing his own intuitive, exhila-
rating touches. HIGHLY RECOMMENDED."

– *Canadian Review of Materials*